CH00894893

Dead Silent

Nina Smith

Copyright © 2013 Nina Smith

All rights reserved.

ISBN-13:
978-1492734659

ISBN-10:
1492734659

Dedicated to Sandra,
for the stories you shared.

CHAPTER ONE

Enda Wilson forced the last white pill into drain holes just too small for it. Water gushed from the taps and flushed it far, far away.

The phone let out a demented shrill. The sound made her jump, but she refused to feel guilty. She turned the taps off, stormed into the lounge room and grabbed the receiver. "Christ Mum, you don't have to check up on me!"

Silence on the other end. Oh shit. Maybe it wasn't Mum at all. "Enda? Enda is that you?"

At first she couldn't place the voice. "Who is this?"

"Chrissake, it's me Selene!"

Enda scowled at the phone. "Why are you ringing me at 3am?"

"I have to get out of here. I'm coming to see you."

"What's happened? Where are you?"

"I'm still in Dead Rock. What's happened is our whole family is really fucked up, okay? I can't talk over the phone. I have to leave, now. I'll be there in three hours." Selene's voice trembled on the last word. A door slammed in the background.

"But Selene why would you-"

"I'll see you soon."

The phone went dead.

Enda stared at the receiver. Then she lay down on the couch and stared up at the fancy lights Mum had installed last year. They were dusty. She swallowed, hard. No. Selene, come here? After all these years? Not now, not when her career was in ruins and the closest thing she had to a friend was a psychiatrist who thought she was delusional. God no.

But Christ, she'd sounded scared.

A cat purred near her ear. The imprint of a paw appeared in the red velour of the couch, but there was nothing there.

Enda closed her eyes and curled up around the phone. Tiny bumps broke out on her skin where the ghost cat passed.

*

The phone went off right next to her ear.

Enda groaned and opened her eyes. The clock on the wall said 9am. She had a cramp in her neck from sleeping on the couch and the phone was practically embedded in her cheek. She peeled it off her skin.

She didn't want to face today. She didn't want to start a stupid new job she was going to hate. She pressed the button to answer the call. "Alright Mum, I'm up."

"Enda, it's me."

It felt like 3am all over again, except she knew exactly whose voice answered her this time.

"Dad?" she sat up and rubbed her eyes. "Hi." She didn't know what else to say. It had been nine years since she and her mother left Dead Rock. He'd called maybe three times in those years.

"It's good to hear your voice," he said.

Enda clutched the phone so hard her knuckles turned white. "How are you?" the question seemed inane.

"I'm – I'm not so good."

Enda thought she heard him drag on a cigarette. Gross. It had taken her a year to get that smell out of her clothes when they left.

"How are you? How's your mum?"

"We're fine. She just got some big new contract. She's been at this conference."

"That's great. I heard you finished uni."

"That was like two years ago."

Awkward silence.

He cleared his throat. "Listen, Enda, something's happened. It's your cousin, Selene."

"I just spoke to her last night."

"She's dead. She–she fell off Dead Rock early this morning."

It felt like all the air had been sucked out of the room. Enda slowly shook her head. "What? No. No, that's not possible. What was she doing up there? How could she fall?"

Her father's voice lowered. "We think–that is, your uncle said she jumped. He's devastated. Everyone is."

There was a lump in her throat that made it hard to talk. She glanced at the front door, half-expecting Selene to walk through it like she'd said she would. "No way. She rang me at 3am and said she was coming here. There must be a mistake. Why would she go up Dead Rock?"

She paused. The 3am phone call seemed like a dream. Selene had said she was at Dead Rock, but had she meant the town, or the rock of the same name?

"I want you to come home," her father said into the silence. "For the funeral. Please come home, just for a few days. Your room's still here, I never changed it. I want to see you. Everybody does."

Enda had her doubts about everybody, but she heard herself say yes. She didn't seem to be in her body. Mum's immaculate lounge room, dusty light fittings and thick carpet felt like a dream. Selene couldn't be dead.

She hung up the phone and slid down to sit on the floor. The mirrored doors of the china cabinet reflected her face. Selene wouldn't have known her. She'd dyed a big lock of her dark brown hair white-blonde and cut the lot straight across the shoulders. Because she could. Because she didn't live in a shit hole town with a population of 600 and she could look as freakish as she wanted to.

She closed her eyes. She didn't want to go back to Dead Rock. She didn't want to see her father.

She wanted to see him desperately.

A key scratched in the front door. Footsteps came up the hall and padded over the carpet.

"Good morning."

Enda opened her eyes. She had to look up and up and up; those damn high heels made Leda Wilson too tall. The hair piled up so high just made the impression worse. She was wearing full makeup and a tailored beige skirt suit. She looked fresh and relaxed, at least for two seconds. Then the familiar concern creased her brow.

"Is everything okay? You look like you've been crying."

"I haven't." Enda fidgeted with her sleeve. Her flannel shirt was creased from sleeping in it.

Leda dumped her bag, kicked off her shoes and crouched in front of her. She had that resigned look on her face. She'd had it a lot lately. "You need to talk to me if I'm going to help you through this, Enda. Have you taken your medication today?"

"Yes." The lie rolled off her tongue like water. She resisted looking at the sink, where she'd flushed her lithium last night right before Selene called.

"Do you need me to call the psychiatrist?"

"I don't need a psychiatrist!" Enda took a deep breath and forced herself to calm down. "I just spoke to Dad. Selene killed herself last night. I have to go back to Dead Rock for the funeral."

Leda collapsed onto the floor next to her. "Are you serious?"

"Yes."

"How long will you go for?"

"Just until the funeral. See how Dad's doing. Look, I know you got me that job and all, but I need to go."

Leda made a quick, tense movement. "Fine. I know you and Selene were close."

"Not really. Are you coming to the funeral?"

"I don't know. No."

"But she's your niece!"

"I don't want to go back to Dead Rock!"

Silence followed Leda's terse statement. She softened her tone and spoke again. "Look, I'll try, okay? I'm just not sure I'm ready to see your father yet. And I want you to be careful out there. I don't want anything to happen to you."

"Nothing's going to happen to me, Mum. It's Dead Rock for God's sake."

"Bipolar disorder is a tricky condition Enda, I'm just worried going back there could be a trigger."

Enda set her teeth. "I'm not crazy."

"I never said you were."

"So drop it."

The crow's feet around Leda's eyes deepened under her

makeup. "I'm sorry. I just want what's best for you."

"Drop it!"

Leda stood up and walked away, every line of her body held in the rigid angles she got when she was angry. That was most of the time.

Enda wondered if she'd remembered to hide the empty lithium box.

*

It was a three hour drive to Dead Rock. The further the highway got from the city, the narrower and more winding it became. Enda was vaguely surprised her mother had agreed so readily to her going. She'd half expected her to hire an escort of doctors in white coats.

Maybe she was just sick of looking after a nutcase.

She slowed at the entrance to the town. Head Rock, two kilometres, the sign said. Someone had spray-painted a D over the H in Head decades ago, and the town had been called Dead Rock ever since, same as the infamous cliff that claimed life after life.

Enda blinked back tears. Surely there'd been a mistake. It couldn't have been Selene that jumped. Selene might have been a prize bitch, but she would never end it like that.

The entry to town had changed little in nine years. The same red-roofed houses, the little hotel and the park with the rusty swing she and Selene used to play on as kids. Then the cliff threw its shadow over the highway and the plain of grey sand that ran from the road to the bush. Broken police tape fluttered at the base of the cliff.

The air went cold so suddenly she checked the sky to see if weather was rolling in, but there wasn't a cloud in sight.

Something flashed in her peripheral vision. Then a woman with long blonde hair and bright red lipstick leaned over from the passenger seat and laid her fingers on the steering wheel. "You shouldn't have come back here." She yanked on the wheel.

Enda screamed. The car left the road and spun out on soft grey sand. She slammed on the brakes. The wheels locked up and the car came to a halt pointing back the way she'd come.

A burst of police siren split the silence that followed.

CHAPTER TWO

Damn it.

Enda leaned on her steering wheel and took a few deep breaths to calm herself. The passenger seat was empty. She'd only got a quick glimpse of the woman, just enough to be very bloody sure it was Selene. Nobody else in Dead Rock wore that shade of red.

There was a rap on her window. Great. Just great. Gone for nine years and the first thing she did on returning was almost crash her car in front of the only cop in Dead Rock. She wound down the window.

"Step out of the car please, miss."

Enda got out of the car. The tall, heavyset man in the blue uniform was red in the face. She couldn't see his eyes under his peaked police hat, but she knew they were dark blue, same as hers and Selene's and her dad's. The paraphernalia of gun and pepper spray and who knew what else at his belt bulked out a slight paunch. His badge said *Sergeant Conrad Wilson*, same as it always had. He'd been Sergeant forever.

He was pissed off. Of course he was. Christ, the poor man had scraped his daughter off the roadside just hours ago and here she was spinning out on the sand. She wasn't game to meet his eyes.

"What the hell do you think you're doing?" his voice came out as a growl.

"I'm sorry." Enda looked at her feet. "I got distracted. I thought I saw –" she hesitated. I thought I saw your dead daughter in my passenger seat. She tried to kill me. Do you mind? "I thought I saw a rabbit, so I swerved," she said.

"A likely story." He held up a white plastic pipe attached to a machine. "I want you to blow into this please."

Christ. He didn't even recognise her. Could today get any better? Enda put her lips around the plastic and blew into it until he told her to stop.

He studied the machine. It beeped. "Your blood alcohol level is zero." He sounded disappointed.

"I know," she said.

"Do you want to explain to me how swerving resulted in your vehicle leaving the road like that?"

"I had a late night, maybe I was a little tired."

"Are you aware that's an offense?"

"What? Being tired?" Enda knew she needed to shut up. The last thing she wanted to do was piss off Selene's dad on her first day back.

"I'm going to need to see your license," he said.

Enda leaned into the car, extracted her license from her bag, handed it over and waited while he glanced over it.

He looked from the license to her. His hand trembled. "Enda? Why didn't you say something?"

"Sorry Uncle Con. It really was an accident."

"Don't worry about that." He wrapped his arms around her and Enda's face was mashed up against a police badge with sharp edges.

He let her go. "What are you doing here?"

"Dad told me what happened. I came straight away. I'm so sorry, if there's anything I can do-"

He shook his head. "You're here, that's enough. Where's Leda?"

"Mum might come for the funeral, but she had to work today."

Uncle Con looked the car over. "You're lucky you only went onto the sand, you know. Doesn't look like there's any damage."

Enda glanced over the shabby old Magna. If she was anyone else, he'd have slapped a yellow sticker on it by now. "Can I go home?"

He sighed. "Are you sure you want to do that? You could stay with me and Betty while you're here if you want. You might be more comfortable."

"I really want to see Dad."

"I'd better come with you."

*

Enda stood in the middle of the waist-high long grass in the front yard, beside the weed-strangled pear tree, the hibiscus and the straggling geraniums. A rusted swing chair leaned at a crazy angle near the veranda. The yellow paint on the front wall of the house was cracked and peeling and one of the windows had a fracture in it. It looked like nobody had even lived here for ages. Uncle Con's hand landed on her shoulder and for a brief second she thought about taking him up on his offer.

"Is Dad okay?"

"Depends how you define okay." The words had a tinge of bitterness.

Enda followed the path trodden through the grass, climbed the three steps to the veranda and walked gingerly over the spongy boards. The door opened at a touch onto the dark hallway.

She stepped into a wall of stale cigarette smell, gagged and left the door wide open. The house was silent. She picked her way over sheets of newspaper lying on the floor, torn cigarette packets and crushed beer cans. Empty green glass bottles lined the edges of the hall. Some had dead or wilting red geranium flowers in them. Uncle Con's heavy footsteps made the floor vibrate behind her.

The familiar patter of invisible little paws preceded her into the kitchen. At least her dead cat had followed her here. She wouldn't be completely alone.

She looked around the kitchen. "Oh my God."

"Like I said, you'd be more comfortable at my house," Uncle Con said.

"I suppose I should have expected this." Enda looked from the kitchen sink piled with dirty dishes to the table cluttered with old newspapers and overflowing ashtrays. The stale smoke smell was worse in here and the floor was covered in a layer of grime. She held her breath, hurried to the windows over the sink, flung them wide open and snatched her hand away from the spider she disturbed in the process. She turned her back on the piled up dishes, but was reluctant to move away from the source of fresh air. "So where's Dad?"

"Why don't you go put your stuff in your room?" Uncle Con disappeared down the hall.

Enda followed him and dumped her suitcase and bag in her old room. It was dusty, but not full of crap like the rest of the house, which was something.

She ventured along the hall, opening doors as she went. She shut the laundry door again very quickly, since the smell was awful. She checked the other two bedrooms and then headed for the sleepout at the back of the house where Uncle Con had gone.

There, afternoon sun shone through dusty louvers, just barely lighting a table spattered with paint, two easels squeezed amid piles of old newspapers and walls covered in half-finished canvases. He'd never been able to finish a painting even when she was a kid. All of these had the same basic shape in the background. He was trying to paint Dead Rock.

Through the open back door she looked into the overgrown garden. That was as bad as the front yard, the grass as high, the trees as strangled. The path to the back fence the property shared with Uncle Con's house was still discernible.

Uncle Con bent over a bed pushed up against the furthest wall of the room, where it was almost dark. There she could just see Leo Wilson on his back, snoring. She tip-toed forward. His hair, blacker than hers, had got long and tangled around his shoulders. Grey streaked through it in places. He hadn't shaved for several days. He stank of stale beer, cigarettes and sweat. Several bottles littered the couch and floor around him and a cigarette stub had burned to nothing between his fingers.

She felt a surge of hatred. This was exactly how she remembered him.

Uncle Con thumped the wall above the bed. "Leo, wake up."

The snoring got louder.

"Wake up Leo!"Uncle Con shook the bed so violently Leo rolled out and landed on the floor at his brother's feet.

Enda winced in sympathy. She didn't think Con should have been quite that nasty.

Leo pushed himself into a sitting position and rubbed his eyes. His voice was rough and cracked. "Hey? What? What are you doing?"

"Get up." Con's voice was clipped and tinged with contempt. "Is this any way to welcome Enda home?"

"Who?" Leo climbed back up to the bed and sat there rubbing his eyes.

There went the sympathy.

"Me," Enda said.

Uncle Con started. He came back to her, put an arm around her shoulder and escorted her to the door. "I didn't realise you came in. Why don't you go unpack or something? I was hoping you wouldn't have to see him like this."

"Why not? It's just how I remember him."

"Just give us a minute." Con opened the door for her.

"Enda?" Leo said from the other side of the room.

Enda looked over her shoulder. Somehow she felt like she'd never left. Same shit, nine years on. "Good guess Dad." She walked out.

*

The kitchen was a pigsty. Enda opened the pantry doors and found the shelves almost bare but for a packet of pasta. She put some water on to boil. She held her breath while she emptied the ashtrays into the bin, then gathered all the newspapers into a single dusty pile and put them near the door. She found a dishcloth with holes in it on the cluttered sink and used it to wipe down the table until the surface at least resembled something hygienic. She kept cleaning and pretended she didn't know Uncle Con was throwing cold water over Leo in the backyard to sober him up. After a while footsteps went up the hall and the shower went on.

She was putting pasta into boiling water when Leo walked into the kitchen. He'd shaved and put on a fresh flannel shirt and torn jeans. His hair was detangled and he no longer smelled. He was thinner than she remembered. He gave her an uncertain smile.

Enda went to her father and hugged him. "Hi Dad."

"It's good to see you." Leo squeezed her briefly, then stepped back and looked at her. "Wow. Look at you, all grown up and glamorous."

"Hardly." Enda pointed at the table. "Why don't you wash some plates? I made some food."

Leo looked at the floor. "I wanted to make you dinner," he said. "Welcome you home, you know. I guess I, um-"

"Had too much to drink and passed out? Yeah, I noticed. Just like old times." She stabbed the fork into the pasta and splashed boiling water on her hand.

Leo shuffled over to the sink and turned on the water. Enda

kept her back to him until the pasta was ready. Then she took the food over to the table and portioned it into the two bowls he'd set out. Plain pasta, not even any tomato sauce. They avoided each other's eyes for a while. Leo ate fast. Enda picked at her food, not really hungry. Finally she pushed it away.

Leo watched her across the table. "It's really good to see you."

"You already said that." Enda folded her arms on the table top. No good asking him how he was doing, he'd obviously been drunk for the last nine years. "Are you working?"

"A bit. I do some gardening here and there."

"Obviously not here."

Leo shrugged. "I'll get around to it."

"I suppose you'll get around to the cleaning, too?"

"You're very like your mother."

Enda almost smiled. "She doesn't think so."

"She rang me today."

"Did she now?" Enda played with her fork and wondered what her mother could possibly have had to say to her father.

"She said you'd had some problems."

Of course she did. Bitch. Enda got up from the table so quickly her chair almost fell over. "Come on. I might only be here for three days, but I'm not living in a pigsty. We'll start with the dishes."

CHAPTER THREE

"Hey look, it's Enda the world."

Selene, at fourteen. Blonde curls rippled over her shoulders. Malice glinted in her dark blue eyes. Three boys hovered at her elbows. The bitch twins from hell stood either side like bookends, all right there between her and her locker. Selene's lips curved and Enda knew what she was going to say before she even opened her mouth.

"My dad put your dad in the jail last night. He was so drunk he picked a fight with his own car."

Enda hitched her schoolbag over one shoulder. She just looked. She knew it infuriated Selene when she didn't rise to the bait.

Selene's voice rose. "Your dad's a drunk!"

Enda raised her eyebrows just the slightest amount. Selene flushed a dull red.

One of the boys looked Enda up and down. "I heard you're so poor you use your dad's empty wine casks for furniture," he said.

Selene's laugh was loud enough to attract attention up and down the hall. "That's because she's white trash."

A flash of white-hot anger. The urge to hurt. She had nothing on Selene, but that didn't matter in high school, people made stuff up all the time. "Do your boyfriends here know you sleep around for crack?"

Selene leaped at her.

Enda clawed at the pillow. The room was dark and close. A cold shadow hovered at her left side, close enough to kiss. Only the familiar weight of the ghost cat, Ivy, at her feet kept a wave of terror at bay. She pulled the blankets over her head and shut her eyes. She'd never realised how comforting it was to hear her dead cat purring.

Darkness. She tried not to inhale the dust from the pillow too deeply. She wondered what kind of woman Selene had become. Neither she nor her cousin had bothered to keep in touch after she left. Why would they? They couldn't stand each other.

"Enda!"

Enda hung upside down from the climbing frame, eyes closed, feeling the sun warm on her face. Her hair hung almost to the ground.

The rusty swing chains creaked back and forth, back and forth. Selene's pigtails flew through the air. "Enda look how high I can go!"

Enda opened her eyes. She looked past Selene to Dead Rock. The shadow of the cliff ended just where the playground began. The sky was her floor and the rock her sky. She swung off the frame, walked to the fence and leaned over it. A tall Aboriginal man wearing a battered hat and old-fashioned braces stood under the rock, staring at the playground.

Enda waved. He tipped his hat at her.

Selene jumped from the swing and landed with a thud in the sand. She joined Enda at the fence. "Who are you waving at?"

"That man over there."

"What man?"

Enda pointed.

"There's nobody there!"

Enda pointed again. "He's right there."

Selene's voice rose. "I'm telling your mum! She said you weren't to make up stories to scare me anymore! There's nobody there!"

Enda punched the pillow into shape. A dust cloud enveloped her face and she sneezed. The heavy blackness of the room absorbed the sound. She kept her eyes squeezed shut and shifted further under the blanket. That cold mass near her shoulder breathed, waited. She couldn't go out there. She just had to stop thinking about Selene.

Stop.

Thinking.

Dead Rock, washed deep purple in the early dawn light.

Stop thinking about it.

Standing at the top of Dead Rock. The first grey light in the sky, picking out the shadows and shapes of houses and trees as far as the eye could see. Vast black space yawning at her feet.

One little step.

A step. Someone behind her left shoulder.

Dark blue eyes, shadowed in the dawn.

She plunged so fast, sickening, body and mind lost in one wave of terror, one scream-

Enda sat bolt upright. The bedsprings squeaked and the mattress bounced as though she really had just fallen from a great height. The darkness suffocated. The cold breathed at her shoulder. Her blood pounded so hard she felt dizzy. Miles of nothing stretched between her and the light switch. Her shallow breaths sounded like thunder. The darkness shifted around her, thick with shapes and mutters.

Her breath sounded like a sob, but she didn't know if that sound even came from her.

Light blazed. Enda squeezed her eyes shut against it.

When she opened them only the bedroom was there. Leo stood in the doorway, one foot in and one foot out as though he wasn't sure he'd done the right thing. "The nightmares?" he said.

Enda nodded. She felt an overwhelming rush of gratitude and familiarity. Only her father had ever really understood about the nightmares. Leda had shrugged them off and said she'd grow out of it. "You remembered."

Leo smiled. "Come on," he said. "It's 3am. Stupid time of the night to be sleeping."

Enda was only too glad to leave the room. She threw her long coat on over her pyjamas for warmth and followed her father into the kitchen, which was a hell of a lot cleaner than it had been when she'd arrived. She filled the rusty old kettle with water and set it to boil.

Leo sat at the kitchen table and took a swig from a bottle of beer.

Enda gave the tiniest sigh and wondered if he'd been up all night drinking. She made her tea black, with plenty of sugar, and joined him.

"I could get you a beer," he said.

"No." The word was more forcible than she'd intended.

He shrugged. "What was the nightmare about?"

"Selene." Enda wished she could take the word back as soon

as she said it, because it made Leo tip back his bottle and drink what was left in one go.

He went to the fridge and came back with another. He sat heavily in the chair and cracked it open. "Selene," he said.

Enda took a sip of her tea. The hot liquid burned her lips. She formed the question carefully in her mind before speaking it. "Are they sure she jumped?" she said. "I mean, how do they know it was suicide? Who's to say there wasn't somebody else there with her?"

"This is Dead Rock. People don't get murdered here." Leo's tone forestalled any more questions. He fidgeted with his beer bottle and looked at her like she wasn't even in the room. His eyes were red-rimmed and bloodshot.

"Dad," she said. "I want you to do something for me."

"What?"

"I want you to stop drinking."

"Don't be a bloody idiot." His voice was low and rough.

Enda flinched.

Leo dropped his face into his hands. "I'm sorry. I'm sorry Enda, I didn't mean it. I can't. I just can't. I know I'm a fuckup. I know I was never a good father, but I have to–I have to–" He took a swig of his drink.

"You have to what?" Enda curled her fingers around the hot mug.

Leo stared into his beer and said nothing.

Enda slid her fingers across the table until they almost touched his. She rested her chin on her arm, tired, and looked up at him. The years and the alcohol had made their mark on his once handsome face. She wondered what had turned him into the man he was. "Please Dad," she said. "It's just three days. Just while I'm here. I want to see you, not some drunk who doesn't know what he's doing."

"It's not that easy. You can't just stop." Leo looked at her fingers.

Enda withdrew her hand and straightened. God, if it was going to be like this, she may as well just get back in her car and go. "Three days, Dad. Three days out of your whole life, for me. You know what? You owe me this. Do you have any idea what it was like to grow up in this shithole town with everyone knowing my dad was the local drunk? It was fifteen years of hell. So I reckon you can give me three days sober."

Leo looked at her. For a moment she thought he was going to yell, or swear, or walk away. She wished he would. Anything to show he wasn't just a piss-weak old wino.

Then the tension drained from him. His hand slackened on the bottle. His shoulders slumped. "How come you never told me?"

"What was I supposed to say?"

"If I do this for you, you need to do something for me."

"What?"

"Tell me what's wrong. Tell me what your mother was talking about."

Enda considered for a moment, but there was really no contest, since Leda would tell him anyway when she got here. "Deal," she said, and stuck out her hand.

Leo shook it. He raised the bottle to his lips.

"Starting now," Enda said.

"Now?" Leo looked rebellious. "Can't I just finish this one?"

"No."

He pushed the bottle across the table to her. "Fine. But you need to help me. Get rid of it. Get rid of it all."

"Okay." Enda took the bottle and emptied it down the sink. She felt Leo's eyes on her back, watching her every move. "Tomorrow we'll get the house sorted out. For now, you go to bed."

"And your side of the bargain?"

Enda threw him a glance over her shoulder. "Tomorrow," she said. "When you're sober."

She heard him leave the kitchen, followed his footsteps down the hall. Best to take him at his word, even if it meant he'd be mad in the morning. She pulled half a carton of beer out of the fridge and emptied each bottle into the sink. The hiss of beer down the plug hole was like music.

There was a bottle of vodka in the top cupboard. A tail end of bourbon under the sink. Why the hell did he still hide them, when he'd lived alone all these years?

Enda put the empty bottles in a box and carried it down the dark hall. Ivy trotted at her feet. Their footsteps echoed together in the darkness.

She walked carefully across the spongy veranda and down to the bin, where she dropped the whole box in.

Ivy purred. Enda moved away from the bin, crouched in the long grass and reached out her hand. Cool air brushed her fingers. She looked up at the clear sky. It was so dark out here, so black. Every star stood out. The half moon was so bright it hurt her eyes to look at. She'd forgotten what the night was like in the country.

A gentle wind skipped across the yard, rustled the grass, carried night fragrances of baked dirt and settling heat. Hibiscus flowers turned their deep pink faces to the moon. Enda closed her eyes and just listened. She didn't want to go back to bed. Not with something in her room.

Blades of grass whispered to each other. The pear tree's leaves sighed. No other sound reached the garden gates. Nothing at all might exist out there, except a blonde woman in a red dress with dark blue eyes.

Enda started back to consciousness. Her neck prickled. The pear tree threw shadows over her. The wind picked up and the long grass bent double. The house glared at her with cracked eyes and peeling skin. She backed away as though it was a wild animal. It didn't want her. It had Leo. She shivered because the night had turned icy cold.

She bumped through the gate. The squeal of rusty hinges cut the night and then creaked into silence. The grass whispered furiously.

She turned her back on all of it, clutched her coat closer around herself and walked away. The air quickly warmed. She had hoped Ivy would follow, but there was no patter of feet, no invisible purr.

White daisies glowed over a tumbledown fence in the path. Enda broke one flower off at the base of the stem. She crossed the road and took a little alley that led between two houses with tall fibro fences. The gravel hurt her bare feet; she walked lightly into the pitch blackness.

The fences gave way to a concrete path that wound through a patch of forest. Balga bushes formed spiny black and green walls on either side. Between them rose towering, rough-barked jarrah and marri, their trunks blackened from some long ago fire. Thick layers of dead leaves crowded the edges of the path. The air was warm and pleasant. Maybe she'd bring her pillow and blanket out here tomorrow night and sleep where there weren't any ghosts.

Enda followed the path until it emerged into a big, bare space. She curled her toes into the cold grey sand and looked up at Dead Rock. It was just a big black shape in the darkness. She couldn't see the rock face, or the fissures, or anything except far, far above where the rock ended and the stars began.

She walked slowly over the sand. She crossed the tracks left by her near-car accident, then the empty road.

Scraps of yellow police tape lay on the ground. A white shape glowed in the darkness near the base of the rock. Enda's stomach contracted. Someone had planted a little cross to mark the place where Selene had fallen. She crouched down to place her daisy with the other tributes. A white petal floated to the ground.

Cold seeped like acid into her muscles. Enda's hands shook. Her teeth chattered. She scrambled out of the cold space. Something moved in her peripheral vision; a flash of red disappeared into the shadows where the path up the rock was hidden.

She closed her eyes. All the anger she'd held at Selene all these years was nothing. There must have been something much bigger at stake for her cousin to do the unthinkable. "Selene?" she whispered into the night.

Nothing.

Enda looked at the top of the rock. What could have driven Selene to suicide? Perhaps it had been the only thing left to do. Perhaps it had been simpler than trying to live.

There was a little alcove at the base of the rock where you had to duck under an overhang and then climb a steep, rocky slope, hang onto elbows of rock and the tough vines that grew near the path. Her feet slipped on sandy slopes, but she curled her toes in and grasped the rock. She wondered if this was the way Selene had come up last night, and why, so soon after calling her and saying she was coming to the city.

She'd forgotten how steep it was. By the time she gained the top of the path, Enda's shoulders burned, her feet were cut and scratched and the knees of her pyjamas were torn. She lay on the bare rock for a few minutes to catch her breath. Then she pushed herself up on her hands, got to her feet and took a few steps toward the edge.

The night spread out before her. The stars cascaded to the

distant horizon. Dead Rock town was all black, with just a few pinpoints of light to relieve the shadow. You forgot, in the city, that there could be darkness like this, or silence broken only by the wind, the hoot of an owl and the whirr of the crickets. She couldn't tell where the drop was. She edged forward. Tried to imagine Selene standing here, hurting so bad she felt no other option than to jump, but she just couldn't. Selene had never in her life just given up. Would never jump. Enda knew it as certainly as she knew the edge was somewhere near her toes.

She inched forward and watched the distant horizon. The faintest ribbon of grey washed the edge of the sky. The stars began to fade. The grey ate up the darkness and turned to a brilliant red that bled from horizon to horizon. The molten tip of the sun set the red on fire.

She'd never seen the sunrise from here. It was beautiful, the way the light crept from horizon to town, unveiled Dead Rock and kept travelling up. The sunlight hit the rock, defined the edge and covered her toes in cold scarlet light.

The sensation of flying whispered through her mind. Wind like a knife. Impact, face first into the ground.

Enda jerked back to herself. She shivered. She shouldn't be standing on the edge of a cliff fighting sleep, but it was too late to go now without being seen. She could hear footsteps coming up behind her. She stayed where she was and watched the sunrise fade and the sky turn pale blue.

The footsteps came to a stop beside her. "You alright?"

Enda turned her head. A woman stood next to her. She was probably in her late fifties, from the smattering of crow's feet around her eyes and the sparse streaks of grey in her long black hair. The planes of her face were hardened, as though life had dealt her some blows, but she didn't look angry about whatever it was. She wore a long green cotton skirt and a black t-shirt with the red, yellow and black Aboriginal flag printed on the front.

"I'm fine," she said.

"You wanna be careful up here," the woman said. "One more step and you'd be a goner."

"I wasn't planning on jumping." Enda tried not to snap the words, or to be too irritated at having her thoughts interrupted while she was in her pyjamas on a cliff top.

"Sometimes you don't have to be." The woman kept her eyes on the horizon. "What's your name?"

"Enda." Enda took a step back from the edge and turned away from the brightening sun.

"Enda? Enda Wilson?" the woman screwed her eyes up and looked closer. "Aren't you Leo's daughter that took off with her mum?"

"Yeah, that's me."

"Come back for your cousin's funeral?"

"Yep."

"Figures." The woman scowled at her. "Best you don't come up here anymore. Hate to see another Wilson go."

A touch of sarcasm in her voice made Enda flinch.

The woman walked in the other direction.

"Wait!" Enda hurried after her.

She turned back.

"Did you know Selene?"

"I met her once or twice. She was alright." She looked down at Enda's clothes.

Enda grabbed her coat shut over her pyjamas. "What's your name?"

"Molly." Molly hesitated for a moment. Her voice was defiant when she spoke again. "Molly Wilson."

"Molly Wilson?" Enda paused, confused. She'd thought she knew all her relatives.

"Never told you, did they?" Molly came a few steps closer.

"Told me what?" Enda saw herself, momentarily, reflected in Molly's eyes; a tiny figure with a white streak in her short hair, a midget city girl out of place and time.

"You won't tell anyone else."

Enda recognised the command in the words. She nodded.

Molly jerked her head. "Come on then." She continued walking away.

Enda ran after her and fell into step. She kept her eyes on the ground, watching out for rocks or bits of glass that might hurt her feet.

Molly only spoke when they were well away from the cliff top and picking their way down a wide, steep slope covered with dried grass and spindly trees. Honkeynuts slipped underfoot. Black cockatoos screeched at them from the tree tops. Already the heat was rising, and with it clouds of black flies.

"Should wear shoes out here," Molly said.

"I didn't have time to put any on."

"Why not?"

"I-" she hesitated. Then she matched Molly's earlier defiant tone. "I got freaked out. I thought there was a ghost in my dad's house."

"Ghosts always freak you out?"

She thought about Ivy. "Not always."

"I'm your aunty, Enda Wilson."

The words were so abrupt that for a moment they didn't sink in. When they did, Enda stopped walking. "What?"

"You heard me. What's the matter, you don't want a Noongar for an aunty?"

"It's not that." Enda searched for the right words, not wanting to offend. "How come Dad and Uncle Con never said they had a sister? How could they not tell us?"

"I was adopted is why." Molly leaned against the nearest tree and folded her arms.

"That's not a reason to pretend you don't exist." Enda cast her mind back, thinking hard about all the things she'd learned in school, adding up the dates. She knew Leo and his brother had grown up in the fifties and sixties, so Molly must have grown up with them. Words she'd barely understood in high school rolled through her mind. Assimilation. Stolen Generation. Concepts so far removed from her own experience they were little more than a historical oddity. She didn't even know how to frame the question. "Molly were you – were you –"

Molly waited, not making the question any easier.

"When you were adopted-" Enda hesitated. Maybe she shouldn't even be asking, but somehow it had become very important in the last three minutes to find out.

Selene's voice echoed down the telephone line at her. *What's happened is our whole family is really fucked up, okay?*

"I never knew any other family when I was a kid," Molly said. "Just the Wilsons. I didn't even know I was a Noongar for years."

"Were you taken from your real family? Like with the Stolen Generation?" There. The words were out, awkward as they sounded.

"Not like, Enda. I was. I was stolen."

They looked at each other. Bees hummed in the dandelions. Flies clung to their shoulders. It was getting too hot for a long coat and pyjamas. Enda could smell her own sweat. A bush rustled and a long black skink darted past them.

"Go home now," Molly said. She pointed down the hill. "Road's just past those trees. Remember your promise."

She walked away.

CHAPTER FOUR

Enda placed her feet carefully on the gravel, heel first, then toes. Rocks skittered. A twig stabbed her left heel. She was glad to reach the bottom of the slope, even if it did mean she was out in the open where anyone could see her. She stopped to check her heel and make sure it wasn't bleeding.

"Hello," a voice said.

A girl of around Enda's age squatted under the trees nearby, poking at the few remaining coals of a campfire with a stick. There was a rumpled sleeping bag and a rucksack by the fire. The girl had dreadlocks and skin tanned from being outdoors a lot. She wore an old cotton dress that had seen better days and no shoes.

"Hi." Enda approached her, uncertain. "What are you doing?"

The girl flashed a grin. "Hiding."

Enda sat down across the fire from her. "Really?"

"Yeah. The cop in this town is a prick." The girl poked at the coals one more time, then heaped sand on them. "I'm Sahara," she said.

"I'm Enda."

Sahara watched over Enda's shoulder for a minute. "What are you doing out here?"

Enda shrugged. "I'm on my way home. Listen do you need a place to stay? You can't just camp out here."

Sahara shook her head. "I'm leaving today. I know when I'm not wanted. That cop's got it in for me, you know."

"Why?"

Sahara gave her a furtive look. "I didn't do anything."

"Of course not."

"I thought maybe if I came here I could camp out and not bother anyone."

"Don't you have anywhere to live?"

Sahara's lip trembled, but only for a second. She tossed her head and gave Enda a big, defiant grin. "I don't need a house. That's just like a big cage. I need my freedom. I'm gonna go east."

"Are you sure you don't want to come over? Just for a little while? I could make you breakfast."

Sahara reached out. Her fingers hovered just over Enda's heart, not touching. The space around them was icy cold.

Enda's neck prickled.

"You're kind," Sahara said. "But you're different. You'll be next."

"What do you mean?" Enda tried to move away from her, but her feet were like lead. She felt cold, so cold.

"He's coming," Sahara whispered.

Enda looked over her shoulder. "Who?"

When she looked back Sahara was gone. There was no campfire, no sleeping bag, nothing but an icy space in the hot morning. She got to her feet and backed out of it. When her heels encountered warm bitumen she bolted across to the sand on the other side of the highway, glad the road was empty. She skirted a flat area where big black bull ants hurried in and out of a hole an inch big and stopped to look at her tyre marks from yesterday. She gave the rock a furtive glance, but there was no woman in red under the cliff and no homeless dreadlocked ghost.

A short, sharp burst of police siren split the emptiness. Great. Just great. Enda looked down at herself. Crap. Bare feet and pyjamas, he was going to think she was nuts. She tightened the coat around herself.

Uncle Con pulled over to the side of the road and got out of the car. He leaned back on the door, arms folded, watching her. He jerked his head at the road in a clear signal to come back.

Enda looked longingly at the bush, the way home. Damn. She wondered if Selene had found the man just a little suffocating. She shuffled back to the road. Grains of warm sand crunched between her toes. Sweat trickled down her back. Black cockatoos screeched up near the rock.

Uncle Con took off his hat when she reached him and wiped sweat off his forehead. His scalp was red. The line between his eyes made him look like a pissed off wombat. "Get in the car," he said.

"Why? I was just going home."

He eyed her jacket. Enda realised it had fallen open again. She blushed.

"Get in the car."

No arguing with the Sergeant. Enda got in the back seat. She watched the buttons and cords and the big black radio until Con started the car and pulled onto the road.

The rock slid by. She glimpsed the little white cross. She caught her breath, because there was Selene, but a minute later there was nothing there. She watched until the cross was out of sight.

Uncle Con only spoke when they'd left the shadow of the rock. "Leo called me an hour ago," he said. "He got up and couldn't find you anywhere. What were you doing?"

Enda heard the crack in his voice. She bit her lip. She could have left a note or something before she left. If the house hadn't looked like a serial killer. "I couldn't sleep," she said. "I just wanted to visit the cross. Pay my respects."

"That's what funerals are for." Con's voice was harsh.

Enda flinched. Tears sprang to her eyes. "I'm sorry."

He shook his head. "It was just–yesterday morning–she was out of her bed that early too. I thought maybe you-"

"I would never." Enda wondered how the hell she could cut this nightmarish conversation off right there. He didn't need it and she didn't want it.

"Just do me and your dad both a favour and stay away from Dead Rock," he said. "It's dangerous."

Enda pressed herself back in the seat. She wished he'd hurry up and drop her off. "No offense Uncle Con, but I'm all grown up now and I do know how to look after myself. I don't need everybody telling me I can't visit the rock."

He glanced over his shoulder at her. "Everybody? Who else were you talking to?"

Oops. Her promise. But she'd only promised not to say anything about Molly's adoption, so that was okay. She wondered if he'd admit to it himself, if she nudged enough.

"Who else?" Con had an edge to his voice.

"Just this woman I saw at the rock earlier," she said. "Her name was Molly. She was as twitchy as you about the place."

"You met Mad Molly?"

"That's a pretty unkind thing to call someone."

There was a short silence. The car cruised down the street towards her father's house and pulled up in the driveway. "Stay away from her too," Con said.

"Whatever, Sergeant." Enda slammed out of the car and stormed up towards the house. The peeling paint and cracked windows looked shabby in the morning light, but not frightening.

Con's door slammed too. He caught up with Enda by the time she had her hand on the door. His boots landed heavily on the spongy veranda. "Just you wait a minute, young lady."

Enda's heart thudded in her chest. She'd always been a little bit scared of Selene's dad. So had Selene, for that matter. It wasn't easy being the Sergeant's niece or daughter. Then she remembered what Molly had said. The fear turned to disgust. "What?"

"Are you and me going to have a problem?"

Enda turned all the way around to face him, her fingertips still touching the door. She almost threw everything Molly had told her in his face, but she'd promised. "Are you threatening me? Like you threatened my mum the day we left? Is that the kind of person you are, Uncle Con?"

He flushed an ugly shade of red. The floorboards creaked loudly and the silence stretched out.

Leo yanked the door open behind her. "Enda, there you are," he said. "What are you doing out there? You coming in, Con? I'd offer you a beer, but she tipped them all out last night." He stomped back down the hall.

"You tipped his beer out?"

"I haven't seen my dad since I was fifteen, I don't want to come home to a drunk."

"You're very like your mother." Con took his hat off and nodded at the hall. "Come on. I don't know how much longer these floorboards are going to hold us."

Enda went inside and straight to her room, where she put on jeans and a blue tank top, brushed her hair and made herself presentable. Then she went back into the kitchen, where Uncle Con cut a formidable figure in his blue police uniform, sitting across from Leo. By the looks of it they were drinking coffee. A third cup waited for her.

Enda sat down at the end of the table. She didn't like coffee, but she pulled the cup toward her. "Morning Dad."

Leo looked better today. He'd shaved again, brushed his hair and tied it back in a ponytail. His clothes were wrinkled, but clean. "Con said you went to Dead Rock."

Enda made a face into her coffee. "Don't you two have anything better to talk about than me?"

Leo's fingers trembled slightly around his mug. He wasn't as together as he looked, then. It was early days, Enda reminded herself. It would take more than a few hours for forty years of hard drinking to make its way out of his system.

"I was worried," he said. "I mean, I figured you must be pretty shocked by what happened, and after what your mother told me-"

Enda put her cup down hard. Scalding liquid splashed onto her fingers. "What the fuck did she say, Dad? Honestly-"

"Language, young lady," Con said.

"Don't you language me, Uncle Con. You two seriously need to lighten up."

"I've seen this kind of thing happen before." Con's glare didn't let up. "A young person commits suicide and others follow. Nobody wants to see another spate of copycat suicides in Dead Rock, Enda."

Enda shuddered as though he'd tipped a bucket of cold water over her head. How could he even talk like that, barely a day after Selene's death?

"Why did you go there?" Leo's voice was gentler than Con's.

Enda would have liked to tell him about the ghosts, about the house at 3am and the wind in the grass, but not in front of Con. Ivy chose that moment to brush up against her legs and yowl. She looked from one man to the other, but they gave no reaction. She shrugged. "I couldn't sleep," she said. "So I went to put a flower there. On the cross. Then I went up to see the sunrise."

"You went to the top?"

Oops. Shouldn't have said that. Enda sighed and matched Con's accusing stare. "Yeah, I went to the top. It's a good view. You ever seen a sunrise from up there? It's like the sky is bleeding."

"Nobody's fool enough to go up there but Mad Molly," Con said. "Just stay down here. You don't want to become a statistic."

Leo looked into his coffee and said nothing.

"She didn't seem mad to me."

"You didn't see her up there talking to herself then."

"No, she talked to me."

"What about?" Con's tone was studied, too casual.

Enda shrugged. "She told me not to go up there."

"Then maybe you'll listen to her," Leo said. "If not your uncle."

"How can you be sure Selene jumped?" Enda bit her lip, but the words were already out.

Con stared at her. "What kind of a question is that?"

"I just want to know. How do you know she jumped? I mean, it seems a bit strange, when she rang me that morning and said she was coming to the city. She sounded upset, maybe scared, but not suicidal. What if there was someone else up there?"

Con's knuckles had gone white. "She rang you? When? What did she say?"

"It was about 3am. She said something was really wrong and she was leaving, right then, and coming to stay with me. That's it." She reached down absently to scratch Ivy.

A fleeting look of relief crossed Con's face. Leo stared into his coffee as though he could turn it into beer through pure willpower.

"Well?" Enda knew she sounded demanding. She didn't care. "Does that sound to you like she was suicidal?"

"Selene had some problems." Con rubbed his temples. "If you'd been around, you would have known, maybe even helped."

Enda fidgeted with her cup. "It's unlikely she would've listened to anything I had to say. What kind of problems?"

Con turned his right arm over to expose the thick veins in his wrist. He made a fist with his left hand and moved his thumb down as though depressing a syringe. His voice was strangled. Grief and rage seemed to be fighting to be heard, but he kept an iron grip on both. "My daughter was a drug addict," he said. "I found her one night injecting speed. I did everything I could to make her stop, to dry up her supply, but she always found a way around me. It took her over. Made her unpredictable. I know she was high when she jumped. She probably shot up right after she called you."

Enda's gut twisted. "I'm sorry," was all she could think of to say.

"So am I." Con got up out of the chair and put his hat on. "I should be going, I'm on duty. I'll see you both at the funeral tomorrow. Betty's looking forward to seeing you, Enda, there's something of Selene's she wants you to have." He walked out of the room.

Enda and Leo sat listening until his footsteps had faded and the front door had opened and closed. Enda wasn't sure she wanted to see Selene's mum, or get any of her things, but she supposed it had to be done. She got up out of her chair to go and pour the coffee down the sink and make some tea, but Leo laid a hand on her wrist. "Sit," he said.

Enda sat and scowled at him. "What, now I'm in trouble with you too?"

"No. I just want you to be more careful. Don't get caught outside in your pyjamas." He gave her a slow grin. "Con's always on the lookout for weirdos and hippies to either run out of town or commit to Doctor Howard's psych room. Don't be his next project."

"Howard? That old coot's still around?"

Leo chuckled. "That old coot is no older than your uncle or your dad, young lady, and yes he's still around."

"He always gave me the creeps. That's why I never got sick. What about my cousins, are they still in town?"

"Chris and Jake moved away, but they're back for the funeral. Alice is still in Dead Rock. The kids are in school now."

Enda sighed into her now cold coffee. "I can't believe she was using drugs," she said.

"Neither can most people," Leo muttered.

"What was that?"

"Nothing." Leo gave her a level look. "I'm sober. You promised me you'd tell me what was wrong in your life."

"Maybe later."

Once again, Leo laid his hand on her wrist. "Now," he said.

Enda looked at her hands folded on the table. They were cut and scratched from climbing to the top of Dead Rock. Her nails were ragged.

"Your mum said you were fired from your job," Leo said.

"Yeah."

"What happened?"

"You remember how sometimes when I was a kid, I'd talk to that old lady next door, and how Mum used to get upset over it?"

Leo rubbed his chin. "You mean the old lady who died before

you were born?"

"Yeah, her."

"I think I know where this is going."

"Well, you know I did nursing, right?"

Leo nodded.

"So I was working in emergency for a bit. I got used to seeing people come in in all states, drunk, on drugs, bleeding, broken bones, you know what it's like. Sometimes there were patients the doctors just didn't get to, but anytime I said something they told me I needed more sleep. One night this man came in. He just kind of staggered through reception and keeled over and bled everywhere. So much blood. I did what I was supposed to do, I got a stretcher for him, I called for the orderlies to help me, called for a doctor, but they all just stared at me and did nothing, and then this man started convulsing on the floor."

Enda paused and swallowed, hard. She couldn't stop a single tear making a track down her face. "I screamed at them to help. Everyone was staring. Then one of the psych doctors came down and I realised. Nobody else could see the patient because he was already dead. Maybe a long time ago. I couldn't begin to understand what I'd done until they stuck me in the psych ward."

Leo reached out and curled his fingers around her hand. "Wankers," he said.

Enda took a deep breath. "Yeah," she said. "Wankers. Lucky for me I studied all the right stuff and I knew what to do get out of there. But it was pretty much the end of my not so brilliant nursing career, not to mention my income and my self respect. Now Mum thinks I'm nuts and the doctors expect me to pop lithium like jellybeans. I was supposed to start some dumbass sales job Mum lined up for me yesterday, but then you rang. I was kind of glad to come back here, in a way."

Leo chuckled. "That's definitely not what she said happened."

"What did she say?"

"She said you had a psychotic episode and the doctors were treating you for acute bipolar disorder."

"I'm not bipolar." The words were close to savage. "You're the only person in the world who ever believed in the ghosts I saw, Dad. Mum just switches off if I so much as mention it, she'd rather I was mentally ill. And I never met anyone who could tell me how to tell the difference between the living and the dead."

Leo glanced around the kitchen. "Any ghosts in here?"

"Just Ivy."

"Ivy?"

"My cat. She got hit by a car a while back. Been hanging around ever since."

"You have a ghost cat?"

Enda grinned. "Yeah, I do."

Leo squeezed her hand. "That explains the meowing I heard last night. Don't you worry, girl, we'll find a way through this together, alright?"

CHAPTER FIVE

Enda figured the best way to make the time pass was to keep busy, so she sent Leo outside to brush the cobwebs off his lawnmower and cut all the long grass. Then she set to work inside with a broom and several garbage bags. Leda would have a fit if she saw the house looking like a squat.

By late afternoon the garbage bins were overflowing and the house looked almost decent, at least from the inside. The back yard looked less like a jungle and more like the yard she used to play in. Even her rusted swing set still leaned against the far corner of the fence.

Enda went out the front and saw Leo hard at work. All of the grass had been cut between the house and the gate. Now he wrestled with the last dense patches in the far corner. His shirt was soaked with sweat and a cloud of little black flies clung to his back.

Enda cupped her hands over her mouth. "Dad!" she yelled.

He turned off the mower, walked back to the steps and wiped sweat from his forehead.

"Yard looks great," she said.

Leo shrugged. "Yeah, s'pose. Could sure use a-"

"Nice cold drink?" she jumped to the bottom step. "Me too. And some decent food. Got any money?"

Leo scowled. "A bit. But it's for-"

Enda raised her eyebrows at him and folded her arms.

"Food. Fine." Leo stomped up the stairs. The floorboards on the veranda creaked ominously under his feet. He went inside and returned a few moments later clutching his wallet.

Enda nodded, satisfied, and got in her car. Leo got in the passenger seat and they set off towards town.

"What happened to your car?" she asked, to distract herself from the sight of the school around the corner.

"Lost my license," Leo said. "So I gave it to Selene to use." He looked at his hands. "They found it near the rock. I think Con took it to the station."

Enda turned the corner and passed the library. "I wonder which way it was pointed."

"Huh?"

"She was supposed to be coming to my place that night. I wonder if she was on her way when she went to the rock?"

Leo shrugged. "Could be. Best not to think about it too much, eh?"

"Why? I'd rather know every single detail so I could be sure of the truth. If it was me, wouldn't you want to know exactly what happened?"

"Stop it Enda." Leo's hand landed heavily on the dashboard. "Just stop it, alright? It wasn't you. It was her, it was suicide, that's the end of it."

"Geez Dad, take a chill pill." Enda jerked her car into a parking space at the front of the supermarket.

They got out and walked into the store. Enda picked up a basket and tugged on Leo's arm when she saw he was lost in contemplation of the bottle shop across the road. "Come on," she said. "What food do you eat?"

"Maybe I should just get a six pack for later." He took a step away.

"No! You promised me!" Enda tugged on his arm again.

Leo blinked a couple of times and turned back to her. "Sorry love, force of habit. Come on, let's buy some food."

They wandered the aisles and filled the basket. By the time they'd been around the whole shop, Enda had swapped the basket for a trolley. She wondered if her father was overcompensating for his lapse in attention by getting so much food. "Can you afford all this?"

Leo glanced into the trolley. "Yeah. It'll keep us going for a while, eh?"

"But how? You hardly work."

He shrugged. "Con looks after me."

Enda stopped the trolley right in front of a shelf full of breakfast cereals and gave him a look.

Leo tipped a massive box of chocolate-flavoured rice puffs in on top of everything else. "What?" he said.

"Does Uncle Con buy your alcohol?"

"Course not. He just tides me over when I'm short."

"And you take his money and use it to buy alcohol?"

The skin around the corners of Leo's eyes crinkled. He leaned closer to her. "Take a chill pill, Enda. Nothing wrong with a man having a drink."

Enda scowled and followed him to the counter with her trolley, where Leo paid for everything. They carried the shopping back to the car in boxes.

"We could go have a meal at the pub," Leo said, once again staring across the street. "They got a good cook there, you know."

"I'll cook." Enda got in the car and slammed her door. Leo took the hint and followed suit.

The short drive home was silent. Leo carried the boxes inside and Enda busied herself cooking them dinner while he went to finish the lawn.

After a while, the silence of the house eased the tension she'd built up watching the way her father had watched the pub. Amber light from the setting sun made the kitchen glow around her. A pot of spaghetti bubbled on the stove. She emptied tomato paste into the bolognaise mix. Footsteps entered the kitchen behind her.

"All finished out there?"

No answer. Enda glanced over her shoulder. The kitchen was empty. A cold prickle ran down her spine. She went back to stirring the sauce.

Movement in the doorway caught her attention. Enda glanced up just in time to see a flicker of blonde hair, blue eyes. The shape disappeared down the hall. She stood poised, the fork halfway to her mouth, her throat apparently unable to work enough to make a noise.

More footsteps.

Enda dropped the fork. She hurried to the door and looked down the hall in time to see the shape disappear into the back room.

She followed, but the back room was empty. The sunlight filtering in through the louvers had deepened to orange. Leo's half-finished drawings of the rock fluttered as though a breeze had gone through.

But the room was still. Enda walked very slowly to the door and opened it. She could see the whole back yard now the grass was cut. Over the fence a tall figure, silhouetted against the setting sun, cracked a cricket bat into a pole so hard the sound echoed in the room. Enda flinched, but couldn't bring herself to look away from the anger Uncle Con must keep hidden from everyone in the world.

He swung the bat around his head. This time the crack echoed like a gunshot.

Heavier footsteps came in behind her. If that wasn't Leo, then this house was even more haunted than she'd thought.

"I turned the stove off," Leo said. "The food was almost burned."

"Oh. Sorry." Enda turned away from the door. "Does he always do that?"

Leo glanced over the fence. "Not always. Come on, I'm starving." He headed back up the hall.

Enda followed and found he'd set out plates on the table. He'd stuck his head under the shower, too; his hair dripped on the floor. For just a second it felt like she was little again and the family was together and everything was just fine. She hid a smile and spooned singed mince into the plates.

They ate in silence. Enda watched her father inhale the food as though he hadn't eaten anything decent in years.

Only when his plate was empty did Leo speak. "So when do you go back?"

Enda wound spaghetti around her fork. "After the funeral."

"Right after? Or the next day? You don't want to drive back at night, do you?"

Enda shrugged. "You're probably right. I'll go back the next day."

"What to?"

She looked up from her food. "What do you mean?"

Leo rested his chin on his hands and watched her. "What are you going back to? It doesn't sound like you've got much going on in the city, except for living with your mum and doing a job you'll hate."

There went her appetite. She pushed aside her unfinished meal. "Who says I'll hate it?"

"I do. You won't last a day selling stuff."

"What's your point?"

"My point is, why are you so keen to go back to all that?"

She shrugged. "It's my life. I've gotta go back and restart it sometime."

"Or you could stay here."

"No."

"Just a bit longer." Leo pushed the plates aside. "Look, I know I fucked up, and I missed out on seeing you grow up for the last nine years. Give me a second chance, Enda. Just a few more days, or weeks, whatever you want. We could be good for each other, you know."

Don't get stuck in Dead Rock.

Enda pushed her mother's advice to the back of her head and stared at her hands. She was tempted. No sense in denying it. She didn't hate being here as much as she'd thought she would, and it was good to see her dad. "I'll think about it," she said.

"Good. Good!" Leo took the plates to the sink and began washing up.

Enda decided it was time to shower and go to sleep, no matter how much she was dreading the darkness in that room. She was so tired after last night, maybe she'd just sleep right through and remember nothing.

"If I do stay longer," she said, "will you keep your promise and not drink?"

"I'll keep my promise," Leo said. "So long as you keep talking to me."

*

The rusty old swing creaked back and forth. It was the only sound. The sky was white with clouds, the road to Dead Rock was empty and not a bird or an insect could be heard.

Enda let the gentle motion of the swing lull her. She was so tired.

A second regular creaking joined the first. Enda turned her head. She hadn't even noticed there was a second swing until now. Selene sat in it, hands wrapped around the chains. Long, untidy blonde hair framed her thin face. She wore a red dress, the kind of lacy, delicate thing she'd always liked to wear, a dress that looked as fragile as the woman herself.

"Hey," she said, and the fragility fled.

Enda recognised the hard-headed, bitchy teen she'd known in this full-grown waif. "Hi Selene."

They sat there for a while and rocked the swings. The clouds moved slowly across the sky.

"Is it true?" Enda finally asked.

"Ask him." Selene pointed through the playground fence.

Enda followed the direction of her finger. A man wearing old-fashioned braces and a big, brimmed hat stood underneath the rock, looking up. "You see him now?" she said.

"You have to go back to the rock." Selene stood up and went to the gate. It creaked open with the same noise Enda's swing made.

Enda followed her out of the playground. They walked along the road and into the shadow of the rock. Selene was just out of reach. Enda quickened her pace and reached out, but Selene's dress evaporated at her touch.

Then they sat in the long grass in the front yard of Leo's house. Selene ducked low, as though hiding. She stared straight through Enda. "He's coming for us."

Enda looked back at her. Selene's blonde hair flowed from a fleshless face. The skull whispered again, and the bones wearing the red dress gestured at the road.

"He's coming for us."

Enda sat bolt upright, panting. The night was hot and close. Invisible claws kneaded the blanket at her feet. Ivy purred.

She slowly calmed her breathing. There was a mile of darkness, a terrifying void, between her and the light switch. She didn't need a clock to know it was 3am, the time Selene had first called her.

She dived under the covers, buried her head under the pillow and prayed for morning to come.

CHAPTER SIX

Enda woke up late with a ghost cat asleep on her back and a good deal of pillow stuffed in her mouth. She removed the pillow and rubbed her eyes. Ivy jumped to the ground and trotted out of the room.

Enda squinted at the sunlight pouring through the window. Finally, she'd managed to oversleep. She stumbled out of bed, remembered it was the day of the funeral and put on the long black dress she'd brought for that purpose. It was a tailored, expensive thing Leda had given her. She normally wouldn't have worn it in a fit, but it seemed right for a funeral. She dabbed on some makeup and went out to the kitchen, feeling almost human except for the growling in her belly.

She stopped halfway across the kitchen. Leda sat at the table with Leo, sipping coffee. She wore a black dress not unlike Enda's and her hair was swept up into a smooth coif. Her makeup was immaculate.

"Good morning Enda," she said. "I was just about to come and wake you."

Enda looked down at herself. At least she wasn't in pyjamas, but her mother only had to be in the room to make her feel scruffy and underdressed. She went and sat down. "Morning." She looked at Leo. He just shrugged and poured her a bowl of chocolate-flavoured breakfast cereal.

"Is that what you're eating?" Leda tapped the silver-painted nail of her index finger against her coffee cup. "It looks revolting."

Enda pulled the bowl towards her. "Mmm, chocolate for breakfast. Thanks Dad."

Leda lifted an eyebrow, but declined to comment further.

"Mum what are you doing here?" Enda swallowed a mouthful of cereal. The sugar woke her up quickly.

"I came for the funeral sweetie, I told you I would."

"You said you'd try."

"Well, I did. Here I am."

Enda ate in silence and watched her parents trying not to look at each other. At least Mum had arrived while Dad was sober. It would make things a lot easier. "What time's the funeral?" she asked, when she'd finished and pushed her bowl away.

"Soon." Leda looked Leo up and down. "Shouldn't you go get ready?"

"I am ready." Leo ran a hand over his hair, which was brushed and tied neatly back. He wore a new-looking flannel shirt and a pair of black jeans.

"You look like a bogan."

"You married me." Leo didn't look the least bit offended. In fact, Enda could have sworn he was enjoying the conversation.

"I also divorced you. Go and put a suit on."

"Don't own one."

Enda put her face in her hands and groaned. "Don't even start, you two. Dad, at least go and put on a black shirt, okay? Mum, the rest of what he's wearing is fine, lay off."

"Selene never had a problem with flannel." Leo left the kitchen.

"Finally." Leda fixed Enda with a piercing stare.

Enda groaned a second time. "What?"

"I saw Conrad on my way in."

"What a surprise. I hope he apologised for what he said when he last saw you."

"Don't be silly, the man hasn't a single social skill. I'd be surprised if he even knew the word sorry."

Enda snorted. "Yeah, sounds about right. What about it?"

"He told me he found you wandering the streets in bare feet and pyjamas yesterday morning."

Oh God.

"So?"

"So he was worried. Sweetie, have you been taking your medication?"

Enda cleared her plate and the empty coffee cups from the table and took them to the sink. She turned the tap on hard and washed everything with as much noise as possible. When she finished, Leda was still watching her.

"Have you been taking your medication?" she repeated.

"I'm not crazy."

"No, you're not crazy. You were diagnosed bipolar, it's a mental illness and it's treatable. You need to take the medication to prevent any more episodes."

"I see ghosts, Mum. That doesn't make me bipolar." Enda wished she hadn't said it as soon as the words came out, because Leda just looked more and more serious.

"There's no such thing as ghosts," she said in a low voice.

Leo saved her from getting into deeper trouble by returning at that moment wearing a black button up shirt with a stiff collar.

"Better go then," Leda said.

Enda grabbed her bag and followed the two of them outside. Leda's four wheel drive was parked behind Enda's car. Enda got in the back seat. She watched her father sit in the front, staring at the newness of the car and the bells and whistles. "You've done alright for yourself," he said.

"Yes. I work for a living." Leda started the car and they reversed onto the street.

Enda watched Dead Rock go by. She ignored the frosty silence in the front seat. It was only a short drive to the church. It was a short drive anywhere in this town. They pulled up outside the stone hall of the Anglican Church. The Wilson clan as a whole weren't exactly religious, but of the three churches in Dead Rock, this was the one they were most likely to go to when one of their number got married or died.

Leda parked under the trees across the road. Enda got out of the car and looked at the church through the overhanging branches of a young jacaranda. The building was neat and well-kept; lavender bushes grew in border gardens down the sides and leafy trees shaded the windows.

Leo's hand landed on her shoulder. "Okay there?"

Enda nodded and swallowed. She generally preferred not to enter churches, an issue neither parent had ever forced. She glanced over her shoulder. Leda was busy locking the car. "Help me out Dad," she whispered. "If you see me talking to someone who's not there, just give me a signal. Shake your head or something."

"Gotcha." Leo gave her shoulder a brief squeeze.

"Come on then." Leda passed them and crossed the road. She didn't look particularly happy about being here either, but there were no surprises there. Who really wanted to face an entire crowd of in-laws you'd long since walked away from?

Leo and Enda caught up to her and they walked into the church as a family.

Enda dropped back a step. The minister, an elderly man with glasses and a white comb over, waited at the door that led from the foyer to the hall. He greeted Leo and Leda and then pressed Enda's hand. He peered at her closely. "Enda?" he said. "I haven't seen you since you were quite little. So sorry for your loss."

Enda nodded and disengaged herself, but going into the hall was hardly an escape. Most of the pews were filled with the semi-familiar faces of the extended Wilson clan. Some she knew instantly, others were complete strangers. Several children leaned over the back of one of the middle pews, whispering to each other.

Leda went straight to an empty pew near the back and sat down. She motioned for Leo and Enda to join her.

Enda patted her on the shoulder. "Just a minute, Mum." She couldn't take her eyes off the gleaming white coffin at the front of the church and the red and white roses spilling out of it.

"Enda no," Leda whispered, catching her wrist. "You don't want to go up there and see that. You don't know how it could affect you."

Enda tugged her wrist free, annoyed. The people in the next pew turned to stare. She looked at her feet, at the gold-patterned, threadbare carpet, and went up the aisle. She was grateful to feel Leo right behind her.

The closer they got to the front of the church, the more people there were. Enda spotted Alice, Selene's older sister. She was blonde too, but that was the only resemblance. Her face was lined and she wore a heavy black skirt and top that put twenty years on her. Three kids sat around her, looking pale and teary. She nodded at Enda, then looked away.

Doctor Howard sat in the third pew back. He looked serious. He'd run the local hospital forever. Not much changed in Dead Rock. Selene must have been a patient. Or maybe he was here for Uncle Con, they'd been friends a long time.

Selene's brothers sat together. Chris she only recognised by the scar on his left hand, a legacy of a snakebite he got before she was born. Jake she knew instantly. They'd been on good terms for years, because outcasts always understood each other. She gave him a little wave. He smiled at her, even though he was crying.

Uncle Con and Aunty Betty sat together in the front pew, holding hands. They got up when Leo and Enda approached. Betty smothered Enda in a hug that smelled of lavender and gin, then burst into tears on her shoulder. "It's good to see you Enda," she said between sobs. "I'm glad you came, Selene always talked about you, she missed you."

Con pressed Leo's hand, but neither man spoke a word. Engaged in removing herself from Betty, Enda glanced at them and caught a look from Leo that made her pause. She could have sworn it was a look of intense dislike he directed at Con's back.

Con turned to her and gave her a brief, awkward hug. "It would have meant the world to Selene to know you came," he said.

Enda squeezed his hand. For all the man could be overbearing, he'd lost his youngest daughter and she figured he must be hurting badly. "I'm so sorry," was all she could think of to say.

"Did you want to–" He glanced at the coffin. "They did a good job. It just looks like she's sleeping." He put his arm around Betty and led her back to the pew.

Enda moved, alone, up the two steps and over to the coffin.

Selene lay peacefully amidst white satin and lace. She held a bouquet of white roses in her hand. More red and white roses were heaped around the coffin. Her eyes were closed and her lips curved upward in the tiniest of smiles. She wore a long blue skirt and white blouse and her hair was carefully arranged on the pillow.

Enda laid her fingers gently on the edge of the coffin. Selene's wrists and the underside of her arms were exposed with the way she held the flowers. They were smooth and clean. No track marks. But then, she'd dealt with enough overdoses in her short time at the hospital to know track marks could be hidden on other parts of the body. Uncle Con knew what he was talking about. He'd been a cop forever.

A sensation of ice cold crept down her neck. She shivered. A set of neatly manicured fingertips rested on the edge of the coffin alongside her hands. Selene looked down into her own coffin with a thoughtful expression. Her hair wisped over her face. She wore the familiar red dress.

Enda supposed she should have expected this.

"I do look like I'm sleeping," Selene said. "Huh."

Enda looked back at the body. It was very quiet around her. She was afraid to look at the church in case everyone else had disappeared.

"The clothes are awful." Selene sounded petulant. "You don't ever think to just say, hey Mum, if I die, let someone else pick what clothes I'll get buried in."

Enda flinched. This was the Selene she remembered, the bitchy one, but the barbs weren't aimed at her. Still, she didn't dare speak, not with Con and her mother both watching for slip ups.

"Come on Enda, I know you can see me." Selene turned her back on her corpse, leaned against the coffin and folded her arms.

Enda glanced at her, then put her head down again and spoke to the satin. "Why didn't you come to my house, like you said?"

"Because I died. Duh."

"Why would you jump?"

"Why would I?" Selene leaned close and spoke in her ear. "Go back to Dead Rock. Find out for yourself."

Enda closed her eyes. The cold spread from her ear to the side of her face, until her skin felt like brittle ice, ready to crack at any moment. "Go away," she breathed.

The air grew uncomfortably warm. When she opened her eyes Selene was gone. The murmuring in the church was just as it had been. Nobody seemed to realise anything at all had happened.

Enda went down the steps. Leo was nowhere to be seen, so she went down the aisle to where Leda was sitting. "Where's Dad?"

"I think he went out for a smoke." Leda patted the seat next to her with an almost pleading expression. "Sit with me, Enda. Please."

"Sorry Mum. In a minute, okay?" Enda hurried out of the church.

She found Leo down the side, crouched against the wall in a cloud of cigarette smoke. He watched her approach. "You didn't say I couldn't smoke."

Enda sank to the ground next to him. "You don't smoke that much anyway."

"Yeah, well, you didn't tell me your mother was going to turn up like this."

"I didn't think she would." Enda studied her blunt fingernails. A minute ago she'd been busting to tell Leo about seeing Selene, but now she couldn't find the words. "Are you okay with it?" she said instead.

He shrugged. "Dunno."

They lapsed into silence for a while. The cigarette smoke curled around Leo's head. Enda wrinkled her nose at the smell.

"See any ghosts yet?" Leo stubbed his cigarette out on the church wall.

"Yeah." Enda pushed herself off the ground. "You know Mum thinks I'm nuts, right?"

"I know." Leo got to his feet. "Don't be too hard on her. She's scared. Come on, let's get this over with."

They went back in the church and sat in the pew with Leda just as the service began.

Enda sat between her parents, self-conscious about the cigarette smell clinging to Leo, watching her mother's expression out of the corner of her eye for the slightest hint of disapproval, watching the various members of her extended family to try and catch some hint of what they were thinking. The minister's speech about death and heaven went right over her head. Try as she might, she couldn't pay enough attention to understand a word. His voice was underlaid by Aunty Betty's quiet sobbing.

She wondered why Selene wanted her to go back to the rock. She'd do no such thing, after everyone came down on her so hard last time.

The minister stepped aside and Alice walked up to the pulpit. Her face was streaked with tears and pinched with nerves. She glanced down at a sheet of paper in front of her and back at the church. "I was going to talk about Selene's life," she said. "Because I know how important my sister was to every person here, but I–but I–" a tear streaked down her face.

Enda swallowed a lump in her throat. She felt sorry for Alice, who'd never liked being the centre of attention, or standing out in any way. The longer she stood there, the more terrified her cousin's pale face became.

Alice took a deep breath. "It's not fair!" her voice cracked, wavered and came back strong. The words rang through the church. "It's not fair that she did this to her family! She was so young, so pretty, she could have done anything, but she just threw it all away! Look, I know I'm supposed to say something nice about her, but it's the truth. She had no right to just end it like that!" She burst into tears.

Uncle Con hurried up to the pulpit, put an arm around Alice's shoulders and led her back to the pews. Alice's sobs echoed through the silent church. She pulled away from her father, ran down the aisle and disappeared. Betty followed her after a few moments. Enda could hear the muted sound of the two of them wailing outside.

Leda dabbed at her eyes with a tissue. Enda stared at her hands, embarrassed and sad. At least Alice could grieve. She didn't think she was going to be able to do any such thing so long as Selene kept hanging around.

The minister stepped back up to the pulpit and cleared his throat. "Some family members have prepared a slide show of happier memories," he said.

The lights dimmed. The screen hanging on the wall at the front of the church lit up, flickered, and filled with a picture of Selene in a long red ball gown. Letters filled the screen; *Selene Violet Wilson, October 22 1986 to January 17, 2008.*

The photo dissolved and was replaced by a series of baby photos. Selene grew before Enda's eyes into a toddler, then a little girl with blonde hair all the way down her back. Soon she was blowing out candles on a tenth birthday cake. Enda spotted herself in the background, dark-haired and awkward against the bright birthday party colours. Then there was the first day of high school, Selene in her crisp new uniform. These photos reflected the cousin Enda remembered best. She was always pretty in a red dress or a neat uniform, but with a sulky set to her mouth and something a little cruel in her eyes.

There were graduation photos, photos with boys Enda barely recognised from school, photos at parties where she grew older, skinnier, blonder and more made up.

The last photo showed Selene in the same red dress her ghost wore. She was still pretty, her hair still waved in all the right places, but she had dark circles under her eyes and she smiled at the camera with the tight expression of somebody wishing they were anywhere but there.

The screen went dark. The minister started a prayer. Enda closed her eyes and tried to pay attention, or at least look a little religious, but it was no good. She opened her eyes. All the heads in the church were bent. Selene was a faint shimmer near her casket, incorporeal, watching the show.

Enda nudged Leo to let her out. She climbed past him and hurried out of the church.

The sun outside rippled through the trees, baked the cars lining the road, wilted the flowers in their neat little beds. Enda took a deep breath of hot air. She was relieved not to see Alice and Betty anywhere. Maybe they'd gone back inside.

She leaned against the cold stone of the church wall, closed her eyes and savoured the temporary solitude. Crows cawed from the shelter of a jacaranda growing on the corner. The repetitive notes soothed her.

"Hey look, it's Enda the world."

Enda's eyes snapped open. God, it was the bitch twins from hell, Selene's friends from school, come out of the church. Both brunettes, supremely confident in their early twenties, acting like they still ruled the playground. "Bite me," she said.

The brunette who'd spoken shrugged, turned her back and walked away. Her sister hesitated. "Sorry about her," she said. She extended a hand. "It's nice to see you, Enda."

Enda hesitantly shook the fingertips. Both girls withdrew from the contact quickly. "You too." She couldn't remember this one's name.

"I guess the circumstances could have been better." The girl looked at her feet, but made no move to follow her sister. "You know Selene really missed you after you left?"

Enda shrugged. "People keep saying that. She didn't really feel like a best buddy in school though, you know." It didn't feel right to be any more specific than that at a funeral.

"But that was all fun. She didn't mean any of it."

"It wasn't much fun for me."

The girl shrugged. "Yeah, well, it doesn't matter now, does it? I just can't believe she did what she did. Nobody ever would have guessed she was that depressed."

Enda tilted her head. "Depressed? Did she have anything to be depressed about?"

"I think her dad was really down on her about stuff, but other than that, who knows? She never really told anyone what was going on at home."

Enda looked past the girl's head at the crows, who were cawing louder. "Did she use drugs?"

"God no!" the girl sounded shocked. "I mean, I dunno, she might have smoked a little pot, but that's hardly enough to go jump-" she stopped. Tears trembled on her eyelashes. "I'm sorry," she said. "It was nice to see you, Enda." She ran after her sister.

"Yeah, you said that," Enda muttered.

More people trickled out of the church in ones and twos, then in larger groups. Leo joined her at the wall and pulled out another cigarette, but quickly put it away again when Leda swept past. They followed her to the car.

Leda's mouth was pinched when she unlocked the doors. "I presume the two of you are going to be good enough to not wander off and leave me alone at the cemetery? I know we haven't been a family for a long time, but I really, really don't feel comfortable taking on the entire Wilson clan on my own and I would appreciate a little support."

"Cemetery?" Enda swallowed hard.

"Yes, Enda, the cemetery, that's the way funerals happen." Leda tossed her bag into the car and jammed the key in the ignition. "Are you two going to get in?"

Enda took a step away from the car. She'd last visited Dead Rock cemetery when she was ten. It had been a crowded, horrible place she'd fled from when too many ghosts pressed in, all demanding her attention at once. Selene hadn't spoken to her for a month and she'd never gone near a cemetery again. "I'm not going."

Leda's mouth tightened still more. "If you give me any more of that ghost rubbish, I swear to God, Enda Wilson, I will call your doctor right now."

Enda's face went hot. She was awfully tempted to scream something vile at her mother, but people were already looking and Leda would never forgive her.

Leo laid a hand on Leda's arm. She looked down at the hand like it was an insect. "Leda, just give me and Enda a minute," he said.

Leda scowled, got in the car and slammed the door.

Leo put an arm around Enda's shoulders and walked with her to the nearest shady tree. Around them, cars reversed and drove away in a well-rehearsed mechanical ballet.

Enda sat down under the tree and stared at her hands. Leo sat next to her.

Enda rubbed at a scratch on her knuckle. Leda's hands were never scratched. She never knew how her mother stayed so well-groomed.

"You know this isn't easy for your mother," Leo said.

"That's funny, because she only has to deal with the Wilsons," Enda said. "I have to deal with the Wilsons and practically everyone who ever got buried in Dead Rock if we go there."

"Everyone?" Leo sounded intrigued. "Don't any of them, you know, move on?"

Enda shrugged. "I dunno. It just seemed like a lot last time I went."

"You scared?"

"No. Yes. I don't know, I can handle one ghost at a time, even two. Big crowds of them are something else."

Leo was silent for a moment. "Selene told me about the time you two went to the cemetery," he said.

"When did she tell you that?"

"Last couple of years, we got to be drinking buddies. She was alright, Selene. She came over to get some breathing space from Con and Betty and give me some company. We used to talk about you a lot."

Enda played with the black fabric of her dress. She wanted to cry, but she choked the feeling back. "I'm sorry," she said. "You must miss her."

"Yeah, I do." Leo plucked a blade of grass. "You don't have to go to the cemetery, Enda, not for your mum or me. But maybe you could go for her. Could make it easier to say goodbye."

Enda was silent. She wasn't so sure Selene was going to accept a goodbye from her just yet.

"And if you do, I'll be there every step of the way," Leo said. "If it's too much, I'll get you out of there and deal with your mother, too."

Enda leaned her head against the smooth bark of the tree. The road was filled with the stench of departing petrol fumes. "In other words, you want me to get my butt to the cemetery like everyone else."

"Yeah, I do, but I'll give you an out if you need it."

CHAPTER SEVEN

The cemetery had the greenest grass in Dead Rock. It was so thick Enda's shoes sank into it at every step. You had to follow the little white markers to stay on the path and walk between the rows of graves. There were more people dead than alive in this town, always had been.

At the front of the procession Uncle Con, Selene's two brothers and five other men bore the closed coffin on their shoulders to the deep, deep hole prepared up ahead. Enda walked between her mother and father at the very end of the crowd, shutting her mind to the babble of voices. She didn't think the noise came from the Wilsons. When she snuck a glance, they all seemed to be wrapped in their own grief, not talking to each other, or yelling, or laughing.

She'd never heard a ghost laugh before. That was enough to make Enda sneak a glance to the right. She saw a kid running alongside, hopping up and down and making faces at a supremely oblivious Leda. She scowled.

The child caught the scowl. Her eyes got big and she ran away.

Shit. Now they knew. Enda returned her eyes to the grass but only a few minutes later, she heard a voice that made the hair on her arms stand on end.

"You go away. We don't need your kind around here."

Enda clenched her jaw and refused to look. He was a ghost. He couldn't do a goddamn thing.

"Hey! I'm talking to you!"

The voice was right in front of her. Enda shuddered violently. She'd just walked right through a man with a bleeding head and a cricket bat. See? He couldn't hurt her.

"Are you alright dear?" Leda asked.

"Fine."

"I know you can hear me!" he roared from behind. "You can't ignore me! I told you to get out!"

Well what did he want, her attention or for her to run away? Enda clenched her fists and thought about coming back when the cemetery was empty to give him a piece of her mind.

A cold wind brushed her back. Great. Now he was swinging that bat at her. "Hey!" he yelled. "Hey, girl, look at me when I talk to you!"

"Piss off!"

Enda's breath hissed out between her teeth. The shouting stopped behind her. Selene shoved in between her and Leda.

"Don't worry about him," Selene said. "He's got issues."

Enda nodded.

"You know you've got to talk to them. You can't just ignore us all forever."

Enda wondered how to explain, sometime, that she just couldn't talk to ghosts in front of her mother unless she wanted the woman shoving lithium down her throat.

"Hey! There's my grave!" Selene sounded quite pleased at the prospect.

The Wilsons formed a circle around the graveside. Interspersed through the family and crowding around the edges, an assortment of ghosts watched with interest, poked each other, made comments and generally acted like this was the most interesting thing to happen all week. Cricket bat man stood on the other side of the open grave, making nasty faces through the blood pouring from his forehead and tapping the cricket bat against one hand.

The minister said a prayer over the grave, but Enda was too far away to hear.

"Christ, it's not very cheerful, is it?" Selene said.

"It's a funeral," Enda said through her teeth. "What do you expect?"

"What's that dear?" Leda plucked a sprig of rosemary from a basket being passed around.

"Nothing Mum." Enda took a sprig of lavender and passed the basket to Leo.

"Yeah, but come on," Selene said. "Listen to that old coot, would you? Valley of the shadow, blah blah blah, what does he even know? I'm not in a valley and I'm definitely not weary. These people don't even know how to have a party!"

Enda winced; Selene had screamed the last word. The other ghosts pointed at her, but not one Wilson so much as twitched.

Selene giggled. "Sorry. I always wanted to yell that at them. And now I can, it doesn't even count. Come on, Enda, can't you liven things up a bit?"

Enda walked toward the grave so she was out of Leda's hearing. "No," she hissed. She dropped her lavender on the coffin. It floated down to join the pile of flowers lying there.

"Christ, you're as boring as the rest of them."

Enda watched four men take hold of the ropes and pulleys. Slowly, smoothly, the coffin was lowered further into the grave.

"That's creepy," Selene said. "I wonder how they'd like to see their own coffin shoved in the ground like that? So they can put you out of sight and just forget about you?" Her voice rose.

"Selene," Enda said. "What else do you expect them to do?"

Alice, who had been standing at the edge of the grave, turned around abruptly. "What's that supposed to mean?"

Enda stared at her in shock. Her heart thumped. Her cheeks flamed.

"Tell her it means her mum," Selene whispered in her ear. "Tell her to piss off and stop pretending to be so bloody superior just because I died. She's as bad as Dad, sneaking around my stuff and telling him anytime I did anything bad."

"Nothing." Enda backed away from Alice's glare and pushed her way through the crowd.

"Chicken." Selene dogged her every step. "Come on Enda, let's blow this shit off and go to Dead Rock."

"No." Enda spotted her parents standing at the edge of the crowd, not talking to each other as usual, and made her way over. "Can we go now please?"

"God yes." Leda looked relieved. "I'm working early in the morning, I need to get back."

They'd only gone a few yards when Uncle Con caught up with them. Enda gave a tiny sigh and waited.

Con shook her mother's hand and kissed her on the cheek. "Leda, it's good to see you," he said. "I know Selene would have appreciated you coming. Will you all be at the wake?"

"The wake?" Leda detached herself from Con as though she'd touched something poisonous. "I really don't know Conrad, I have to get back to the city."

"It would mean a lot to Betty to have you there," Con said, as though she hadn't even spoken. "Leo, you're coming?"

Leo nodded. "Course."

"And you, Enda?"

"Blow it off," Selene hissed. "Unless you want to watch our dads get drunk and my mum crying all over the place."

"I'll come," Enda said.

Selene gave her a dirty look and walked away.

Enda breathed a sigh of relief.

"Good, good. We'll see you all at home in ten then." Con went back into the crowd.

Leda headed toward the car with as angry a walk as her high heels would allow. "One hour," she said. "That's it."

*

Uncle Con's house hadn't changed much over the years. It was always immaculately kept, from the roses in the front garden to the spotless floors and gleaming tiles. Enda supposed Betty had little else to do, since she'd never worked.

She stuck close to Leo. Not drinking was going to be tough for him here. The living room was the biggest room in the house, but it filled up quickly. As far as Enda could tell everyone there was very much alive except for Selene, who sat on the table in the middle of the salads and plates of cold chicken and glared at her.

Enda ignored her. She stuck with her parents and avoided Alice, who also glared at her at every opportunity. People milled in groups around the room, eating and drinking. The noise level quickly grew uncomfortable. Time crawled.

Aunty Betty wove her way through the crowd towards them after a while, looking pale, but at least not crying now. "Leda, so good to see you," she said. She kissed the other woman on both cheeks and left lipstick marks. "Leo, you look well, Enda must be a good influence. Enda would you come with me for one minute, please?"

She couldn't refuse, so Enda got up, hoping her mother's

presence would be enough to keep her father from drinking.

Betty seized her hand and led her through the crowd. Selene followed them.

Enda breathed easier once they were in the hall and the noise was muted. She followed Betty past several closed doors and into the room at the end, which still had Selene's name glued over the door in fancy pink letters. The final e had fallen off years ago. Selene had replaced it with permanent marker and been grounded for it, but the letter remained.

Betty sat down on the neatly made bed and put her head in her hands. She took a deep breath. "I'm sorry sweetheart, this is really difficult for me."

Enda sat next to her and patted her on the back. She'd never had a problem with Betty, really; nobody did, because mostly nobody noticed her.

Selene wandered around the room and reached out for things, but her fingers never quite touched.

Betty finally got up and opened the top drawer of the dressing table. "I thought you might like to have something to remember Selene by," she said.

"Tell her you want the massive dooby I rolled last week. It's in the shoebox under the bed," Selene said.

Enda snorted and quickly turned the sound into a cough.

Betty took a small velvet box from the drawer and held it out to her. "Con gave this to Selene when she graduated high school. It was precious to her. Take good care of it."

Enda opened the box. Inside was a big, polished amethyst pendant on a heavy silver chain. The purple jewel shone and sparkled.

Selene appeared at her shoulder so suddenly she jumped. "You can throw it off Dead Rock for all I care," she said, and there was so much bitterness in her voice Enda almost dropped the box then and there.

"Thanks Aunty Betty," she said. "I'll look after it."

"Good girl. Come on, we'd best get back." Betty opened the door and they went down the hall.

"Poor Leda," Betty sighed, before they reached the door.

Enda stopped. "Why?"

"Anyone can see how uncomfortable she is. Maybe I should

sit and talk with her a while. We used to be friends, you know."

"She'd probably like that."

They went back into the crowded lounge room, which now seemed even noisier. Enda slipped the box into her bag. She quickly lost sight of Betty and suddenly found herself passed from one cousin to the next, each one wanting a hug and a kiss and a long conversation about how terrible it was to lose Selene that way, or worse, what Enda was up to nowadays.

When she finally detached herself from a particularly emotional second cousin, Enda bumped into Alice. She sighed inwardly.

Alice looked her up and down. Her face was pinched and unhappy. "I'm surprised you came back," she said.

Enda looked back at her and didn't answer. She didn't think Alice had ever liked her. Neither she nor Selene had fit her definition of normal.

"You haven't changed." Alice brushed a hand through her hair. "Why won't you say something? You were all talkative at the cemetery. Still babbling away to our imaginary friends, are we?"

Enda made to step past her, but Alice blocked her way. She leaned close and spoke in a low voice. "I hope you're going back to the city soon, Enda Wilson, because this is hard enough for the rest of us without having to deal with Selene's freaky little friend hanging around."

"Tell her to piss off," Selene said in her ear.

"Bite me." Enda pushed past her.

"Hey! Don't you talk to me like that!" Alice grabbed her shoulder.

Another hand grabbed her other shoulder. "Lay off, sis," said a calm, slightly amused voice. "She's done nothing to you."

"Why don't you go and have another cheap wine, Jake. I'm sure her father could pour you one." Alice turned her back and walked away.

Jake Wilson's hand tightened on Enda's shoulder when she tried to run after her. The rest was fine, but the comment about her father made her want to slap the woman silly.

"She's just grieving," Jake said. "Don't mind her. Alice is never nice to anyone."

Enda sighed and turned to face him. Jake had filled out from

59

the skinny teen she remembered, but not much. He had the muscles and deep tan of someone who worked outdoors, but he also looked pinched, like he didn't eat enough. His dirty blonde hair was scruffy and needed cutting. His good black clothes were too big for him. "Hey," she said. "Thanks for the rescue."

"Anytime. Wanna get out of here?"

Enda looked at Alice's retreating back, at Uncle Con drinking and talking loudly with the doctor, at the knots of now slightly drunk Wilsons all yelling at each other to be heard, at her father boring a hole in the nearest bottle of wine with his eyes and her mother checking her watch every thirty seconds while Betty tried to carry on a conversation with her. "Yeah, I really do," she said. "Just give me a sec." She headed over to her parents.

"Enda!" Leda looked immensely relieved. "There you are. Listen, we really need to go now."

"You go Mum, I'm just going for a little walk with Jake to catch up. I'll see you back at Dad's."

Leda   sighed.   "Fine,   don't   be   long."

Enda put her hand on Leo's shoulder. "Dad, why don't you go home with Mum. It'll be easier."

Leo flushed and looked guilty. He tore his gaze away from the wine bottle. "Yeah, alright then."

Enda crouched in front of him. "You're doing really well," she said.

Leo shrugged. "Whatever you reckon."

"Go home with Mum now. Promise me."

"Just don't be too long. She does my head in."

Enda grinned. "Deal."

*

Jake drove a rusty white ute that rattled violently on every corner and pothole. It was hot inside and the air conditioning didn't work, so they wound the windows down all the way and drove away from Con's house as fast as they could.

"What's with the hair?" Jake adjusted the mirrors while he was driving and shoved a Billy Idol CD in the player.

"It grows on my head. Happens to most people." Enda checked her reflection in the side mirror, just in case, but her hair looked normal.

"That blonde bit. You look like Cruella de Ville."

Enda made a face at him. "I just felt like it, okay? What's with you, anyway? You look like you've been living on the street."

"Can't live on the street so long as I've got my car," Jake said. "I travel a lot these days. Get jobs in different towns. I like it. Makes me hard to track down."

"Hard for who?"

Jake turned a corner. "Dad," he said, after a pause. "Kinda hard to breathe around him these days, or hadn't you noticed?"

"Yeah, I noticed." Enda watched Dead Rock get closer and closer. She thought maybe they were going to the other side of town, but Jake parked in the shadow of the cliff.

"Thought we should give her a proper send off," he said, and got out of the car.

Enda got out too and leaned on the bonnet. She looked up and up and up at the top of the rock. "What kind of send off?"

Jake went straight to the base of the rock and disappeared up the steep path.

Enda thought she saw a man on top of the rock, looking down. She couldn't make out much about him, except for his old-fashioned hat. She frowned, trying to remember where she'd seen that recently, then followed Jake up the path.

Climbing it by day, with shoes on, was marginally easier than at night wearing pyjamas. The dress didn't help. It was torn in three places before she was even halfway up.

Selene sat on the path ahead of her. "Nice," she said. "You won't come up with me, but you will with my deadbeat brother."

"I'm here aren't I?" Enda paused to catch her breath and then climbed the next part of the path, choosing with care where to place her feet and hands. More than one rock slipped away underneath her shoes and skittered all the way to the ground. Uncle Con was going to have puppies if he found out about this.

Selene was not on the path next time she looked. Enda pulled herself up over the last steep part. Jake grabbed her arm and hauled her onto the cliff top, where they sat and caught their breath.

Jake moved to a spot near the cliff edge. He sat down on the grass and stared out at the distant blue horizon.

Enda went and sat next to him. It was cooler up here. A crisp breeze whipped her hair back from her face. She closed her eyes and tried to imagine the vast space between the two of them and the horizon.

"It should have been me," Jake said.

Enda opened her eyes. "What?"

"It should have been me that jumped. Not her. She was the best of us, the one with all the talent, all the potential. The only one who had a hope of standing up to Dad." Jake rubbed his eyes like a little boy after crying.

Enda looked from him to the edge. She curled her hand around his arm as if she could hold him to the ground, and heard Uncle Con say something about copycat suicides in the back of her head. "You wouldn't do it Jake, would you? You wouldn't jump?"

"Why not?" Jake got to his feet and stood with his back to the cliff top, his arms spread wide against the floating sky. He tipped his head back. "She had the guts, why not me?"

Enda got up slowly. She felt sick. "Is this why you brought me up here? What's wrong, Jake? Why would you want to jump?"

"Why did Selene jump? Maybe she hated her life so much she just couldn't stand it anymore. Maybe she couldn't get away from Dad and jumping was the only way out of the prison. Maybe even when she got out she couldn't get away from fucking Dead Rock!" His voice rose to a shout. "Selene!" he roared at the sky. "Selene!" Then he collapsed to his knees and buried his head in his hands. His shoulders shook.

Enda approached cautiously. She put an arm around him and said nothing, because what could you say to pure grief?

After a while Jake calmed and they sat together on the cliff top. The sunset turned the grass crimson and cast the town below in shadow.

"I'm sorry if I scared you," Jake said.

"You'd better be." Enda nudged him. "Psycho."

Jake nudged her back. "That's charming, coming from the girl who talks to herself while climbing up a cliff."

Enda watched the colour of her hands change while the sunset deepened.

"I should've stayed," Jake said. "I should've been around to look out for my little sister, but I wasn't. I didn't have the guts to stick around, like she did. Maybe I could have made a difference."

"Nothing would have made a difference." Enda spoke the words softly, thinking about that first dream, where two people had struggled on a cliff top.

"I guess you never know." Jake got to his feet and held out a hand. "Come on. I'll take you home."

Enda shook her head. "I'll go in a while. I can walk from here."

"But it's getting dark."

She shrugged. "I know my way."

The wind caught Jake's hair and tumbled it around his face. He was framed in the fading light while he looked out at the horizon. "I'll see you then," he said. "Don't know when. I won't come back to Dead Rock if I can help it."

"Look after yourself, Jake."

He walked away. The twilight was so dim his shape was swallowed up in moments.

Enda watched the light fade from the sky. The air grew colder and pinpoints of light across the town appeared in an awkward counterpoint to the first stars.

Selene walked the edge of the cliff, arms out, balancing like a little girl on a tight rope.

"Why'd you do it?" Enda asked.

"Why did I do what?" Selene turned around and went back the other way.

"Jump."

Selene looked out over the cliff edge and swayed. She jumped back. "I don't know."

"What do you mean?" Enda got to her feet and stretched.

"I don't remember it," Selene said. "I mean, sure, I remember falling, and landing, that was pretty nasty. Then I thought I was okay, except nobody could see me. The other man told me I was dead. Said it happened to him, too. Bitch of a thing to happen first thing in the morning."

"Other man?" Enda began to follow her progress, up and down, but she stayed further from the edge. It felt like they were six and playing hopscotch again.

"Yeah, he's always here."

"Selene, why did you want me to come here?"

"Because I want you to find out what happened to me."

"And how am I supposed to do that?" Enda stopped walking up and down. "Who do you think I am, Nancy Drew?"

"Everything you need to know is here." Selene leaned out over the edge, reaching into the void, eyes closed. "Just let go, Enda, it's easy."

Enda took several steps further back from the edge. "What, are you trying to kill me now? Is that why you made me go off the road the other day?"

"That?" Selene balanced on one foot, right on the edge. "I just saw you and freaked. I don't really remember why. All I know is you have to let go so you can see what I saw."

It was completely dark. Enda's heart pounded. Selene's hair looked like mercury in the starlight. Her face was cold and hard. "Go away!" she yelled. "Stop it Selene! Leave me alone!"

Silence. Darkness. God, her parents were alone together and probably calling Uncle Con to go look for her.

Enda cursed under her breath. She'd intended to go back down the way Molly showed her, but the path was quicker. She dropped to her hands and knees and crawled toward it, then felt around until she found the top of the path. She dropped down onto the narrow rocky slope and skidded several feet. Her dress tore on a tree root. She grabbed at a branch to stop her slide, missed and scraped her palms across jagged rocks. Finally her feet found a flat spot. She jammed her arms into either side of the path and stopped, breathing hard. Pebbles rattled past her shoulders and down the path. The noise went on for a long time.

The darkness was thick. There wasn't a sound apart from the whirr of crickets to be heard, but Enda knew she wasn't alone. She hoped the eyes she could feel were Selene's and not some other faceless spirit who belonged to the rock. She couldn't go forwards for fear of tripping, or backwards for fear of sliding. What an idiot. She should have gone back with Jake. Something brushed her hand and she almost screamed. She'd been so caught up with ghosts she'd completely forgotten about spiders and snakes and centipedes and God knew what else that must live on the rock.

"Shit," she said aloud. Her voice wavered, high and uncertain, in the darkness.

Then there were footsteps up above. Enda buried her forehead in her shoulder. Sweat trickled down her neck. "Selene I'm not doing it," she said aloud. "Stop messing around and help me, will you?"

A bright light slid over her hands and stopped at her feet. Enda almost sobbed aloud, but she couldn't twist to see how Selene had found a light.

"Enda Wilson, is that you?"

Enda almost let go in shock at hearing a voice she knew was good and alive. More stones skittered under her feet and she steadied herself. "Molly?" she tried to keep the hysteria from her voice and failed miserably.

"What are you doing? Come up here right now!"

"Can't. I'm stuck." Enda followed the progress of the torchlight. It moved from her feet to the walls beside her and failed to spill into the darkness below.

"Look, you're standing on a ledge." Molly sounded impatient. "I'm shining the torch there, see? Just turn yourself around and face me."

Enda kept her eyes on the light around her feet. She shuffled around to face the other way and quickly grabbed hold of the sides of the path again.

"Right," Molly said. "You need to climb back up." The light came closer. Molly leaned over the top of the path, shining the torch down on the wall.

Enda found the handholds and pulled herself up the steep, twisting track, then dragged herself up the last and most difficult part of the slope. Her hands burned, but she gritted her teeth and didn't mention it, since Molly already seemed to think her enough of a nuisance. She grabbed onto Molly's hand and clambered back onto the top of the cliff. There she lay for a minute, catching her breath and trying not to think about what would have happened if she'd been found by anybody else.

When she opened her eyes she realised Molly wasn't alone. A young Aboriginal man stood watching them. He wore an old-fashioned, wide-brimmed hat, braces over a white shirt and grey shorts. Much more she couldn't tell in the dark, but she was sure she'd seen him somewhere.

"Are you crazy?" Molly said.

Enda sat up and scowled. "No."

"What are you doing trying to go down that path in the dark?"

Molly flicked off the torch, leaving them with only the light of the rising moon.

Enda was relieved. The torchlight had been hurting her eyes. "I didn't realise how late it got. I thought the path would be the quickest way home."

"Huh." Molly flicked the torch back on. "Come on then. I'll show you the way. Again."

Enda got up and followed the light away from the rock edge. "Who's your friend?"

Molly stopped dead and shone the torch light straight in her face. "Are you taking the piss?"

Enda squinted. "No. I was just wondering who that man over there was. I think I've seen him before."

Molly directed the torch at the ground and started walking again. "That's Tom," she said. Her voice sounded odd. "He's an old friend."

"Is he coming with us?" Enda couldn't penetrate the darkness around the torchlight anymore. She couldn't see where Tom had got to.

"No." Molly cleared her throat. "It was Tom who told me you were here. I thought I'd better come and find you."

"I appreciate it." Enda stepped carefully over a cluster of rocks. Something shone in the passing light. "Wait," she said, and crouched down.

Molly directed the light at the rocks. "What is it?"

Enda explored the rocks with her fingers, then the sand underneath them. She found a cold, sand-encrusted chain and pulled on it, but it wouldn't budge. She followed it to its end and moved aside a small rock to free it. Then she tugged free a small rectangular object.

Molly crouched next to her. "Is that a purse?"

Enda brushed the sand off the pink leather and unsnapped the clasp. "Yeah, it is. Weird. Wonder how it ended up here." She opened it up and plucked out a piece of paper lying on the top.

Molly directed the light at it. "What the hell?"

Enda stared at the scratchy black writing on the paper; *Enda,* it said, and underneath her address and phone number. Her hand trembled. She felt in the purse again and this time pulled out a driver's license, from which Selene stared, looking bored.

Molly dropped the torch. She scrabbled for it and retrieved it. "Take that home," she said. "Keep it safe."

Enda put the paper and license back in the purse and stowed it in her pocket with Selene's necklace. "I should give it to Uncle Con," she said. "Maybe then he'll believe –" she paused and squinted when Molly shone the light in her eyes again.

"Believe what? Conrad won't believe anything."

"She wasn't planning on killing herself that night," Enda said. "She was coming to see me."

"Come on." Molly got up and headed down the hill.

Enda ran to keep up with the bobbing light. "What, you don't think I'm right?"

"I know you're right." Molly skirted a tree and lit Enda's way past several thorn bushes. "I just don't think you should go to Conrad with it."

"Why not? He's her dad and he's the police, surely he'd want to know the truth."

"Just how well do you know your uncle?"

Enda followed the light in silence for a few minutes, thinking about this. She thought about Jake, standing at the cliff edge, arms out like he could fly. He had some father issues with Uncle Con, that much was obvious. Everyone in the family did, but surely, surely any father would want to know the truth about what happened to his daughter? If there was one thing Enda was becoming sure of, it was that Selene's death wasn't simple in any way.

Molly's voice cut through the dark. "Who were you talking to just before I found you up there?"

"Selene," Enda said without thinking. She pressed a hand to her mouth and almost tripped over a branch.

Molly stopped and sat on a fallen tree. She turned off the torch. Moonlight bathed a wall of thick, high bushes that hid them from the highway.

Enda sat on the cold sand in front of her. "I'm not crazy."

Molly shrugged. "Me neither, but that doesn't stop people from saying it. So how is Selene?"

Enda took a moment to work up a reply. She was too shocked at being believed to make her brain function. Then she had to think about how to answer. "I think she's confused," she said. "She doesn't remember why she died."

"She ask you to help?"

"Yeah, but then I think she asked me to jump off Dead Rock to find out what happened," Enda said. "It kind of freaked me out."

Molly appeared to mull this over. "She used to come and see me sometimes," she said. "Once she knew I was her aunty. She was alright." She picked up a stick and drew a picture in the sand between her feet and Enda's, a square house with a window and a door. Then she drew lines radiating out from the house. "I told her how I came to live with the Wilsons," she said. "I don't remember anything that happened before it. I was five, I think. Maybe six. I remember being in the back of a car. It was hot, and I felt sick, but I knew I wasn't supposed to talk or ask for my mum." Molly paused. Enda thought she was crying, but her voice came back on a harsher note. "Those two white people in the front of the car said my mum didn't want me anymore, so I was going to a new home. A better home, they said, where I would have a white family and learn how to work. They said I was lucky to be chosen to go to a family. I had to be good, they said, or I'd be sent to the mission instead."

Molly wiped the picture in the sand out with one swipe of her hand. "I was scared of those two. I still can't remember why. Maybe they were the ones who stole me from my mum. No matter how hard I've tried, I've never been able to remember anything else about it. I just remember how sick I felt. They took me to the Wilson's house in Dead Rock and left me there, and I was supposed to just be part of this whole new family." Molly stared down at her hands for a few minutes, saying nothing. "You'd best get home."

Enda got to her feet, not sure what to say. An owl hooted behind her. It must be very late, but right now Leda being mad at her seemed to be just that much less important. "I'm sorry," she said.

Molly made a sound that was half laugh, half snort. "Are you?" She shook her head. "You sticking around?"

"Maybe."

"Then come and see me sometimes. I live up there." She pointed at the top of Dead Rock. "Just walk back a bit. You'll find it."

"Alright. I will." Enda walked through the trees onto the highway. She checked both ways for signs of the police car before she came out of the shadows. When she was sure the road was empty, she bolted across and over the sand beyond. She didn't stop running until she reached the bush track. Then she had to go slow to try and pick her way over the path in the moonlight.

Molly's story tumbled through her mind while she hurried home. She prayed that at the very least, Mum and Dad would be there on their own and that they hadn't called Uncle Con.

CHAPTER EIGHT

Enda pushed through the gate. The house squinted at her through broken eyes. Leda's four wheel drive glowered down on her rusty blue Magna. She trod softly on the grass, as though by sneaking up she could lessen the impact of being this late.

The creak of the veranda underfoot sounded like a tormented scream. Enda pushed open the door. A cold wind brushed her legs and Ivy yowled. She bent down to scratch the cat, but as usual, her fingers met cold air.

Raised voices echoed down the hallway. Enda tiptoed forward. If Mum and Dad needed to have it out, maybe she could sneak past and make it to her bedroom before they noticed she was home.

Leda appeared in the kitchen door. Her face was flushed and wet with sweat. Strands of hair had escaped from her coif. "Enda? Is that you?"

"Yeah." Enda walked into the kitchen and dumped her bag on the table. "Sorry, thought I'd be back sooner."

Leo scowled at her from the opposite corner of the room. His hair fell loose and untidy over his face. A growth of stubble had appeared since morning, making it hard to tell if he looked angry or just untidy. "Where were you?" his voice was level.

"Out with Jake." Enda put the kettle on to boil.

"Where?" Leda demanded.

"Cuppa, Mum?"

"No I do not want a cuppa!" Leda's open hand landed hard on the table. "Enda I told you I had to go back early today, why would you stay out so late? Now I'm going to have to drive home for three hours in the dark!"

"You could have gone. I would have understood." Enda poured water onto a tea bag and heaped in sugar. She kept her voice nice and level in the hope things would simmer down in here.

"I was hoping you would follow me home."

Enda took her tea to the table and sat opposite her mother. "Why?"

"Because the job I organised for you is not going to wait forever. I told them you'd start tomorrow."

Enda took a sip of her tea and tried not to be too angry. Leda was only doing what she thought was the right thing.

"It didn't occur to you to ask Enda before you told them that?" Leo said.

Enda winced. He'd said exactly what she'd wanted to say, but it was entirely the wrong thing.

"Enda agreed to take the job," Leda said. "She's got to start work sometime. Enda, I want you to get ready to go when you've finished that drink. If you don't want to drive back in the dark you can come with me and your father can drive your car up tomorrow. *If* he can stay sober long enough."

"Shut up!" Enda made an involuntary motion with her hand and knocked her tea across the table. She jumped to her feet, got a cloth and threw it over the spreading liquid.

"Don't you tell me to shut up!" Leda went red in the face.

"No! I mean it Mum, shut the hell up!" Enda righted her cup and mopped at the table furiously. "I'm sick and tired of hearing bitchy little comments about Dad! He hasn't had a drink since I got here, alright? And I'm not coming back with you!" She paused, blinked at her own words. She didn't know she'd made the decision, but really, she couldn't possibly go back yet.

"What do you mean you're not coming back with me?"

Enda calmed her tone. "I'm going to stay in Dead Rock for a while. Maybe a couple of weeks. Me and Dad have a lot of catching up to do."

"I don't think that's a good idea," Leda said. "Sweetheart, you need to be close to a hospital. What if-"

"I'm not crazy!" Enda threw the dishcloth at the sink and missed. It splattered mopped up tea all over the floor. Her voice hurt from the scream the three words had ripped from her throat.

All the colour drained from Leda's face.

Enda took a deep breath and once again forced her voice into normal patterns. "Mum, I love you, and I appreciate you're trying to do the right thing, but there's nothing wrong with me. I'm not sick, I'm not crazy, I don't need to be near hospitals. I want you to back off and stop trying to control my life."

Leda looked past her to where Leo still stood in his corner, watching them. "This is your doing," she said. "You've been encouraging this ghost business to get her to stay. I knew this would happen."

"Don't talk about me like I'm not here," Enda said.

"It's alright." Leo shifted from his corner and went to stand next to her. Leda glared balefully at them both. "Enda will be fine here," he said. "You don't need to worry."

"Until your little dry stint comes to an end and she has to scrape you off the floor of the Dead Rock pub," Leda snapped. "No, I'm sorry, but it's out of the question. Enda, you're coming home with me."

"No I'm not."

Leda looked her up and down. "Look at you. Four hours on your own, God knows where you were, but you look a fright. Your dress is torn. Do you know how much that dress cost me?"

Enda smoothed over the tears in her dress as though she could make them disappear.

"And what have you done to your hands? And elbows?

Enda hid her hands behind her back. Leda was around the table in a second. She pulled an arm out and looked at the grazes on her palms. "Christ, anyone would think you'd been climbing Dead Rock in the dark!"

Enda's cheeks burned.

Leda stared. "That's exactly where you were, isn't it? And you say there's nothing wrong with you? Enda, honey, you've got to see sense and come home. You're going to end up a statistic, just like Selene!"

Enda snatched her hand back. "For your information, I went up there with Jake, and he was the one talking about jumping!" she yelled. "Give me a little credit, Mother!"

Leda rubbed her temples and retreated across the kitchen. "I'm sorry," she said. "I just can't deal with this right now. I didn't want to have to do it, Enda, but you leave me no choice. If you don't come home with me tonight I'm calling your doctor in the morning to check your medication. Maybe they need to increase the dose."

"Leda, that's enough." Leo's voice was rough and angry. "Listen to yourself. Our daughter is an adult who is legally entitled to make her own decisions about her medication and where she wants to spend her time. You need to back the hell off and get out of my house!"

"Enda!" Leda went, if possible, whiter still.

Enda folded her arms. "I'm with Dad on this one."

"So that's the way it is. Fine." Leda snatched her bag off the sideboard. "You know where I am when everything goes wrong."

Her back very straight and her head held high, Leda headed for the door. She stopped abruptly when a man cleared his throat. "Conrad," she said, her voice high and unnatural. "How long have you been standing there?"

Uncle Con stepped into the kitchen. His frame seemed to fill the room. He still had on his black and white suit from the funeral. "Long enough," he said. He nodded at Leo and Enda. "Just came to see if Enda knew where Jake got to."

"He left," Enda said.

Con shrugged. "Leda, I'll walk you out. I wanted a word."

"Fine." Leda cast one last death glare at Leo. "I'll be seeing you both." She walked out ahead of Uncle Con.

Enda exchanged a glance with Leo, who shrugged. She hurried to the doorway and peered around it.

Con stood over her mother at the end of the hall. A proprietary hand rested on her waist. "Don't worry, I'll keep an eye on her," he was saying.

She made a face at his back and returned to the kitchen, where she gave her dad a hug. "Thanks," she said. "I have no idea what just happened, but you were awesome."

Leo grinned. "You're really staying?"

"Yeah." Enda went to make herself a fresh cup of tea. She put coffee in a mug for Leo. "Is Uncle Con coming back?"

"Probably."

She added a third cup, sloshed in boiling water and milk and set them out on the table.

Con returned to the kitchen after a few minutes and sat with them. The flickering fluorescent light gleamed on his scalp. He sipped the coffee. "Your mum's pretty upset, Enda," he said.

"She'll get over it. We fight all the time." Enda wondered just how much Leda had told him. She hoped she'd retained her dislike of the man enough to not tell him about the hospital.

"But I really came over to look for Jake," Con said. "Enda you went off with him. What happened? Where did you go?"

Enda hid her face in her mug. "Dead Rock," she muttered.

Con went red. "What did I tell you about going up there?"

"Hey!" Enda held up a hand. "Jake wanted to go there, not me. He just wanted to say goodbye in his own way."

"And where is he now?"

"He left. He said he wasn't coming back."

The wrinkles between Con's eyebrows deepened. "He say anything else?"

Enda shook her head. She wasn't going to be the one to tell Con another of his children was bordering on suicidal because of father issues. "Oh!" she said, remembering. "I found something up there." She took Selene's purse out of her pocket and pushed it across the table. "It was under a rock, almost like someone hid it on purpose. I mean, you must have searched the area-" she trailed off. It wouldn't do to criticise his policing skills right now.

Con stared dumbly at the frivolous pink object in front of him. "What is this, Enda?"

"It's Selene's purse," she said. "Her license is in there. And my address and phone number. Take a look, Uncle Con, it could be important, right? It proves she was really intending to come and see me that night, not to – to go anywhere else."

Con didn't touch the purse. He looked from it to Enda. "How do I know you didn't put your address and phone number in there yourself to further some ridiculous theory of yours my daughter didn't jump? What are you trying to say, Enda? That she was murdered? You think that's going to make things any better? Maybe you think Mad Molly pushed her off the cliff, since she's the only other person who's ever up there?"

Enda's cheeks burned so hot they hurt. "Why don't you just go-"

Leo spoke before she could finish the sentence. "That's a bit harsh, Con," he said. "And that is Selene's purse. Why don't you take a look? I'm sure you'd recognise your daughter's handwriting."

Uncle Con grunted. He fumbled with the catch and upended

the purse on the table. The scrap of paper fell out, along with the license, a few coins, a bank card and a newspaper clipping.

Enda drew the clipping toward her. It was old and very yellow. It had a tiny black and white picture of an Aboriginal man in the corner. "Tom Nickel," she said aloud, squinting at the caption.

Leo took the clipping from her fingers and slid it back to Con, whose face had gone completely blank. "Evidence," he mumbled at Enda's questioning look. "Best not to handle it."

Con put the contents of the purse back together and then slipped it into his inside pocket. "I'll look into it," he said. "I appreciate you bringing this to me, Enda."

Enda looked from one man to the other, unsure what had brought on the sudden tension in the air. "Are you two okay?"

"I've got to go." Con scraped his chair back. "Maybe I can still catch up with Jake before he gets too far. Enda, stay away from Dead Rock. I'm serious. There's no need to go looking for trouble."

Without another word, he left.

Enda watched the empty kitchen door until Uncle Con's heavy footsteps had faded down the hall. She listened to the door click shut. "I wonder who Tom Nickel is?" she said.

Leo got up quickly and took the cups off the table. "I'll make some dinner," he said. "Would've done it earlier, but your mum was pretty keen on picking a fight with me. You know you should listen to Con, Enda. It's not safe to keep going up Dead Rock."

"Yeah, I got that." Enda studied the grazes on her hands, which were weeping. "Got any antiseptic?"

"Yeah." Leo disappeared for a moment and came back with a tube of antiseptic cream. "Show me your hands."

Enda waited patiently while Leo smeared cold salve into her grazes.

"How'd you get these?" he said.

"I tried to go down the path in the dark." She winced when the cream went into a cut. "Pretty dumb."

"Very." Leo gave her a hard look. "Tell me about this medication your mum keeps going on about. You been taking it?"

Enda rubbed her hands together to spread the salve a little more. "I flushed it down the sink," she said.

Leo chuckled. "I'm supposed to frown at you now and tell you you're bad, right?"

"Yeah, I guess." Enda sank into the chair. "I didn't like what it did to me."

"What did it do?"

Enda stared at her hands. The grazes were red raw. She remembered how her head had felt thick and everything had been so quiet. She'd gone home that first day and looked and looked for Ivy, but the house had been empty and silent. "I couldn't see the ghosts anymore."

"And was that a good thing or a bad thing?"

She shrugged. "I didn't like it much."

*

Selene walked up and down the edge of Dead Rock, her arms out for balance. Her fingertips trailed a sky the colour of blood. A pink purse dangled from one wrist.

Enda walked slowly towards her. "Come away from the edge," she said.

Selene looked right through her. Her face twisted with the old bitterness. She stormed away from the edge and pushed someone. "I know what you did," she said. "I'm never coming back here! I'll go where you can't find me!"

Enda looked around for the person Selene spoke to, but the sky blurred and she fell to her knees. When she looked down, she wore a lacy red dress and her hands were not her own. Below her knees was a dizzying drop. The red sky went on forever.

A hand clamped over the back of her neck.

"Just let go," Selene said, but the voice came out of Enda's mouth.

The hand shoved. Enda plunged into the sky, screaming.

She landed hard in her bed and sat upright, staring into the darkness of the room. The springs squeaked underneath her, swaying as though she really had just landed. The darkness closed in like a hand around the throat. Something gripped her shoulders. A lightning bolt of fear shot through her head, leaving her shaking all over. She didn't even know in which direction the light switch lay.

Enda took a deep breath. She clenched her teeth. "Get off me," she hissed. "Leave me alone."

The thing on her shoulders gripped her harder. A loud meow erupted from behind the curtain. The fabric parted and Ivy jumped onto the bed. Moonlight spilled into the room, illuminating the dark form of the cat.

Enda had never seen anything so beautiful. She leaped at the window and yanked open the curtains. Moonlight flooded the room in silver light. Ivy stood in the middle of the bed, pure black, arching her back and spitting. Another form fell onto the bed.

Enda pressed her back to the window and faced it. "Who are you?"

"Nothing," Selene's voice said from across the room.

Enda looked from the shadow to the wardrobe, where Selene leaned, studying her nails. She was immaterial in the moonlight. Enda could see the grain of the wood though her red dress. "What do you mean, nothing?"

The shadow moved toward her. Ivy hissed.

"Well, not nothing. It's one of the shadow things," Selene said. "They feed on fear and anger and guilt. It's lived in this room a long time. Probably since our dads were kids, or before."

Enda's heart thumped. The shadow grew bigger. The edge of its darkness crept toward her. She flattened herself against the window. Ivy's fur stood on end and she hissed again.

"See, now you're feeding it." Selene's tone was bored. "You've been feeding it every night you ever slept in this room. No wonder you were always so weird, Enda the World."

A flash of anger. She hated that name. "Shut up!" she hissed.

The shadow got bigger. It bled towards her knee.

"Go away!" Enda's voice broke.

"They hate light," Selene said. "And you're blocking the window."

Enda sprang away from the window. Moonlight streamed across the bed and the dark thing melted into the shadows. Ivy's fur went back down. Enda reached out a hand to stroke her. It was the first time she'd seen the cat since she was run over. Before, she'd always just felt and heard her. Her hand touched only air, but Ivy purred and rubbed her head on her fingers.

"It hasn't gone," Selene said.

"I know." Enda wrapped the blanket around her shoulders and sat on the bed, watching Ivy. "How come I never saw it before?"

"I dunno. I'm not your witchdoctor." Selene crossed the room and sat under the window. Moonlight filtered through her head. "They're everywhere, you know. You see them on bad people."

"Am I a bad person?" Enda put her arms around her pillow and hugged it to her like a shield.

"If you were a bad person, it could go everywhere you do," Selene said. "But you're not, so it only attaches itself while you're sleeping. That's when you're vulnerable. I've been watching it."

"How do I stop it?"

"Get a nightlight, dumbass."

Enda leaned back against the bed head. She closed her eyes. "How come you don't remember anything from that night, Selene?"

"Don't know."

"What if you weren't alone up there?"

Silence.

Enda opened her eyes. The room was empty. Moonlight spilled through the open curtains onto a black cat sleeping in the middle of the bed.

CHAPTER NINE

Sunlight poured into the bedroom. Enda smiled at the sight, because today was hers. No work, no funeral, no responsibilities. She could be reasonably sure Leda wouldn't be in the kitchen and if she was lucky she could dodge Uncle Con all day too.

Enda got up and dressed. She put on a little bit of makeup and brushed her hair into place. She felt so much better this morning, despite the awful dreams.

She paused and looked at the open curtains. They'd been closed when she'd gone to bed. Great. Unable to distinguish between dreams and reality, the psychiatrist would love that. A shadow on the bed, some awful, frightening thing that fed on her fear and anger. Nightmare. Surely a nightmare. If such a thing existed she'd have seen it before.

A black shape trotted into the room, jumped onto the bed and purred. Enda stared. "Ivy?" she whispered.

Ivy stretched out one paw and raked the air, then settled down again. Enda moved across to her and sat on the bed. She could see every separate hair, every whisker, even the placid expression in the eyes.

"Did you see the dark thing, Ivy?" she whispered.

Ivy licked her front paw.

Enda drew her legs up. When she was a kid she'd been convinced there was something under the bed. Maybe she'd been right. She shifted onto her belly and dropped down to look, but there was nothing there but dust balls and shadows.

So much for that.

She went out into the kitchen, but her father wasn't there. A hastily scrawled note lay on the table.

Called out for a job. Back for dinner. Stay out of trouble. Love Dad.

The chocolate cereal and an empty bowl sat on the table.

Enda poured herself a bowl of cereal and ate it dry, while standing at the window and looking out over the back yard. When she was done she found the texta Leo had used and scrawled a note back, although she was reasonably sure she'd be back before he was.

Gone to the library. Love Enda.

She grabbed her purse and headed out on foot, since it was a nice day. The library definitely classed as staying out of trouble. She wondered if Dead Rock had discovered the internet yet.

Two corners later, she walked through the sliding door–that was new–into the old stone building she'd haunted as a kid on the many occasions Selene wasn't talking to her. Inside was quite different to what she remembered. All of the shelves had been rearranged and a shiny new check out desk dominated the entrance. Apparently Dead Rock had discovered the internet, because there was a whole row of computers down one wall.

Enda hesitated. One of the bitch twins was behind the desk. Her name tag said *Skye.* That jogged her memory. Skye Thomas.

Skye leaned on the desk, apparently quite at home. "Hi Enda."

That was a promising start. She must have got the nice one. Enda tried a smile. It couldn't hurt to make friends, right?

Skye smiled back.

"Can I use a computer?"

"Sure. Just grab any one."

Enda headed over to the computers. Only one was occupied, and that by a teenage boy. She picked the computer furthest away from him, opened a search engine and stared at the screen, thinking.

Tom Nickel, she typed in, and pressed enter. The list of responses wasn't much help. She didn't want to hook up with Tom Nickel on facebook, and she didn't think a list of obituary notices from England was any help either.

There was nothing for *Dead Rock History,* and the only listing about the town itself was one paragraph in Wikipedia. Enda stared at the screen. Her fingers hovered over the keys. Really, she had no idea how to find out what she needed to know. She barely even knew what she was looking for, or how a man in an old newspaper had any connection to Selene's death. She didn't even know what question to ask to find the answer she wanted.

"You look stuck."

Enda jumped. She hadn't realised Skye was standing behind her, books piled in one arm, watching her stare at a blank screen. She spun the chair around to face the other girl. "Yeah, kinda."

"I'm here to help, you know." Skye put her pile of books down on a desk.

"Do you know who Tom Nickel was?"

Skye stared at the roof, thinking. "Tom Nickel. Familiar name. Did he go to our school?"

"No," Enda said. "He'd be old."

"I've definitely heard the name. No, wait." A little furrow appeared between Skye's eyes. "I could almost swear Selene was looking him up a couple of weeks ago. Hang on."

Enda followed her back to the desk, where Skye typed a name into her database. "Yeah," she said after a minute. "We've got a pile of old papers, essays and reports and stuff. There was this one report about suicides in Dead Rock. I remember now, Tom Nickel was the first recorded one. He jumped way back in the 60s." She went silent and pressed a hand to her mouth. "Oh my God," she said. "I never even thought about it. She must have been planning it."

"Do you still have that report?" Enda asked. "Can I see it?"

Skye shook her head. "It's checked out to Selene," she said. "She never returned it, but someone since put in a complaint about it, so it's restricted now until a review can be carried out."

"Restricted? Who made the complaint?"

Skye leaned across the desk and lowered her voice. "There's only one person in Dead Rock who could make a complaint like that and get a result. You tell me, who has that much influence?"

Enda thought about it. "Are you saying it was my uncle? Selene's dad?"

"Exactly. So why do you want it?"

"I just want to know what was going on in her head."

Skye looked unhappy with that answer. "Do you really think that's a good idea? People say Dead Rock's cursed. Something up there wants people to jump. Maybe it would just be better to leave the whole thing alone."

"Maybe," Enda said. "Or maybe someone needs to find out what really happened, on the off chance that knowing stops it from happening again."

Skye looked at her for what felt like a long time. Her face was blank, but Enda felt like the woman was trying to make a decision. Finally, her fingers moved over the keyboard again. "You got an email?"

"Yes."

"We have electronic copies of all those documents. I'm not supposed to, but I'm going to send it to you. You got a computer at your dad's house?"

"No."

"So give me your address. Then come back tomorrow and check your emails. And don't tell."

*

Enda walked away from the library as fast as she could. Her heart pounded against her ribcage, but not from the exercise. No, her brain had thrown at her a little scene from last night that she'd barely noticed at the time. She'd had that newspaper clipping under her fingers, she'd said Tom Nickel's name aloud, and everything had gone strange from that moment. Leo had taken it from her. Uncle Con had shoved everything back in the purse and brushed her off with some bullshit about looking into it. He wasn't going to look into it. He and Leo were keeping something from her, something important, something that had to do with Tom Nickel and with Selene.

The thought was like a punch in the gut. Things had been going so well with Dad. She'd thought they could make up for lost time. She'd thought she could trust him. Damn it. Well, she'd find out. She'd confront him when he got home from work.

She stopped in the middle of the footpath, insensible to the bees in the bottlebrushes next to her, or the traffic that crawled past. He'd evaded her questions about Tom Nickel even after Con left. And Con was dead against anyone knowing anything, apparently.

She started walking again. Maybe it was like Skye said, maybe they thought there was something up there making people jump, maybe they were just trying to protect her.

But that was stupid. People were trying to put her in a mental hospital for believing things like that. Which begged the question, what if there was something up there?

Enda rubbed her temples. She was missing something. She must be missing something.

A beat up old blue ford slowed and pulled in at the curb near her. The passenger window was down. "Hey," a voice said. "Hey Enda, you okay?"

Enda went over to the car and looked in the window. Molly peered back at her. Her long hair was tied out of the way and a bag of groceries rested in the back seat.

"Who's Tom Nickel?" Enda said.

Molly gave her the faintest of smiles. "You'd better get in."

*

Enda sat on the edge of a blue couch. All the furniture in the room was old and faded, some with broken springs and buttons, but the little lounge room was neatly kept and comfortable. A vase of pink geraniums sat in the middle of the glass coffee table and an Aboriginal flag covered one wall. The black, red and yellow dominated the room. Through the window all that could be seen was a thick stand of bush, where balgas grew in the spaces between the taller ghost gums. Beyond that, Enda knew, was the slope leading to Dead Rock. She'd glimpsed the cliff on the winding drive up the hill.

Molly returned to the room with two glasses of water. She placed them on the coffee table and sat in the easy chair across from Enda.

Enda looked at her hands, unsure what to say now she was here.

"Where'd you hear about Tom Nickel?" Molly said.

"There was a newspaper clipping in Selene's purse." Enda reached for her glass and held it between her hands. "I saw the name on it, but my dad and Uncle Con took it away before I could read it."

"Didn't I tell you to keep that purse to yourself?"

"I'm sorry."

Molly shook her head. "Maybe you'll listen to me next time."

Enda's cheeks burned. "So who was he?"

"Tom." Molly's voice softened.

Enda looked up quickly. She couldn't believe she hadn't made the connection already. "Tom? The man you were with up on Dead Rock? But I thought he was the first one to–"

Molly raised her eyebrows.

"Jump," Enda finished.

"He didn't jump." Molly's voice was so harsh Enda flinched away from her.

"But he is a ghost."

Molly just nodded. "And he's not the only ghost you see, is he?"

"No, he's not." Enda settled back into the couch. "What about you?"

"I just see Tom." Molly drew her legs up and sat cross-legged on the chair. "So this is awkward. I never met anyone else who could see him before."

Enda looked out of the window at the bush and imagined Tom wandering around out there, alone, on the cliff. "What happened to him?"

"I could answer that question, but it would take days," Molly said. "You can't start a story at the end."

"I've got time."

"Really?"

"I decided to stick around for a while in Dead Rock with my dad."

Molly fixed her with an unnerving stare. Finally, she spoke. "Everything I tell you stays between us."

"I can live with that."

"I'm serious. You can't go running to Leo or Con with this. You can't breathe a word."

"I swear, I won't tell a soul." Enda had no idea how a story could be this serious, but Molly didn't look like she was ready to be messed with on that point.

"Alright then." Molly settled back and half-closed her eyes.

*

1956

Molly was lucky.

All the grown-ups said so. How lucky she was to be adopted

by a good family, a family with money, so she could learn how to work and live properly.

She kicked the table leg.

Kick. Kick. Kick.

The sound was dull and rhythmic. Soon Mum Wilson would yell. Her yellow hair would fling about and her red lips would stretch back over her teeth.

Kick. Kick. Kick.

The yellow linen tablecloth was almost the colour of sand. When the grown-ups stopped telling her she was lucky, they'd say how she was too short to be much use yet. Her head barely reached the top of the table. When she took her hand away, there were finger-shaped smudges on the yellow cloth. Mum Wilson didn't like fingerprints.

Molly peered around the tablecloth. Mum Wilson was busy at the stove. She scrubbed everything until it was whiter than white, and told Molly all the time she'd learn to how to scrub too when she got taller.

There didn't seem to be much of a point to all that scrubbing. The boys would just come home and make everything dirty again.

Mum Wilson's back was like the fence around the back yard. It blocked out everything.

Molly made her footsteps soft, like she was walking on sand. Outside the kitchen, she took off the shiny black shoes, because Mum Wilson really liked them and would probably get mad if she took them away.

~

Dead leaves crackled under her bare feet. Cold, fresh air stung her face. Big black birds screamed in the trees high, high over her head. She didn't know what to call those big birds, or if they would come swooping down like the magpies at her real home. Didn't matter. She veered off the road and ran into the bush, because she could hear a car roaring up the road behind her.

Molly squatted under a Balga tree, in amongst the long, needle-like leaves. Her hands were the same colour as the burned trunk. She didn't think Mum Wilson was really her mum at all. Her hands were pink like the flowers that grew around the veranda steps.

She watched the car go by. It was all covered in brown dust.

The noise made the birds go quiet.

~

Molly's feet were coated in cool grey sand by the time she reached the road. It was all dirt, and went for miles and miles to somewhere else in both directions. She didn't want to go somewhere else. She wanted to go home, but she didn't know which way. She sat down by the roadside and stuck her knuckles in her mouth. Mum Wilson got mad if she cried, because she was lucky to live with a white family and had nothing to cry about, but Mum Wilson wasn't here. Her eyes watered. A tear made a track down her dusty face.

Across the road was a rock that climbed up and up into the sky, so high Molly couldn't even see the top of it. She tried and almost fell over backward. When she looked back at the road, there was a boy standing on the other side. He looked like her, but he was a little bit taller, and wore only a pair of grey shorts and no shirt.

Molly stood up and took her fist out of her mouth.

The boy reached out a hand and beckoned to her. Molly darted across the road. When the boy ran toward the rock, she followed him.

~

The boy climbed a steep, narrow path that went up the side of the rock, hidden from view of the road. He grabbed fistfuls of grass and clung to the rock like a big lizard. Molly copied what he did, determined not to say anything or to fall.

When they reached the top she was so tired and thirsty she just laid there for a little while watching the clouds sail past. She'd thought up here she might be so close to the clouds she could touch one, but they seemed as far away as ever.

Finally she sat up. The boy watched the sky out over the cliff. He didn't turn around, but he seemed to know she'd recovered. "What's your name?" he said.

"Molly." Molly inched closer to him.

"I'm Tom." Tom was all hunched up, his arms around his knees. "Where you from?"

Molly sniffed. Tears prickled her eyes again. "Don't know," she said.

"I come from out there." Tom pointed his finger at the

horizon.

Molly tried to see where he pointed, but there was just a long, long line of blue. "Where?" she demanded.

"Out there." Tom dropped his hand and shrugged. "But I got to stay here now."

Molly squared her shoulders. "I'm running away. I'm going home."

Tom looked at her with all the wisdom his extra two years could muster. "How you gonna go home if you don't know where you're   from?"

Molly glared at him. "I don't like it here."

Bright white teeth gleamed out of Tom's face. "Come on," he said. "I'll go too."

~

So many pale, chalky ghost gums climbed the slope it looked like the hilltop had hair. Molly's eyes were wide. She'd never seen forest like this. Tom held her hand. They were almost there when somebody shouted behind them.

They both turned around. Molly clutched Tom's hand harder.

"Who's that?" Tom said.

"That's my white brothers." Molly tugged on his hand. She wanted to get into the forest and hide until Con and Leo went away.

Tom understood. They both ran for the trees, but the boys were older and faster.

Leo hit Molly in the back before she even got to the first tree. When she saw Con tackle Tom to the ground she screamed. Tom yelled and bit him and the two boys tumbled around the slope, kicking and hitting each other.

Molly kicked Leo in the shin and bit his hand. She broke free, but he grabbed both her arms and held her so tight it hurt. She howled.

Con was twice the size of Tom. In the end he held him down and punched him in the ribs. Something cracked. Molly howled louder. All at once she was free, but she just fell to the ground and kept howling, because Tom was lying on the ground not moving and Con kept hitting him.

Leo raced over to Con and although he wasn't as big as his brother, he grabbed his arms and hauled him back. Molly couldn't hear what they said over her own wails.

Con kicked the ground and sent up a great spray of dirt. He directed a nasty look at her. "You shut up," he said.

Molly stopped instantly, in case Con took it into his head to start punching her too. She got up and ran towards Tom, but both boys grabbed her arms and carried her in the opposite direction.

*

Molly looked out of the window at the forest of ghost gums crowding the fence down the side of the house. "Best we get you home," she said.

Enda sat up, startled, disoriented. "What happened? What about Tom? Was he okay?"

"Yeah." Molly got to her feet. "Tom was tough, he never let Con really get to him. I saw him in school the next week anyway."

Enda followed her out of the back door, her mind racing with thoughts of Leo and Con as kids, of her Nan as a young woman yelling at a little girl she'd helped to steal. "Did you say they got you so you would work? That was all they wanted you for?"

Molly snorted. "What do you think? That's what they mostly took us Noongar kids away for. They didn't really care about making us white. They just wanted cheap labour."

*

Enda stared out of the car window all the way home, thinking about Nan taking a little girl from her family and training her up to be a maid. She'd grown up in that very same house, but all her nightmares had been different.

What's happened is our family's really fucked up, okay?

Enda sighed. They'd been almost Selene's last words to her, at least while she was living. Maybe this was what she'd been talking about.

"Did you tell the story to Selene?" she asked.

"Yeah. Yeah, I did." Molly turned from the bumpy gravel back road onto the smoother highway.

Enda watched the shadow of Dead Rock creep across them. "Do you think bad things that happen in a place leave, you know, traces?"

"What kind of traces?"

"Dark things. Things that want the same kind of bad thing to happen again."

"You talking about the cliff?" Molly turned down the road into town. The shadow receded behind them.

"Yeah. But more about things in my dad's house."

Molly thought about it for a few moments. "Maybe. Why do you ask?"

"I saw something new last night." Enda looked at her fingers. They were still scratched from her last climb up Dead Rock. "But it's kind of hard to tell sometimes if something's a dream or if it's real."

"Most things are real," Molly said. "You of all people should know that."

"But that's the question, isn't it? The minute I mention ghosts my mum calls in doctors and starts shoving lithium down my throat."

Molly laughed. "I was good friends with your mum a long time ago. Maybe she needs reminding she was a bit wild at your age too."

CHAPTER TEN

Enda walked home from town after stopping to buy a nightlight. There wasn't that much to choose from in Dead Rock's poky supermarket, but in the chemist she found a glitter lamp in the gift section that if nothing else would be pretty.

Molly's story made her look at Dead Rock through new eyes. It must have been different in the 1950s. The bitumen she walked over would have been all grey dirt and most of the houses not even built. All those neighbourhoods she walked through now had been bush.

She stopped at the front gate and looked at the ramshackle house. Pop had built it for his wife, for Nan, when she was pregnant with Uncle Con. It would have been new and immaculate when Molly was brought there. Now it was old and haunted with the memories of a little stolen child.

Enda stepped over the gate and walked across the grass. Going inside got harder every time she came back here, but she'd do it for her dad. She went carefully across the creaking veranda and made a mental note to talk to Leo about fixing it. Those boards weren't going to last another six months.

The front door was open, so Leo must be home. Enda went down the two halls to her bedroom to set up the lamp. She was vaguely surprised to find Leo not in the kitchen waiting for her. She checked the other rooms, but he was nowhere in them, either. She went last to the back room and found an easel set up with one of his Dead Rock paintings leaning against it. The painting itself hadn't changed much. Dead Rock dominated the canvas, a great black shadow. There were smudges of sky above it. What was new was the tiny human figure silhouetted against the rock, arms out, just like Jake had stood the other night when he'd talked about jumping.

Enda took a step back from the painting, unsettled. Leo

couldn't be far away, since the paint was still wet.

Raised voices caught her attention. She went to the back door, stood on her toes and looked over the fence. Dad and Uncle Con were yelling at each other in Con's back yard.

Oh God.

Enda bolted across the lawn. She squeezed through the gap between the end of the fibro fence and the crooked post and stayed for a moment in the shadow of Con's big olive tree. The light was fading, leaving the two men to argue in a greying twilight. Con was at least a head taller than Leo, and broader across the chest. Leo was too thin. He could never stand up to his brother in a fight.

But he had, Enda reminded herself. He'd pulled Con away from Tom Nickel when they were kids. Con had been twice his size then, too.

"She's old enough to know, she has to be told!" Leo yelled.

Enda tuned in to the fight, startled. They were talking about *her*.

"It's out of the question!" Con sliced a hand through the air, as though just by speaking, his word became law. In Dead Rock it probably did. "Think of what you're asking. Think of Betty and the other kids. We made a deal, Leo, you, me and Leda, and we're keeping it!"

"And look what it's doing to us!" Leo's fist clenched, but it stayed by his side. "What's going to happen when she finds out on her own like Selene did, Conrad? What then?"

"You don't let her find out on her own," Conrad said through clenched teeth. "You don't let her find out. She's unstable enough already, don't you think?"

"She's not unstable!" Leo roared. His face went scarlet.

Time to put an end to this. Enda crossed the distance to the two men swiftly, put herself between them and pushed them apart. Both of them, she was pleased to note, looked stunned to see her. "Quit it, the both of you," she said. "If you're going to keep secrets from me, it generally helps if you don't yell about it at the top of your voices."

"How long were you listening?" Con folded his arms.

"Long enough. Anything you want to share?"

"Just stay out of it, Enda."

Enda turned her back on him and put her hand on Leo's arm.

"Come on Dad, let's go home."

Leo cast Con a look of pure dislike. She didn't blame him. She could hardly stand to be within ten feet of the man right now. She glanced back once when they reached the fence.

A last ray of sunlight cut across the yard behind Con, lighting up his profile. On his shoulders sat a dark thing, a shapeless shadow. Somehow it had no beginning and no end, but it was bound to the man's form so tightly it seemed a part of him.

Enda squeezed through the gap in the fence and stumbled into her dad's yard. She leaned against the fence, breathing hard. Her heart hammered against her ribs. She was afraid to peer through the gap and see if Con and the shadow were both still watching.

"Are you okay?"

Enda turned her head to Leo. The light had almost gone. Maybe it was playing tricks on her. There was a shadow on him too, but not on his shoulders. It was attached to his ribcage. It pulsed slightly, as though feeding. She pressed a hand to her mouth. His face was almost skeletal. How had she never seen the despair in his eyes? He looked half-dead.

Leo took a step towards her. "Seriously, everything's fine, Enda, don't worry about me and Con fighting, we do it all the time."

Enda dodged around him, ran inside and shut herself in her room with the light blazing. She sat on the bed with her back to the wall, breathing hard.

Selene appeared right in front of her. "You look like you've seen a ghost."

Enda jumped, hard. "Do you have to do that?"

"Do what?"

Selene's face was so close Enda could see every strand of hair that lay across her eyes. A network of faint scratches marred her skin. Even as Enda watched, the scratches grew deeper and became cuts. Blood beaded across each one and trickled over her face. She shrank back, but there was little room left to put any distance between herself and her cousin's ghost. "I mean, do you have to turn up so suddenly? And why are you bleeding like that?"

Selene tilted her head to one side and smiled. It was a colder expression than Enda remembered her wearing even when she was alive. "Seems you're on the right track to finding out what happened to me. I thought my dead head might encourage you to work a little faster."

"Your dead head?"

"Yeah. That's what the others call it. Apparently this is what I look like now, but I've been keeping a prettier face on for your benefit. Not every ghost can do it, you know. I'm one of the strong ones." She sounded smug.

Enda eyed the rivulets of blood. "Charming. Now would you back off?"

Selene slid off the bed and went to sit on the dresser. "What's got your knickers in a twist then?"

She rubbed her eyes, suddenly tired. "It's the shadow things. I thought maybe that was a dream, but then I saw them tonight on both our dads. It was really horrible."

Selene shrugged. "Get used to it. Lots of people have them. They're like leeches."

"But it's feeding off my dad!"

"Course it is, that's what leeches do. It'll kill him soon. Maybe your dad'll stick around and me and him can get drunk in the cemetery every night."

"No!" Enda threw herself off the bed and across the room, but when she tried to grab Selene, make her shut up, her hands closed on thin air.

Selene laughed. The sound was unkind, just like it had been in high school. "You have to go to Dead Rock, Enda. The answers are all there."

Enda collapsed against her closet door and eyed the ghost. "How do I get rid of the shadow things?"

"You can't."

"Come on, there must be a way."

"*You* can't." Selene turned her head to look at her own reflection in the mirror. "I was pretty, wasn't I? Can't think why I would have thrown it all away like that. Maybe I had a shadow thing too." She pushed the hair out of her face. "You can't get rid of your dad's shadow thing because he has to do it himself. He has to want to."

Enda turned her head at the sound of a gentle tap at the door.

"Enda?" Leo said from the other side. "Come out and have some dinner."

Enda listened to his footsteps retreat down the hall. When she looked back, Selene was gone. She sighed, went out into the kitchen and sat at the table. She watched silently while Leo spooned sausages and mashed potatoes onto two plates, then sat across from her.

He didn't seem to know what to say, so they ate in silence for a while.

"I'm sorry about before," Leo said. "I never meant for you to see any of that."

"What is it?" Enda pushed her plate away. "What doesn't he want me to know?"

Leo shook his head. "I'm sorry, I can't tell you."

"Yes you can. I know there's a secret, you have to tell me now."

"Whatever else happens, Enda, I just want you to know that I love you and I will always be your father."

"That's not an answer." Enda grabbed the plates and took them to the sink, but when she got there a horrible thought occurred to her. She dropped the plates and went back to Leo. "Are you sick? Is that it? Are you dying?"

"Where would you get an idea like that?" Leo gave her a slow grin. "I'm not sick."

Enda dropped her gaze to his ribs. The shadow thing pulsed and fed from him. "Are you sure?"

The grin dropped from his face. "What do you mean?"

"Dad-" Enda dropped into the chair next to him and fixed him with her most serious look. "There's a thing attached to you. Right there." She pointed to his ribcage. "It's feeding from you."

"What kind of a thing?" his face remained expressionless.

"It's a kind of a shadow thing. They feed on anger and fear and maybe stuff like guilt, too, I don't know. They're everywhere." Enda hesitated. "You don't believe me."

Leo closed both of his hands around hers. "You've got to be careful," he said in a low voice. "Please, Enda, think about what you're saying. Ghosts I can handle, they're fine, I've heard footsteps and I've heard your cat, but this? You can't let people hear you talking like this. Not with things the way they are."

"It's real," Enda said. "I saw them. I see it right now. Selene said you were the only one who could get rid of it. Please, Dad, you have to listen, this thing is killing you."

94

"You see Selene?"

Enda nodded, desperate to bring her dad back. This man with the skeptical, almost frightened eyes seemed a stranger. "She wants me to find out what happened," she whispered. "She doesn't remember, but I know I'm on the right track. I think it's all linked together, Selene, Tom Nickel-"

Leo dropped her hand and strode across the kitchen. He stood at the sink with his back to her. "Don't go digging up the past, Enda, you'll just end up hurting people. It's not connected. Any of it. Selene jumped because she was high, no other reason. And there are no shadow things, so just drop it, alright? I've been telling everyone you're fine, I need you to back me up and act like it."

Enda's eyes prickled with tears. He'd never spoken to her in that hard voice, never. She blinked back the tears and stood up. Her chair clattered to the floor. "Whatever." She slammed out of the kitchen and into her room, threw herself on the bed and buried her face in her pillow.

The bed sank next to her. "That went well," Selene said.

The hairs on the back of Enda's neck stood up. "Go away."

"No." Selene laughed, a bubbling, girlish sound Enda found gruesome. "You need me as much as I need you. You've got nobody else to talk to now. Admit it. Everybody else thinks you're crazy."

Enda lifted her head from the pillow and looked at Selene. She had her normal face back on. No scars, no blood. Her blue eyes held the familiar spark of malevolence. "Molly doesn't think I'm crazy," she said.

"Then go see her," Selene said. "Go to Dead Rock. All the answers are right there. Go, Enda. Go now. Nobody will ever know. What else are you going to do, stay here and wait for the monster to come out from under the bed?"

"Get out," Enda said.

"Make me."

Enda growled under her breath. She would have preferred to have a screaming match with Selene, but things were bad enough with Leo already without something like that. So she turned on her glitter lamp, turned out the light, stuck her head under the pillow and clamped it down with both hands.

The bed bounced beside her. Selene must be jumping up and

down on it. The bitch didn't give up easily.

Enda shut her eyes and willed sleep to come.

"I know you want to go to Dead Rock," Selene said. "It's all you can think about. It calls you, doesn't it, like it used to call me. Come on Enda, I know you can hear me, get up. Let's go now. All you've got to do is follow me. Wake up, Enda. Wake up! Let's go to Dead Rock!"

Enda forced herself to unclench her jaw, unscrew her eyes and tune out the shouting. Life must be so nice and peaceful for all those people who couldn't see or hear ghosts.

She must have fallen asleep, she thought, when she looked down to find her bare feet crunching over dry summer grass. A pebble dislodged by her toes skittered off the edge and plummeted into nothingness.

She hoped she was asleep.

Selene stood beside her, her red dress whipped around her legs by the breeze. Moonlight made her blonde hair glow. "I know," she said. "I know everything. I'm leaving and I'm going to take her too, somewhere you'll never find us."

"She'll never go," Enda said.

"She will once she knows the truth. You can't stop us. You can't control everything." Selene grabbed Enda by the front of the shirt and jerked.

Enda went over the edge like she was diving into a deep, black river. Wind rushed past her face. She heard screaming, but it wasn't her own. Selene fell with her, down, down, until she disappeared into the nothingness.

Enda landed on her hands and knees. The ground shook around her and grey dust flew into the air. She looked up into the face of Tom Nickel. He was young, maybe no more than seventeen or eighteen. She rose slowly to her feet.

Tom reached out a hand and placed it over her ribcage. He curled it around something she couldn't see and drew his hand back. Enda watched, fascinated. A shadowy mass struggled furiously in his hand. "Don't believe everyone you see," he said. Then he crouched down and plunged his hand into the dirt.

Enda burst out from under her pillow like a diver surfacing for air. She gasped, curled over and breathed deeply. The glitter lamp made watery patterns on the walls. The room glowed in its gentle light. Behind her on the bed, Ivy purred, awake and watchful.

A darker mass edged toward her along the floor. Enda eyed it. She set her jaw. She swung her legs off the bed, leaned down and placed her hand over it.

The shadow jumped onto her hand instantly and clung there. Her skin went ice cold. She gingerly carried the thing out of the room and down the hall.

Lights blazed in the back room. Leo sat hunched on a chair, paintbrush in one hand, staring at his painting. He shook himself when she came in. "What's the matter?"

Enda's reply was curt. She didn't want to talk to him right now. "Spider," she said, pushed through the back door and went down the three steps into the yard. She carried the thing into the moonlight and walked around until she felt dirt under her feet. She crouched down.

There was a problem. Where Tom had simply plunged his hand into the dirt in her dream, her hand wouldn't go. The dirt was, unsurprisingly, not that liquid.

Enda dug at it with her other hand. Dead Rock was built on soft grey sand, so it wasn't difficult to make a hole. When it was big enough she stuck her ice-cold hand in there and piled sand back on top of it. "I don't want you anymore," she whispered. "I don't need you. Leave me alone."

She withdrew her hand from the dirt. Her skin was warm and her fingers tingled. She felt extraordinarily proud, like she'd just achieved something huge. She walked back to the house. The tingling spread to both hands. She felt strong. Maybe it was time she took charge of things, instead of letting other people push her around all the time.

"Is it gone?" Leo asked when she walked inside.

"What?"

"The spider. Is it gone?"

"Yes." Enda went right past him.

"Enda, wait," he said, when she got to the door.

Enda looked over her shoulder. "Don't talk to me." She left the room.

CHAPTER ELEVEN

Enda slept late the next morning and barely ate before leaving the house. She felt like she should make things up with Leo first, but he was still snoring and she wanted to go to the library and check her emails.

She walked there fast, head down, praying Uncle Con wouldn't go past and ask what she was doing. Not that he could read anything he didn't like into a visit to the library. Surely.

When she got there Skye gave her a little wave, then went back to whatever she was working on. Enda went straight to the computers and signed in to her email account. She didn't normally check it because the only people who emailed her were spammers. This morning however, there was a shiny new email in there from the Dead Rock Library. She opened it up. Skye had left no message, just attached a document.

It took an age to load. Enda tapped her fingers on the desk and waited. There, finally; a title filled the screen. *Dead Silent: Fifty Years of Suicides in Dead Rock.* The document was dated 1999 and written by a Sadie Thorne. She scanned the introduction.

This report was compiled as an investigation into the alarming suicide toll in the town of Head Rock, known to locals as Dead Rock. The town's name is attributed, according to local legend, to the cliff that towers over it. That same cliff has been the site of no less than fifteen recorded suicides and one murder since 1968: a heavy toll for a town with a population of little more than three hundred prior to 1980, and approaching six hundred by 1999.

Enda read the numbers over again. Fifteen suicides? No wonder people were freaked out. She continued reading.

A culture of silence has grown up around the deaths in the town itself, possibly arising from the belief that dialogue about suicide will encourage young people to commit the act. Each time a suicide happens, concerns about copycat suicides have arisen and in some cases been borne out.

Interestingly, the majority of the victims were aged between 18 and 33.

It is the belief of the author that, contrary to popular opinion, dialogue about suicide in small communities is vital to prevent the act. Suicide happens when young people feel isolated and depressed. The causes of these conditions must be discussed, identified and brought out in order for these people to gain the help they need.

Enda read through several pages of statistics and technical speak she could barely understand. Finally she got to the information she wanted: a list of names, pictures and information about the fifteen suicides. The list started in 1968 with Tom Nickel. An old black and white picture of the face she had seen so clearly in her dream last night stared out of the screen at her.

Tom Nickel, 19. Died October 16, 1968. Adopted son of John and Mavis Nickel, worked at their pear orchard as picker and storeman. Taken at a young age from his birth family under government Aboriginal assimilation policies, and placed with the Nickels: it is possible Tom suffered depression as a result of the trauma of his removal, however, no records from the time are available to provide any kind of evidence.

Beth Thomas, 28. Died September 23, 1971. Wife of Evan Thomas. Police records show numerous complaints of domestic violence, none acted on by then Constable C. Wilson and Sergeant A. Page, which was not unusual for the era. Coroner's report showed Beth overdosed on painkillers before jumping from Dead Rock.

Enda paused. Constable C. Wilson? That had to be Uncle Con. He must have been new to the police then. Not that that was any excuse for acting like an asshole.

Dean Thomas, 18. Son of Beth Thomas. Died September 23, 1979. Medical records identified depression, suspected abuse never acted on. Believed to be a copycat suicide, after mother Beth Thomas.

Felicity and David Brown, 34 and 38. Died July 16, 1974. Medical and police records unavailable, but local legend says they came from out of town. Felicity drove their car off Dead Rock in an apparent murder suicide. According to the local newspaper at the time it was an act of revenge on Felicity's part for her husband's infidelity.

Ada Winter, 38. Died January 1, 1983. Suffered from a depressive disorder. Police records indicate she was an alcoholic, ejected from the local tavern frequently. Lived alone. Referred to Dr E. Howard for psychiatric help by Sgt C. Wilson shortly before her death.

George Herald, 36. Died March 16, 1985. Police records indicate several convictions for possession of marijuana. Referred to Dr E. Howard for psychiatric assessment for symptoms of paranoia by Sgt C. Wilson three months before death.

Leigh Herald, 19. Died April 1, 1985. Niece of George Herald; listed as a copycat suicide. No known psychiatric condition or police records.

Nicholas Humble, 23. Died April 3, 1985. Engaged to Leigh Herald; Listed as copycat suicide, or possibly an act of grief. No known psychiatric condition or police records. NOTE: Following these three deaths, there was talk of blocking access to Dead Rock, but no action was taken.

Sahara Shanti, 23. Died December 3, 1989. Out of towner locals remember as being "different." Police records indicate numerous move on notices and warnings for vagrancy. No medical records available. Report from Sgt C. Wilson suggests frequent drug use.

Sahara. Enda bit her lip. The ghost of the homeless girl she'd encountered briefly the morning Uncle Con had picked her up in her pyjamas. Christ, this was getting creepy.

Penelope Wall, 27. Died May 17, 1993. Diagnosed with severe depression by Dr E. Howard. No police records.

Jack Salter, 38. Died June 28, 1995. Police records indicate chronic alcoholism and periods of homelessness. Referred to Dr E. Howard for psychiatric assessment four months before death.

Tina Knight, 19. Died February 14, 1998. Medical records indicated Tina suffered from depression and anorexia nervosa.

Amanda Althiere, 18. Died February 20, 1998. No records of psychiatric conditions. Police records indicate one drug conviction. Possible copycat suicide.

Alyssa Simpson, 19. Died February 26, 1998. Police records indicate drug possession and specify copycat suicide.

Kelvin Fraser, 36. Died October 1, 1999. Diagnosed with bipolar disorder by Dr. E. Howard three weeks before death.

Enda leaned back in the chair and stared at the screen, shocked beyond words. She knew some of those names. She'd heard about some of those deaths at school, but had never connected them with anything as a child. Maybe she'd been too sheltered. Those last girls who'd all jumped within days of each other, she remembered all three. They'd died within weeks of her and Leda leaving town.

The words under Kelvin Fraser's picture disturbed her the most. *Diagnosed with bipolar disorder.*

No wonder people were freaked out about her. She read the list over and over again, looking for common threads. There were a few. Uncle Con and Doctor Howard featured a fair few times, but that was natural, having the jobs they did. It must have got difficult. Maybe that was why Uncle Con was the way he was, having to deal with so much death over the years. She almost felt sorry for him.

Enda sent the document to the printer.

Skye pulled up a chair next to her. "How'd you go? Did you find what you were looking for?"

"I found Tom Nickel." Enda scrolled back to the top of the document. "This Sadie Thorne. Does she still live in Dead Rock?"

Skye shifted on her chair. "She, ah-"

"What?" Enda gave Skye her full attention. "What's wrong?"

"She jumped off Dead Rock," Skye said in a voice so low Enda had to lean forward to hear her. "I think it was back in 2001."

Enda stared. "Are you serious? After writing something like this? Why?"

"Yeah. I think it said in the newspaper she was depressed. Funny how so many people get depressed in Dead Rock."

"Yeah. Strange." Enda shut down the document and logged out of her emails. "What about since then? Anyone else jump?"

"No. There was nobody else until Selene." Skye looked at her hands. "Sometimes it's hard living here. It's horrible, wondering who's going to go up there next, wondering if it'll be someone you love."

Enda patted her hand, a little awkwardly. "Do you really think there's something up there?"

Skye shrugged. "I don't know, it's just what people say. So

much death, it must cause some kind of bad karma, don't you think?

"Yeah, maybe." Enda wondered if there was a great big shadow thing up there that latched onto people and made them depressed. "Listen, do you have any books on ghosts and stuff? I need something to read."

"Sure." Skye pointed her to an aisle in the far corner.

*

Enda took her pile of books home, but Leo was out and the empty house groaned around her. She left the books on the bed and went straight out again, the list of suicides tucked into her bag. She walked quickly into the shelter of the bush path. At the end of that she darted across the sand to Dead Rock, expecting Uncle Con to turn up with his siren at any moment.

When she reached the deeper shadows at the bottom of the rock she stopped and looked up. The rock made an endless black shape against the brightness. She thought she could see someone moving about up the top. She hoped it was Molly.

She skirted Selene's cross and headed for the path, wondering if the other seventeen suicide ghosts were all hanging around too. Surely she'd have seen them by now.

Enda started up the narrow path, hanging onto rocks and foliage. The safer handholds were becoming familiar to her by this time. Admittedly it was a lot easier in daylight. She wondered what had possessed her to try to come down here in the dark.

"Finally," Selene said.

Enda looked up the path to find Selene lounged across it, her red dress fluttering in a non-existent breeze. "What do you mean, finally?"

"I mean, finally. I've been waiting and waiting for you to come back."

"Why?" Enda thought she probably knew the answer. She continued her climb. Selene moved higher up the path whenever she got close.

"Because time's running out and you haven't found out what happened yet."

"I found out about all the others," Enda said. "You were the eighteenth suicide since 1968."

"The others?" Selene smirked. "Try telling them that."

"Where are they?"

She shrugged. "There's some in the graveyard. Some here. Some went to the other place when they died."

Enda paused in her climbing to catch her breath. "Good on them. Why didn't you go?"

The question made Selene freeze for a split second. A shaft of errant sunlight lit up her hair. Then she threw her fist at the nearest rock, but it went right through. "I stayed for you!" she yelled, and disappeared.

Enda stared at the space where she'd been. "Hey!" she said. "Selene, come back!"

No reply.

Enda muttered under her breath about crazy ghosts and kept climbing until she came out on top of the cliff. She sat on the grass and rested. A little way away she could see Molly and Tom sitting on the grass, talking. She waved when Molly looked around at her.

Molly came over, but Tom went to the edge of the cliff and stared out at the horizon.

"What are you doing up here again?" Molly said.

Enda scowled at the abrasive question. "Looking for the other ghosts."

Molly sat down next to her. "Other ghosts?"

Enda handed her the list of suicides, now creased from being in her purse. "I got this at the library."

Molly's brow furrowed while she scanned the list. She handed it back. "Selene came to me with this," she said.

"She did?" Enda placed the list back in her bag.

"A week before she died." Molly hugged her legs and looked into the distance. "You need to be careful, Enda."

"People keep saying that as though I'm going to be the next one to jump. I'm not, you know. But you must remember all these, Molly."

Molly shrugged. "I left Dead Rock for years and years after Tom died. I went to find my real family."

"Did you find them?"

"Yes, although it took a lot of searching. My dad was long gone. He was a farmer. He got my mum pregnant and never talked

to her again. My mum lived a year after we found each other."
Molly's voice wavered. She wiped a tear from one eye. "My sister
got taken too and we never found where she went. After Mum
died, I came back here. I knew Tom was waiting for me."

Enda was silent. She was keenly aware of being a descendant
of the people who'd contributed to Molly's family falling apart.
She had no idea if Molly held that against her, if she should
apologise or just stay silent, or somehow try and make things right,
even though that could never be done.

"I remember when the three girls went, and that journalist
who wrote that list," Molly said after a while. "It was horrible. It
reminded me of Tom." She plucked grass with her fingers and
shredded each blade. "That journalist came to talk to me, you
know. I think that was what caused the problems for her."

"What do you mean?"

"It's no good telling you that until you understand me and
Tom." Molly glanced over at the cliff top, where the tall, thin
shape of the ghost still looked over the horizon.

*

1961

A blanket of heat smothered the classroom. Two blowflies
droned around the windows. The only other noise was the reluctant
scratch of pencils on paper. All the kids were too sleepy to play up
or make any noise. Even moving your hand across the page was an
effort in the stifling afternoon.

Molly's gaze slid from her maths problems to the second desk
along from her. Tom looked back at the same moment. She gave
him a little smile.

Tom looked quickly back at his paper. The bruise Con had
given him in the playground was still fresh and raw.

Molly blinked rapidly. It was no good crying in the classroom,
but the tears would threaten. Her eyes slid to the seat two rows up
and three to the left, where she could see the back of Con's head.
His blonde hair was matted and untidy. Next year he wouldn't be
in school anymore.

~

One of the year tens bashed the big chunk of railway iron that served for a school bell, bringing the interminable day to an end. Everyone had to pack up and sit quietly until the teacher was satisfied they'd leave in nice neat lines, but there was little will to rebel today. There was barely enough energy between the class of seventeen years six to ten students to even leave the building.

Molly waited until she was sure Con was out of the room before she moved. Leo followed close on his heels. So much for her brothers.

Tom walked two steps behind her, both of them deliberately drawing out each step. The heat outside the classroom hit them with the radiant force only an impending February storm could summon up. The pair waited until the last of the other kids had cleared the verandas and made it out to the street. Today, nobody lingered.

They headed down the wooden steps and onto the grey sand outside the classroom. Molly brushed grains of grey sand from Tom's cheek, carefully avoiding the dark, angry imprint of Con's fist. There was another bruise on Tom's arm where Con had grabbed him during the game of British Bulldogs, but it wasn't as bad.

Tom had left a few marks on the bully in return.

They went quickly away from the school and headed for Molly's street, where the shade under the jacarandas was deep and cool. Molly had to go straight home and do the floors and the washing or Mum Wilson would get mad and Dad Wilson would ask what was the good of sending a black girl to school anyway, when she was learning everything she needed to know at home.

Molly didn't like school, but she liked the thought of always being at home less. They walked slower and slower when the gate came in sight, not speaking because it was too hot to talk about anything.

There was no warning. Con could be very, very quiet when he wanted to. He sprang out from behind the tree closest to the gate, grabbed Tom around the neck and pinned him against the next door neighbour's high asbestos fence. He punched Tom in the stomach. Behind the fence the big dog that lived there barked as though he'd rip through the asbestos himself.

"I told you to stay away from her!" Con punched Tom in the ribs this time.

Molly didn't know whether to be more frightened of the dog or of Con, but she was so angry she didn't care. She wished Con would get bit by the dugite that lived under the schoolroom and die. She sprang at his back, dug her fingers into his shirt and tried to tear him away from Tom. "You leave him alone! I'm allowed to have a friend!" she yelled.

Con batted her off like she was a fly and this time gave Tom a black eye. Tom pushed at him, fought back, but Con was twice as big as any of them and knew how to use brute strength.

Molly got up from where she'd fallen and ran at Con again. She balled her fists, punched him in the side, tried to drag his arm away from Tom's neck, and kicked him in the shins.

One of the kicks must have finally hurt him, because he stopped hitting Tom and turned on her. Her grabbed her arm, twisted it behind her back, shoved her into the fence and then knocked her to the ground.

Tom leaped on his back and closed his hands around Con's neck. The two boys spun round and round, each trying to get at the other. Before Molly could get up Con's boot came down on her already wrenched arm, hard. There was an audible crack. She screamed at the top of her lungs.

"Shut up stupid!" Con roared. He finally managed to throw Tom off and headed for Molly again.

A skinny shape flung himself over the gate and between Molly and Con. Molly kept screaming because her arm hurt so bad.

"Move, Leo!" Con yelled. "I'm going to fix this brat once and for all! She kicked me!"

"Dad's coming," Leo said.

Tom darted around Con and Leo and knelt by Molly. He helped her to sit up. They both looked at her arm, which dangled awkward and useless from her side. Molly's screams subsided to sobs.

Dad Wilson stormed through the gate and into their midst. "What happened?" his words were like thunder. Dad Wilson could be a lot worse than Con when he was mad.

"Those two just started hitting me!" the words fired from Con's mouth, rapid, like bullets from a gun. "See?" He pulled up a sleeve and showed a bruise on his arm.

Dad Wilson clipped him across the back of the head. "What

have I told you about telling lies, son? What happened to her?" he pointed to Molly. "You, boy, tell me." He looked at Leo.

"I only just got here," Leo muttered, with a nervous look at Con.

"You." Dad Wilson scowled at Tom.

"He broke her arm while he was fighting me," Tom said. He didn't need to say anything else. His half-swollen eye and bruises told the rest of the story.

"Conrad, get inside. I'll deal with you later." Dad Wilson stooped and picked Molly up off the ground.

"You're going to take his word over mine?" Con demanded. "He's a-"

"How's she supposed to earn her keep with a broken arm?" Dad Wilson roared. "You touch her again I'll break both your legs, boy! Get inside!"

Con turned scarlet. He stormed inside, followed by Leo.

"Go get the doctor," Dad said to Tom in clipped tones. "Then go home. I expect you've got work to do too."

~

Molly lay on her bed in the back room, her broken arm all bound up in plaster and bandages. It still hurt a lot. The doctor had been very kind to her and given her a sweet after he'd set it. Even Mum Wilson had been nice, but right now she was ranting at Leo in the other room about how much work she was going to have to do until the arm healed and how he should have got to his brother earlier.

Molly closed her eyes. Nothing could block out the sound of Dad Wilson's belt cracking into Con's back, over and over again. Con never made a sound. He never did, but later he'd take out the whole thing on her or Tom. She didn't know if Dad Wilson's threats would stop him or not.

~

Molly crept out of the house at midnight, like she always did after something really bad happened. The path through the bush she'd first run at the age of five was as familiar to her as her own hands now, even at night. She went slowly so as not to jar her arm and finally came out on the big sandy area. She went quickly across it and over the dirt road.

Tom was waiting for her on the other side. Normally they met at the top of Dead Rock, but Tom knew she wasn't climbing that for a while.

They stood in the moonlight, side by side, hands just touching, and looked at the space where the road disappeared into the distance. Tom laced his fingers through hers. "One day Molly," he said.

Molly nodded. They both know running away now was no good. The welfare would catch up with them in a jiffy. She'd been on the receiving end of Dad Wilson's belt enough times not to wish another round. "When?" she always asked the question, in the hope sometime the answer would be soon or now.

"When you're eighteen," Tom said. "We can get married and then they can't stop us going away."

Molly's eyes prickled. "That's still eight years. That's forever."

CHAPTER TWELVE

An unforgiving midafternoon sun blazed over Dead Rock. Enda didn't go straight home after Molly walked her down to the road. She needed time to think about the story. She needed time to decide whether school bully Con bore any relation to Uncle Con or Sergeant Conrad Wilson. Of course he did. The man was still a bully, but that didn't mean he'd victimise people for the sake of it now.

Did it?

Her aimless ramble down the highway and over roads she was less familiar with took her to the cemetery. Enda stood at the entrance thinking about the angry man with the cricket bat. She took a deep breath and decided she wasn't scared of him. Maybe some of the ghosts she wanted to find were in here. If they were, she was reasonably safe to talk to them because there wasn't a living soul in sight. She stooped to pick some dandelions from the kerb.

She walked very, very softly on the grass, as though by doing so she could somehow disturb the dead less.

Red geraniums wilted in jam jars by the headstones. At first the place seemed as empty as it had looked from outside the gate. Then, one by one, she spotted them. On one headstone sat a girl with pigtails in a long shapeless dress, swinging her feet. Down the road an old, old woman in black took slow painful steps. A man in a straw hat and checked shirt sat under a tree and talked to himself. Further away, amongst the rows of headstones, other figures moved and spoke.

Enda set her feet towards Selene's grave, still the freshest one here. From the corner of her eyes she watched the angry man storm toward her. He had a way to come, but he was fast. His strides ate up the ground and he simply stomped over or through any headstones that got in his way.

"Hey!" he yelled. "Hey you! I thought I told you not to come here anymore!"

Enda stopped and looked at him. He'd been a big man when he was alive, at least six foot and running to fat. His shirt was torn and his pants had holes in the knees. Blood poured from his receding hairline. What had Selene called all that blood? His dead head?

He swung his cricket bat through the air. "Get out of here girly! You don't belong!"

Enda folded her arms and scowled at him. "Damn right I don't belong. What are you planning to do with that bat, mess my hair?"

His lip went back over his teeth and he snarled. "Get out!"

"No." Enda turned her back on him and continued toward Selene's grave.

He lumbered after her, as she'd suspected he would, still swinging his immaterial bat. "Don't you ignore me!"

Enda sat on a stone bench by the grassy path and looked the ghost in the eyes. "Fine," she said. "You have my undivided attention. What's your problem?"

He shook the bat. "You are! You need to go!"

"Why?"

That stumped him. The bat lowered half an inch and he appeared to be thinking. "Because you don't belong here," he finally said.

"Yes, I think we established that, but I'm certainly not planning on staying forever. I just came to visit. So what's your problem?"

"I don't like your type!"

"What's my type? You don't even know me."

This confused him into silence.

"What's your name?" Enda asked, trying to make her words a little kinder.

"Kelvin."

Enda's heart thumped with excitement. She pulled the list out of her purse and glanced at the bottom name. "Fraser? Kelvin Fraser?"

"What about it?"

"I want to talk to you." Enda leaned forward. "Kelvin can you tell me why you're still here?"

His eyes darted from her to the rest of the graveyard, checking every corner. "Because I live here," he said.

"But why? Why didn't you go to the other place?"

Kelvin sank into a crouch. The bat hung limp from his fingers. "It never seemed right," he said. "It wasn't the right time, see, I wasn't ready."

"What happened to you?"

"I was drunk," he said. "So I just lay down out the back of the pub for a rest, I wasn't right enough to walk home. I closed my eyes, next thing I know someone smashes me in the head with a cricket bat. So I gets up and I catches the bat, but by then I can't see for the blood, so I just starts swinging."

"And then what happened?" Enda felt sick. She wondered if Uncle Con knew any of this about Kelvin.

"Then he smacks me in the back of the head with something else. That was it, lights out."

"What do you mean lights out? You jumped off Dead Rock."

"I'm a Catholic and suicide is a sin," Kelvin said. "I would never." A troubled look crossed his face. "Course, I never knew another thing until I was standing at the bottom of Dead Rock and some boy was telling me I was dead. But I never jumped." He looked at Enda. "Reckon I was dead before I got to the top."

Enda's heart thudded harder. Did Uncle Con even bother to investigate these deaths at all? "You were murdered," she said.

Kelvin drew a finger across his throat. "Murdered dead," he said. "And nobody to cry for me."

"Yeah, blah, blah, blah. Piss off."

Enda stiffened at the voice beside her. "Selene!" she said. "That's unkind!"

Kelvin gave Selene a nasty look. "Like you're any different." He picked up his bat and stormed away.

Selene looked at the wilting flowers in Enda's hand. "They for me?"

"Yeah, they were going to be. But maybe I should go put them on Kelvin's grave." Enda stood up and flung the flowers away. "Why do you have to be such a bitch?"

"Just in my nature." Selene shadowed her across the cemetery. "Why'd you want to talk to him anyway?"

"I wanted to find out why anybody would jump, much less

seventeen of you. He remembers his death, Selene, why can't you?"

"Dunno."

"And why me? Why am I the one who has to find out for you?"

"You can see and hear me. Duh."

Enda scowled. "But you hated me, Selene. Remember school? You made my life hell!"

Selene sighed. "Yeah, that was nothing to do with you, really. I was just kind of angry about stuff."

"So you took it out on your best friend? You were half the reason I went with my mum when she left my dad."

Selene stopped walking. "I'm sorry," she said. "I missed you when you left. I wanted to write to you, but I knew you hated me. I was going to explain it all to you when I got to your house that night."

"Explain what to me?"

"You'll find out soon enough." Selene walked away into the cemetery.

Enda watched her go, frustrated. She wasn't in the mood to play Nancy Drew anymore. She headed home.

*

There were noises coming from inside the house. Enda eyed the cracked windows doubtfully. She slowed her walk, reluctant to actually go inside, even though it sounded like Leo was home and maybe building something.

Or wrecking something.

She trod carefully over the veranda and went quickly down the hall. She left her bag on the kitchen table. Her sneakers crunched on broken glass. Enda scowled and wondered why Leo hadn't cleaned it up. She went for the dustpan and brush.

A crash from the back room stopped her in her tracks. She dropped the dustpan and bolted down the hall.

Leo stood in the middle of the back room. His hair hung wild over his shoulders and stubble shadowed his face. A thin film of sweat covered his skin. He reeked of the sickly sweet stench of rum mingled with cigarette smoke. Around him, canvases lay strewn on the floor. The easel was broken.

Leo wobbled, then made a deep, courtly bow. His out swept arm knocked the paints off the table. "Welcome home, milady." His voice was gravelly and snide. "And what time do you call this?"

Enda took a step into the room. "You're drunk!"

"Why, so I am." He picked up a bottle of rum and took a swig. "Now I'm drunker. Join me, daughter, and we can toast the skeletons in the closet."

"You promised me!" Enda blinked back tears of hurt. "Dad you promised me you'd stay sober if I stayed. It hasn't even been a week!"

"You'd get off your high horse and get drunk too if you knew what I knew!" Leo took three steps towards her and thrust the bottle in her face. "You dunno what you're asking, girl. Stay sober, she says. Be a good dad, she says. How the fuck am I supposed to be your dad anyway?" He staggered away and swept a hand across the table, sending a dirty glass and an ashtray flying.

"Dad stop it!" Enda edged along the wall.

"Stop what? I'm just being myself! The same pathetic waste of space you and your mother couldn't stand to be around!" Leo kicked the nearest canvas, then picked up a lamp from the shelf and ditched it at the wall over the bed. It shattered over the blankets. He whirled back and thrust his face near hers. "What are you even doing here? You hate Dead Rock! You're only here to stop your mother pouring drugs down your throat. We're not that different, Enda. Just a different kind of crazy."

Enda pushed him away and moved towards the back door. The shadow thing on his chest wrapped dark tentacles around his ribs. "Stay away from me."

"No! Stay, and we'll get drunk and talk about skeletons!"

Enda backed down the three steps and then bolted across the yard. She squeezed through the gap in the fence and pelted across Uncle Con's yard, where the setting sun lengthened the shadows of tall gum trees. She hammered on the back door.

Footsteps approached. Enda's heart sank when Alice yanked the door open and looked her up and down. "What are you doing?"

Enda took a minute to catch her breath. "I need to see – I need Uncle Con. Please."

"Oh, let me guess. Your dad is blind drunk and smashing the house up."

Enda's cheeks burned. She hated Alice in that moment. She wished she dared to smack her in the face. "Yes," she said.

"For Christ's sake. One of these days I'll get to spend some time with *my* family." Alice disappeared.

Enda waited and wondered about the way Alice had said *my family* as though there were some significance she should get, but didn't.

Alice was back a moment later. Uncle Con towered over her, his face red from the evening humidity. "Enda?" he said. "What's the matter?"

So Alice was going to make her repeat it out loud. No wonder she was smirking. Enda was terribly tempted to leave them here and just go lock Leo in until he sobered up, but it was too late now. "Dad's really drunk," she said. "Please come and help."

Con sighed. "Alright. You come too, Alice, Enda might need some company. Your mum can watch the kids."

Alice looked like she'd swallowed a lemon. Enda made a nasty face right back at her. They both followed Con through the yard.

He barely fit through the gap in the fence. A few pieces of asbestos broke off with his passage. Alice and Enda slipped through more easily.

Uncle Con went through the back door first. The girls went up the steps behind him.

"Conrad!" Leo staggered against the wall and regarded him with a blurry sneer. "Come to look after me, brother? Our good little girl go and fetch you, did she?"

"Now Leo," Con said in neutral tones. "You're very drunk. Come on, you need to sit down and get a grip."

"You get a grip!" Leo roared. "Why don't you tell her, huh? I swear to God that closet is so full I can't keep it shut any longer! The skeletons are coming out to play, Conrad!" He ditched the now empty bottle of rum. Con ducked and it smashed on the wall beside his head. Alice screamed.

Con gave them a jaded look. "Why don't you girls go into the kitchen? And Enda, bring us some water."

Enda and Alice edged through the room and hurried down the

hall into the kitchen.

Alice dropped into a chair at the table. "Great," she said. "Thanks a heap, Enda. Tonight was supposed to be quality time for the kids with their Nan and Pop, and where do I end up? Babysitting you while your dad fucks up your house. Why is there glass on your floor?"

"Bite me." Enda quickly swept up the broken glass, then got a tumbler from the sink and filled it with water. "I didn't ask you to come."

"Yeah but you took my dad away!"

Enda paused in the middle of the floor, water in hand. "Get the fuck over yourself, Alice!"

Alice sprang to her feet. Her voice shook. "How dare you talk to me like that? You left, Enda! You gallivanted off to the city with your mum, leaving the rest of us to deal with him!" Her finger jabbed in the direction of the hall. "And now you come back all weird and up yourself, like you're better than us, like you've got a right to-" She cut off, folded her arms and sat down again. "Go and give him the water."

Enda turned her back on her cousin and hurried down the hall. She slowed when she got closer to Leo and Con, who were arguing in low, fierce voices.

"She'll find out, just like your daughters did!" Leo's voice sounded awful, like he'd been smoking too much. "How's she going to feel if we're not the ones to tell her?"

"I don't see why you're suddenly so obsessed with this!" Con ran a frustrated hand over his scalp. "She's grown up so far thinking you're her dad, let's just leave things as they are! Think of Betty, Leo. What if Enda said something to her?"

"Were you thinking of Betty when you fucked my wife?" Leo's lip drew back over his teeth. "I *am* her dad, always have been, always will be. Biology is nothing. But she's an adult now, she's got a right to know."

The glass slipped from Enda's fingers and bounced on the lino. Water splashed her sneakers. Leo and Con both turned to look at her.

The look on Leo's face was terrible. His eyes glazed over with a guilt she'd seen there only in his darkest moments in the past. The shadow thing swelled. "Enda," he said.

Enda went back down the hall. For a minute she couldn't even get her breath. By the time she made it into the kitchen her left fist had curled so tight her nails dug into her palm. She smashed her fist into the scratched up mirror that hung at head height near the door. Glass smashed. Pain split her knuckles and blood spurted from her hand.

"Like father like daughter, huh?" Alice said.

"Fuck you!" Enda could hardly believe the scream came from her mouth. She took a breath, staggered and pulled a shard of glass from her skin.

Alice stood up. She was very white. "Shit Enda, are you okay?"

"No I'm not okay!" Enda lurched over to the kitchen sink and turned on the tap. Cold water mixed with blood. It always amazed her how much a hand could bleed.

"What have you done?" Alice hurried over to join her at the sink. "Jesus, this is going to need stitches!"

"Did you know?" Enda demanded.

Alice went, if anything, paler. "Know what?"

Heavy footsteps thumped down the hall. Uncle Con loomed in the doorway. "Enda," he said. "I didn't want to-"

"Get the fuck out of my dad's kitchen!" Enda yelled.

"Oh my God," Alice said. "You told her!"

"You did know!" Enda pushed Alice away from the sink. "How long? Is this why you and Selene decided to hate me so much?"

Tears sprang to Alice's eyes. "You don't know what it's like having to keep a secret like that, when *you* never had to care about anything!"

"Enda what have you done to your hand?" Con crossed the kitchen.

"You stay the hell away from me," Enda said, unable to control the deep tremor in her voice. The blood still spurted out under the water. She was starting to feel dizzy. "You're not my father. You need to leave me and my dad alone."

Con grabbed her hand out of the water and studied it. Blood spurted from Enda's gashes and made thick rivulets over the hairs and veins on the back of his hands.

"Is she going to faint?" Alice's voice came from far away.

"We have to get her to hospital. Alice, you get Leo down there. I'll take Enda in the squad car, it's quicker." Con grabbed a tea towel and wrapped it tight around the hand.

*

Enda lay on the back seat of the police car. She knew from how wet the tea towel was she was bleeding on the leather. Somewhere above her sirens wailed. She wondered if Uncle Con was supposed to use the siren to drive five minutes to the hospital.

They pulled straight into emergency. She walked through the sliding doors on her own and pulled away every time he tried to touch or assist her. By now her rational mind was starting to reassert itself and tell her punching a mirror was really, really dumb, and she'd probably copped a shard of glass in an artery. She stopped just inside emergency, frozen.

This was the first hospital she'd been in since getting out of psych. Sure it was a lot smaller and definitely friendlier than the big, sterile, city hospital, but that didn't stop the walls closing in. Her eyes darted over the three waiting patients and she tried to decide if they were ghosts or not. Best to ignore them all, just in case, until she saw somebody else talk to them.

A nurse approached with a clipboard. "Hello Sergeant Wilson," she said in a bright voice. "What do we have here?"

Enda tuned out of their conversation. She ignored Con while he filled all her details in on the form. Finally, they lay her down on a plastic-covered bed and drew curtains around her.

She had barely a moment of solitude before Doctor Howard appeared through the curtains. He was a small man with a receding hairline, a paunch and little square glasses.

"Hello Enda," he said. "My, you've grown since I last saw you. Conrad tells me you had a little accident. Let's have a look at that hand." He peeled away the sodden tea towel. "My goodness, that's nasty. We'll need to get some stitches in that. What on earth did you do?"

"Punched a mirror," Enda said.

Doctor Howard gave her a sharp look. "Why?"

"My dad pissed me off." The words sounded sardonic, even to her. She shut out the doctor, closed her eyes and did her best to ignore the sting of the needle.

*

Much later, the sterile smells of the hospital woke her up. Enda blinked at the olive green curtains. Her hand didn't hurt nearly as much, probably because she'd been given a bunch of painkillers. It was all bandaged up, but she could feel the stitches.

She turned her head. Leo sat on a chair by the bed, his head in his hands, a curtain of hair falling over them. "Hey," she said.

He looked up. "Hey."

Silence stretched out, awkward. He appeared to have sobered up, although the sickly sweet smell of rum remained.

"I'm sorry," Leo said. "I'm really, really sorry Enda, I fucked up, I know I did. But I promise you things are going to change now. I'm going clean myself up. I know I can do it if you just stay. Please don't go because of this."

Enda regarded him soberly. "Skeletons in the closet, huh?"

Leo looked at his hands. "You should have been told. Not that it makes any difference. I'm your dad, not him. I raised you. I love you."

"Anything else I should know about while you're dropping bombshells?"

Leo looked at her. Again that guilt, eating him from the inside. The shadow thing on his chest pulsed and fed. "No," he said.

"Bullshit."

Leo shook his head.

"Tell me how it happened. How come Mum cheated on you?"

His shoulders rose and fell. "Not really a place I want to go back to."

"Tell me."

Leo rubbed his forehead. He looked tired. "I can't have children, Enda. I think Leda always blamed me for that. She wanted three kids when we first got married. Two girls and a boy. But we couldn't. So when it happened and she fell pregnant, we all just agreed to pretend so everything would stay like it was, so nobody's marriage would break up. Con wanted to protect Betty, Leda got to have a baby, I got to be your dad. Everyone was happy. And miserable."

Enda took this in for a moment. "Wow," she said. "Yay me. What about Selene and Alice? How come they knew?"

"Alice walked in on Con and Leda. She was fifteen, she knew what they were doing and she put two and two together when the baby came. She let it slip to Selene years later."

Enda closed her eyes. The pillow was starchy against her cheek. It smelled of detergent. "When do I get out of here?"

"In the morning." Leo's voice was quiet. "Sleep now. I'll be here."

CHAPTER THIRTEEN

The sound of a vacuum cleaner woke Enda early in the morning. Sunlight poured through the big windows onto the bright white walls and floor. She was in a ward with three other beds, all empty. The vacuum whined outside the door. Leo snored in the chair beside her.

Enda sat up and stretched. She studied her bandaged hand. They'd done a decent job. She could probably do a still better one later, even one-handed. She leaned over and touched Leo on the arm. "Hey Dad. Wake up."

Leo started, blinked at the room, then groaned. He dropped his head into his hands. "Man, I feel like crap."

"Don't think you're getting any sympathy from me. Do they have tea and coffee here?"

Leo nodded. "Yeah, there's a machine. I'll get us some coffee."

"Tea for me. Black, sweet." Enda watched him leave, then got out of bed. Some fresh clothes were neatly folded on the bedside table. She sighed in relief and changed quickly, while the ward was empty, and before anyone could see her in the paper hospital nightie. Then she raked her fingers through her hair and looked around for a mirror.

"Not so fast there Miss," Doctor Howard said from the door.

Enda jumped. "Jesus! You startled me! Can't I go yet?"

Doctor Howard came into the room and laid a clipboard on the end of the bed. "Let me have a look at that hand. Yes I'll be discharging you Enda, but I wanted to have a quick word first."

Enda gave him her hand and watched him examine the dressing. He partially unwrapped the bandage, checked the stitches and then rewrapped it. When he'd finished, he motioned for her to sit down.

Enda sat on the edge of the bed. "What is it? My hand going to fall off?"

He chuckled. "No, it's not that." He sat in the chair by the bed. Lines appeared in his forehead. "I checked your medical record last night, Enda. It gave me some cause for concern."

She folded her arms and looked at the door, willing Leo to come back and tell him to piss off.

"You said you punched a mirror," he said.

"Yes."

"Do you experience these violent outbursts often?"

"Christ," Enda said. "What, I'm not even allowed to be angry now? I lost my temper. Trust me, I had good reason."

Doctor Howard took his glasses off and polished them on his shirt. "I'm sure your psychiatrist explained to you how to watch for mood swings and other symptoms," he said.

Enda grit her teeth and looked at the door again.

"An incident this serious suggests to me your medication is either not working, or you're not taking it."

"I don't need medication," she said in a low voice. "So back off."

"Enda you've been diagnosed with bipolar disorder by some very reputable doctors. I'm afraid I'm going to have to insist you go back on your medication. I don't want to see you end up in a bad way. I've already arranged for a nurse to bring you a dose in a few minutes, and I'll write you out a prescription for more."

"No, screw you. I'm not spending the rest of my life shoving drugs down my throat because a bunch of crackpot doctors think I'm a weirdo!" Enda's voice cracked.

She didn't hear Leo come in, but the next moment, he handed her a cup of hot tea. "What's going on here?"

"I'm very concerned about your daughter's attitude to her condition," Doctor Howard said. He'd gone red in the face at Enda's last words. "I'm afraid I'll have to insist on seeing her take her medication."

"I'm sure that won't be necessary," Leo said.

Enda edged closer to her dad.

"Just write out the script, Eric. I'll see she takes her pills."

Doctor Howard looked as though he were going to argue, but Leo wasn't looking particularly friendly this morning. He capitulated and scribbled out a prescription. "See she does, Leo.

We've had enough tragedy around here already." He handed Leo the prescription and left.

Enda followed Leo out of the hospital without a word. She sipped tea from her polystyrene cup and didn't breathe easy until they were out on the street and a block away from the place. They walked home slowly.

When they were well away from town and walking down a street lined with big, shady sheoaks, Leo took the bit of paper out of his pocket and read it. "Lithium, huh?"

"You're not going to make me take that shit," Enda said.

Leo chuckled. "I thought you were going to say that. What do you want me to do with this?"

"Burn it."

Leo took a lighter out of his pocket and held the flame to the corner of the paper. It flared and caught. Fire crept over Doctor Howard's scrawls. When the flames neared his fingers, Leo dropped it on the footpath. They watched it burn.

"This thing with Mum and Uncle Con," Enda said.

"Do we have to talk about that?"

"Is it why you drink?"

Leo looked up at the trees for a minute. His hair blew across his face in the breeze. Something unspoken hovered. Then his chest rose and fell and he shook his head. "No."

The last of the prescription burned away. Enda stomped on the ashes. "Thanks Dad."

"Anytime." Leo linked arms with her and they walked the rest of the way home.

*

The phone was ringing frantically when they got inside. Leo walked into the kitchen and picked it up while Enda put the kettle on. She watched him make a face, then wince, then hold the phone away from his ear. She could hear the tiny yelling voice clear across the room.

"It's for you," he said. "It's your mother."

"I'm not home."

"Yes you are."

Enda grimaced and took the phone. "Hi Mum."

"Enda are you okay?" Leda sounded seriously rattled. Static crackled over the line.

"I'm fine, seriously, just a couple of stitches."

"Stitches? What the hell? I leave you alone there for three days, *three days,* and you end up in hospital! I knew this would happen!"

"Who told you?"

"Conrad rang me this morning and said you'd put your fist through a mirror. This is what happens when you go off your medication and you're not properly looked after. I'm coming up there tomorrow to pick you up."

"Jesus Christ Mum!" Enda took a deep breath and lowered her voice. "Don't you dare come up here just because I threw a goddamn tantrum and hurt myself."

"Tantrum? What are you, three?"

"Look, you can just back off. I'm not the one who slept with my brother-in-law!"

There was silence on the other end of the line. Then, defensive, "Enda-"

"Don't you Enda me. I mean, ew, how could you? It's beyond repulsive."

"You don't understand-"

"I understand you were prepared to lie to me my whole life about who my father was."

"That's not how it was!"

"Then tell me how it was, Mum, that you fucked around?"

"Just drop it!" Leda yelled. "Why do you insist on dragging up the past at every opportunity? This is why I didn't want you to stay in Dead Rock, I knew you'd get this way!"

"What way? All I want is to know the truth!"

There was a long silence. When she spoke again, Leda's voice was back to normal. "Sometimes the truth can hurt people, Enda. Look, we can talk about this when you come home, I'd rather not over the phone. Besides that, it'll upset your father too much."

Enda glanced across the room at Leo, who was making coffee and pretending not to listen. She suddenly felt really, really bad. "Okay," she said. "But don't come up here. I'll come home when I'm ready."

"Just don't be too long, honey. Don't get stuck in Dead Rock."

"Okay Mum."

"Look, I know we have our differences, but I love you and I'm worried every second you're out there."

"Don't be. I'll be fine. Bye." Enda hung up before Leda could start on anything else. She joined Leo at the kitchen table, where a cup of tea waited. "Sorry."

"For what?" Leo sipped his coffee.

"Having a screaming match with Mum."

He shrugged. "You had to have that conversation with her one day. At least now it's out of the way."

Enda watched Ivy prowl across the kitchen floor. She wondered if she was stalking ghost mice.

"What are you looking at?" Leo asked.

"My cat. She's hunting."

"What are they like, these ghosts you see?"

"These days, really clear. It can be hard to tell the living from the dead."

"There must be ways, though."

Enda watched Leo over her cup and wondered how he could be so smart and down to earth and understanding one minute and hurling bottles in a drunken rage the next. "Sometimes they have their dead heads on."

Leo almost choked on his coffee. "Their what?"

"They look like they did when they died. Like-" she decided not to tell him about Selene's dead head. "Like this guy down at the cemetery, he's got blood pouring out of his forehead and he always carries a cricket bat. He took it from the guy who murdered him just before he died. It's really sad."

"Murder?" Leo pushed aside his coffee. "People don't get murdered in Dead Rock."

Enda sipped her tea. "Wanna bet? Kelvin was murdered. Whoever did it then threw his body off Dead Rock to make it look like a suicide."

Leo's hands started to shake. He hid them under the table.

"Are you okay, Dad?"

"Are you sure about Kelvin?"

"Absolutely. He told me himself, after he stopped trying to hit me with the bat."

A single tear shivered on Leo's lower eyelash.

Enda leaned forward. "Oh my God Dad, what is it? Are you okay? Did I say something?"

Leo shook his head. "Kelvin was my friend," he said. "My drinking buddy. I left the pub early the night he jumped. For years I wondered if I'd stayed, if he might have not gone up there, and now you're saying- now you're saying-" he sat up and squared his shoulders. "Why would I believe this?"

Enda bit back a stab of anger. "Why would I make it up? Or are you just going to turn out like everyone else and call me crazy the second you don't like what I'm saying?" She shoved back her chair, yanked the cups off the table and took them to the sink.

"I don't know what to believe anymore." Leo's chair clattered to the floor and he left the room.

Enda leaned her forehead against the tiles over the sink and closed her eyes. Great. She was getting really good at screwing things up with him. Maybe if she'd brought up some bad memories it would be better to leave him alone for a while. As for washing the cups she could hardly do it one-handed, so she may as well just give that idea up.

A knock at the front door caught her attention. Enda sighed, pushed herself upright and went down the long hall. She really had to get rid of that long line of empty beer bottles along the floor, now that important rooms like the kitchen and bathroom were livable.

She opened the front door. Alice stood on the other side of the fly wire shuffling her feet.

"Hi." Enda waited for an insult.

"Hi." Alice avoided her eyes. "Listen, I just came to see if everything was okay, you know, after last night."

"It's fine." Enda waved her bandaged hand. "All fixed up. I have stitches, you have a story to tell your friends."

"Don't be a bitch, Enda."

"Why not? Seems to run in the family."

Alice took a step back. "Guess I shouldn't have come. I'm glad you're okay." She turned to leave.

"No wait." Enda opened the screen door and took a step out. The veranda squealed alarmingly under her weight. "I'm sorry Alice. It's just you haven't exactly been, you know, welcoming."

"Now you know why."

"Do you want to come in and have some tea?"

Alice shook her head. "I don't like your house. It's creepy. Full of ghosts or something."

"Only my cat, really."

Alice gave her a look. "You wanna go for a walk?"

Enda glanced inside; the house was silent. She hoped Leo was painting. He probably needed some space. "Alright." She closed the screen door behind her. They walked out of the front yard and through the garden gate.

Alice took small steps, as though she was used to matching her pace to children.

"Where are the kids?" Enda asked.

"Home with their dad." Alice ambled over the carpet of dried up jacaranda flowers lining the footpath. "I told him I wanted some time to myself."

Enda nodded. She remembered Alice's husband from before she and Leda left as a thin, spectacled man who mostly did what he was told.

They walked around the corner in silence. Alice turned into the alley that led to the bush path. Soon they were away from the houses and in among the scrub and tall trees.

"I guess we're sisters then," Enda said after a while. "You, me and Selene."

"Yeah." Alice looked sour, but the moment passed. "Somehow I can deal with it better now you know."

"When did Selene find out?"

"Do we have to talk about this?"

"Yes." Enda stopped walking. "Please, Alice, I need to know this stuff. I can't just leave everything all messed up and not know."

Alice stopped, folded her arms and looked up at the nearest tree, where three black cockatoos sat in the branches cracking seeds in their big curved beaks. "I think she was 13," she said. "I was jealous of her friendship with you, really jealous. You two had each other, you were more like her sister than I was. I was too old for her to hang out with. I never really felt like I had a proper sister, only two brothers who were too wrapped up in boy stuff to give a shit about a sister who got married and had kids and never had a life again."

The last bitter note faded into the crisp air. A cockatoo shrieked and exploded out of the tree. Enda saw a shadow thing pulsate on Alice's shoulder, but it was faint and small, not like Leo's or Con's.

"She used to fight like cats and dogs with Dad. You remember," Alice said.

Enda nodded. She used to put as much distance as she could between herself and Selene when she and her father started.

"One day she had this huge fight with Dad. She came to my house afterwards while he cooled down. She was furious because he hit her on the arm and left a massive bruise. I put ice on it for her and listened while she ranted and raved, never minding how I was feeling or that I had problems of my own. She was making my head hurt, just going on and on and on. Then she said she wished she was your sister and Leo was her dad because he didn't give a shit what you did so long as he had a drink in his hand. Well I just snapped, and I told her right then."

Enda was silent. She could imagine how Selene would have felt, finding out the truth so unceremoniously.

"I didn't mean to," Alice continued in a small voice. "I was mortified when I realised what I'd done. I swore her to secrecy, but I knew I messed up because she was different after that. Her relationship with Dad got worse. She barely spoke to me for years. But she protected Mum from the truth, from everyone. And you too. She started getting into fights with people who said anything about you. One time she just about scratched my eyes out when I said something about you turning out like Leo."

Enda shook her head. "Seriously? Are you sure we're talking about the same Selene? She spent high school making my life hell. She and her friends made a career out of making fun of me and my Dad."

Alice shrugged. "I had an idea she was, but I can't account for it. I guess it was her way of dealing with it. All I know is after you and your mum left she became almost impossible. She had screaming matches with Dad every day. She used to drink down the park with her friends, then when she was 18 and Dad couldn't stop her, she started drinking with Uncle Leo a lot. She always talked about moving to the city with you but she never got her act together or saved any money. Then she lost all this weight. She said it was a diet and she wanted to move to the city and be a model, but I guess-" Alice shrugged. "I guess it was the drugs."

"You guess?" Enda wished like hell she'd made the effort to keep in touch with this stranger, this Selene she never knew.

"That was what Dad said, and he should know, he deals with that kind of stuff all the time."

"But?"

"But what?" Alice scowled and started walking again. "There's no more to tell. She got high, she jumped off Dead Rock. Maybe if I'd never told her about you it wouldn't have happened. You never knew and you seem to have turned out okay."

Enda suppressed the inappropriate urge to laugh, since Alice probably wasn't joking. "You don't believe she was on drugs," she said. "I can tell."

"It doesn't matter what I believed or didn't believe. Dad said she was on drugs, he would know, alright?"

Alice stopped walking again because the path had come to an end. The two women stood at the edge of the bush. A river of grey sand ran from their feet to Dead Rock. Alice gazed at it with an inscrutable expression. Then she turned around and walked back, fast.

Enda hurried to keep up. "What about my mum and Uncle Con?"

"What about them?"

"You saw them. Dad said you did."

"You want to know about that? Gross."

"I want to know why my mum would do something like that! I'm just trying to understand, Alice. My mum can't stand your dad, why would she have an affair with him?"

Alice's pace ate up the ground under them. They reached the end of the bush track and were back on the roads before she stopped under a jacaranda tree and looked Enda in the eyes. The words she spoke sounded like they were dragged from under six feet deep of concrete.

*

1984

Alice's heart was beating fast and she felt a little sick. She eased open the front door as quietly as she could, snuck inside and clicked it shut. She carried her shoes in her left hand and her bag in her right, and even though she was terrified, she felt like she'd just had the best night of her life. Ever.

She tiptoed down the hall. Mum was away visiting her sister, which only left Dad to contend with. If he found her sneaking in now she'd probably be grounded until she was old enough to leave home, but if she could just make it to her room unnoticed-

A sound came from Mum and Dad's room. Alice froze. Nobody came out, so she took another step down the hall.

Another sound. Oh. Ew. That was her dad doing something old people just shouldn't do. Alice made a face and kept going.

But two steps later, she stopped again. This time she almost did throw up. Mum wasn't home. That wasn't Mum's voice either. She recognised the voice but couldn't place it.

She could swear the woman was crying.

Alice dropped her shoes. The sound echoed down the hall but did not disturb what was going on in the room. She tip-toed to the door and eased it open, just a few inches.

She had to put her hand over her mouth to stop herself screaming or running in there yelling. Dad was on top of Aunty Leda, his pants around his ankles, her dress torn and bunched up over her hips. One of his hands pinned her wrists over her head and the other was splayed carelessly over her face, muffling her sobs.

Alice eased the door shut. She picked her shoes up, ran back to her room and stood in the darkness trembling. Then she went into the bathroom and dry retched into the sink.

She opened the bathroom door a crack and peered out when she heard footsteps.

Leda stood in the hallway, barefoot, dress torn, swaying. Blood trickled from her mouth and bruises stood out on one cheek. A single, violent sound escaped her before she fled barefoot down the hall. Doors slammed in her wake.

Alice darted across the hall to her bedroom. She locked the door behind her, pushed a chair up against it and sat in the dark, terrified to move or make a sound.

*

Enda doubled over and gripped the nearest tree for support. Her stomach heaved.

Alice watched, her face expressionless, her arms folded.

When Enda got a grip on her stomach they walked home in absolute silence. Only when they got to the house and stood on the creaking, spongy veranda did she find words. "Did you ever tell anyone else?"

"No," Alice said. "And you won't either."

"Why not?"

"Because it was a long time ago. Why drag all that up now? Things are going along just fine."

Enda's voice shook. "But your dad raped my mum."

"Listen to me Enda," Alice said in a low voice. "I love my dad. *Our* dad. He plays a really important role in this town. There's a zero crime rate because of him. He's a husband and a father and a grandfather. He made one mistake, alright? It's a long way in the past. I told you this stuff because you asked and you had a right to know. Now I'm telling you, let it go. If you can't deal with it go back to the city. Nobody wants you upsetting things. Dead Rock's too small a town."

"But how can you live with it?"

"I live for my kids, for the future, not for the past." Alice nodded at the door. "Are you going to let me in? I'll go through the back way and go see my mum before I go home."

"Thought you were afraid of the ghosts." Enda stood back to let her in the hall, then followed her down it.

"Don't be stupid. There's no such thing as ghosts." Enda raised her eyebrows at Alice's back. If only she knew. They went through the kitchen, down the next hall and into the back room. Alice stopped. "Whoa."

Enda squeezed past to see what she was looking at. Leo had cleaned up in here, fixed the broken easel and set up his painting on there, the one of Dead Rock with the little figure with the outstretched arms. Only he'd added to it. Now the outstretched arms balanced the shape of a man, poised to throw him off the rock. A kitchen knife was buried in the middle of the canvas.

Alice's words dropped into the room like artillery shells. "That's fucking creepy."

Enda was gripped by a wave of terror. "Where's my dad?"

CHAPTER FOURTEEN

For the first time since she'd come here Enda truly felt the isolation of being in trouble in a small country town with nothing but miles and miles of bush between her and the safety of the city. There you couldn't get lost, because you were always being watched. There you could call the police or the ambulance and trust them to look after you because they didn't know you. She made up her mind to take Leo back to the city with her. He'd be safer there. He'd be looked after.

Her lungs squeezed like a bellows. Her feet pounded down the bush path she'd just walked with Alice, who'd gone to alert Uncle Con, even though Enda had begged her not to, at least not yet.

Selene kept pace with her. Sometimes she ran beside her. Sometimes she waited up ahead, under a tree. Sometimes she just disappeared.

Enda pelted out from the bush and over the grey sand. She stopped before the highway. Once again she could see a distant figure on top of Dead Rock, but this time she knew it wasn't Molly or Tom.

"I told you," Selene said. "I told you time was running out."

Enda glanced at her bandaged hand. It was no good trying to climb the rock with that. She darted across the road, ran a little way further and started up the hill the way Molly had shown her.

The slope was steep. Her leg muscles burned. She pushed herself to keep climbing until she reached the top. Then she ran along the track, through the balgas and stopped a little way from where Leo stood framed against the sky. He was close to the edge, too close, but he didn't move or shake or fall. He just stood perfectly still.

Enda went slowly toward him. She cleared her throat to avoid startling him and made her voice calm. "Dad? Dad what are you doing up here?"

He didn't answer. When Enda got closer, she saw his face was stained with tears and his eyes were red. She didn't think he was drunk, but he wasn't exactly right either. She curled her fingers around his sleeve. "Dad, come away from the edge."

Leo came to life so abruptly it was like another person had taken him over. He snapped around to look at her, shook her hand off and grabbed her wrist instead. "What would they say if I jumped, Enda?" he demanded. "What would the newspaper write? Copycat suicide, they'd say. Tragic waste of a life. How many other times did they write those words? How many times was it a lie?"

Enda took a step back, trying to pull him with her, but he wouldn't budge. "Please Dad, come away from the edge."

"I've been so blind!" Leo let her go and put his hands to his head. He crouched down, face buried, and let out a roar that started low and ended so loud it echoed down the cliff side.

Enda crouched down in front of him and took his hands from his face. She looked into his reddened eyes and was frightened to see the rage that had added itself to the guilt.

"All these years I protected him," Leo whispered. "I believed him. I needed him. Does that make me as bad? How many other times?" He rose to his feet again and looked out over the town of Dead Rock. "How many more?" he roared.

"Dad!" Enda caught the back of his shirt, terrified he was just going to step off and plummet.

Leo reached back and grabbed her hand. "Stand with me Enda," he said. "Stand here and look at this place. This hole in the universe. I wasted my life here."

Enda stood beside him and looked out over Dead Rock sprawled beneath them in the mid-afternoon sun, dusty tree tops, dusty rooves and a loose network of roads.

"There are things you need to know," Leo said.

*

1999
8pm
Tuesday night. Not that it mattered. Bright lights, blurry neon signs and the click of pool cues in the far corner. Kelvin thumped the juke box and the speakers hammered out the first chords of

some old ACDC number.

"Yeah!" Leo drew out the word until it hurt his throat. He knocked his glass, cursed and righted it before the beer went everywhere. The Dead Rock Hotel smelled like stale beer and the cheap perfume of the girl behind the bar with the short black dress on. The long, black surface of the bar belonged to him and Kelvin. Old man Simpson nursed his red wine at the corner booth and two boys who looked underage huddled over the pool table. Angus Young gave a gravelly scream. The ceiling fans barely stirred the heavy air.

Kelvin lurched back to the bar and landed on the stool next to Leo. He poured the dregs of his beer down his throat and thumped on the bar.

The girl refilled their drinks. She was a fluffy blonde with big green plastic bubble earrings.

Kelvin leered at her. "How you goin' love?"

"I'm just great," she said, took their money and disappeared before the conversation could go any further.

"She thinks I'm alright," Kelvin said.

Leo snorted. "Mate, you're old enough to be her dad. Forget it."

"Did you see how she looked at me?" Kelvin insisted. Beer disappeared down his throat. "One of these days mate, she's gonna go home with me. You wait. I'm gonna get me that girl."

Leo stared into his glass. His good mood was leaking away the longer Kelvin talked shit. He took a drink. The beer was cold, but it did nothing to stop the sweat pouring down his back. "Women," he said. "Forget 'em mate, nothing but trouble."

Kelvin slapped him on the back. "Your missus left because you were a pisshead mate! If I had a girl like that-" he pointed at the barmaid "-I'd stop drinking today. Just like that."

"Nah you wouldn't." Leo considered, for a bare second, the prospect of drinking alone every night while Kelvin played house with a blonde. "You'd be down here talking shit with me."

~

9pm

Kelvin leaned against the bar and stared morosely into a half-glass of beer. Leo refilled his glass from the jug. The smell of sweat and stale beer overpowered the last traces of perfume. The night seemed to be getting hotter.

"Doctor said I got bipolar," Kelvin said. His words slurred. He swayed a second, then sat up straight. "Useless prick. That's the last time I go to him."

"Yeah mate, that guy's a wanker," Leo said. "Get a second opinion."

"Yeah. Yeah I will." Kelvin lurched to his feet and thumped on the bar. "Hey! Hey darling! Come over here!"

The blonde glanced at them from the other end of the bar, where she was talking with a younger man. She stayed where she was.

Kelvin hammered on the bar with his fist. "Blondie!" he yelled.

Leo buried his face in his glass and pretended he didn't know the guy. When he looked again, Blondie's friend was flexing his muscles. Blondie was red and flustered. She said something to her friend and then came over to them.

"Hey Blondie," Kelvin said when she got near. "I need a second opinion. Do you think I'm bipolar?"

She didn't look as friendly as she had earlier. Her lips compressed. "Look sweetheart, I'm going to have to cut you off. Either drink some water and calm down or leave."

Kelvin leaned across the bar and made a grab for her wrist. She jerked out of the way. "Will you come home with me?"

"Off you go Mr Fraser." Her voice was colder than the frost on the freezers behind her.

"But it's still early!" Kelvin poured the rest of the drink down his throat and belched. "Come on Blondie, have a heart."

Blondie glanced at her friend, who nodded at her and headed for the phone behind the bar. She took the jug with its dregs of beer and rinsed it under the tap. "You've had enough and you've been asked to leave," she said. She glanced at Leo. "Take him home, Mr Wilson. You look like you've got a skinful too."

Leo slammed his glass down. "Come on love, he'll be right," he said. "Just pour us one more. Please?"

Blondie shook her head. "Don't make me have you both removed."

"She's an ice queen!" Kelvin stood up on the lower rungs of the stool and waved his empty glass in the air. "Come on Blondie,

I can show you a good time!"

"No thank you," she said. "Goodbye, Mr Fraser."

"I'm not leaving!" he roared. "I want another drink!"

The pub door opened. Conrad walked in in full uniform. He seemed to fill the entire space, to suck all of the air in the room into himself. The pub fell silent, except for the gravelly strains of Bob Dylan coming from the jukebox. Leo watched him through heavy-lidded eyes and wished Kelvin would shut up.

"Problems?" Con said to Blondie. He took his hat off.

"Sergeant I've asked these two men to leave," she said. "This is the third time this week. I'm going to request they be barred if it happens again."

"Barred from the bar." Kelvin swayed where he stood, but Conrad's presence seemed to have penetrated even his drunken haze.

Con looked over the two of them. He shook his head slightly at Leo, as though to say he was disappointed, but expected no better. He jerked his head at the door. "Out."

"Come on." Leo grabbed Kelvin's shoulder. "They don't want us here."

"I'm not nuts!" Kelvin bawled when they went past Conrad. At the door he turned and waved. "Hey Blondie! The offer still stands!"

Leo yanked him into the night. The air was sultry and damp even out here. The footpath was littered with cigarette butts. Neither of them could walk straight.

"Your brothers a fuckin' wanker." Kelvin bumped a wall. "I reckon he's got it in for me!"

Leo snorted. "You, mate? Nah, not you. He's just tryin' not to be embarrassed by his family members, eh. But you're right, he's a wanker."

"Blood's thicker than – than –" Kelvin veered off down an alley. "I gotta take a piss."

Leo stopped in the middle of the alley and leaned against a wall while Kelvin went round behind the pub. "Blood's thicker than what?" his own voice echoed in his ears, hoarse, unsteady. Silence greeted him. Then a shadow fell across him.

Leo pushed himself off the wall. "What?"

"Leo what are you doing?" Conrad sounded tired. He blocked

the alley.

"Waitin' for me mate," Leo said. "He's taking a piss. Is that illegal?"

"You need to go home."

"I'm fine. Seriously I'm fine." Leo put out his hands and walked in a less than straight line, foot over foot, toward his brother. "See? I'm fuckin' sober as an empty beer bottle. I gotta see me mate home, alright?"

Conrad caught him by the shoulders. His face got real close, so close it blurred. "You're not fine, Leo," he said in a low voice. "You've been acting like the town drunk for weeks, drinking with that asshole. I want you to go home and sober up."

"Go home to what?" Leo roared.

"Look, I know it's hard," Con said. "But it's been a year since they left. Man up and get over it."

"What would you know?" Leo got in his brother's face and snarled. Even to himself he sounded like an animal, but he couldn't stop now. "You go home every night to your family, your kids. They don't have a clue what you are. It's your fault I lost my family. So don't you fucking lecture me!"

Conrad grabbed his shoulders and pinned him to the alley wall. "I'm not a drunken asshole who can't keep his mouth shut," he said in Leo's ear. "That's why I've still got my family. Don't blame your shit on me, little brother."

"I've kept my mouth shut for thirty years!" Leo balled a fist and drove it into Conrad's stomach, but it was like punching steel. The man didn't even notice. "And you went and fucked my wife. You fuck everything!"

Conrad grabbed him off the wall and shoved him down the alley. Leo stumbled over his feet and fell to the ground. Conrad hauled him up and shoved him again, this time onto the footpath. He stood over him. "Go home, Leo. And be grateful I'm here to clean up your messes. Again. As for your wife, don't forget you never would have had a family if I didn't fix that for you too."

Leo got to his feet and turned his back on his brother. One foot after the other. Rage pumped through his blood. The alcohol made him stupid and sluggish. When he turned back, the alleyway and the street were both empty.

*

Leo's grip on her good hand hurt. Enda stared at him. "What are you saying?"

"I'm saying if Kelvin didn't jump, there was nobody else around that night."

"But surely that doesn't mean-" Enda swallowed. An image of Leda spitting blood flashed through her mind. She steeled herself. "Uncle Con's an asshole, I'll give you that, but he's not a murderer."

Leo was silent.

"Is there another reason for you to think that?"

His face crumpled. He let her hand go. Something shook his whole body and made him curl over, fists to his face.

A hand landed on Enda's shoulder and made her jump. Then she saw the hand belonged to Molly, who gently moved her away from the edge. Enda walked back and stood next to Tom, who didn't look at her. All of his attention was fixed on Leo.

Molly grabbed Leo's face and made him look at her. Enda couldn't hear what they said, except that the words were low and intense. Then Leo broke down on her shoulder. Molly patted him on the back and moved him away from the edge. When they got closer, Enda finally made out the words Leo sobbed over and over again.

"I'm sorry," he said. "I'm sorry Molly, I'm sorry-"

Molly glanced at Enda. There was an odd look on her face, a mixture of regret and satisfaction and absolute sadness. Then she stiffened. "Did you bring him here?"

Enda glanced over her shoulder. Parked away near the tree line was an ambulance. Uncle Con strode toward them, his eyes fixed on Molly. Alice followed. She grit her teeth. "No," she said. "Alice did."

Leo lifted his head. "Make him go," he said. "I can't face him right now, I can't-"

Enda felt much the same way, but there was nobody else to take control, so she barred Con's way. "Everything's fine," she said. "There's no need for all that." She jerked her head at the ambulance.

Con looked down on her as though she were a gnat. "I'll be

the judge of that," he said. "Alice told me about the painting, Enda. That kind of thing doesn't sound remotely fine in my book. Leo is unwell. He needs to be looked after."

Enda folded her arms. "Then I'll look after him. He's just upset is all. Please leave us here, we'll come down later."

"Do you think I'm going to risk losing you and my brother to Dead Rock days after my daughter?" Con went around her. "And what's Mad Molly doing here?"

"Helping." Enda ran after him. "Uncle Con, please-"

Con put an arm around Leo's shoulders. He looked Molly up and down. "I told you to stay away from my family."

Molly's eyes filled with such complete, unforgiving hatred Enda took a step back as though pushed by a physical force. "I just saved his life," she said. Then she let Leo go and walked over to Tom.

Tom's attention was all fixed on Con. Enda thought he was shaking. She desperately wanted Tom to talk to her, tell her why, but he never seemed to know she was there.

Con guided Leo to the ambulance. "Come on Enda," he said.

Enda looked at Molly, who shook her head. "Go," she said.

Enda ran after Leo, who walked along as though hypnotised, just staring at his feet. Con helped him into the back of the ambulance, where a nurse sat him down.

Con glanced back at Molly. "Now you see why I told you to stay away from her," he said. "Stupid crazy bitch, wandering around up here talking to herself."

Red flashed across Enda's vision. She shoved Uncle Con, even though it was like trying to move a mountain. "She's not talking to herself you son of a bitch! She's talking to Tom Nickel!"

She knew she shouldn't have said it as soon as the words were out of her mouth. Uncle Con's face contorted. There was a sadness that didn't reach his eyes. His fingers curled around Enda's upper arm like a vice and he all but shoved her into the ambulance. Then he closed the doors on them.

CHAPTER FIFTEEN

The bright lights in the hospital made her eyes hurt. Doctor Howard and Uncle Con manhandled Leo into a sterile bed. Enda ran after them when a nurse wheeled it away. "Wait. Wait! Where are you taking my dad?"

Leo didn't look at her. He just stared at his hands like they were the only thing in the world.

Uncle Con caught her by the shoulders and held her back. A flash of fury electrified her. She twisted out of his grasp, balled a fist, swung it at his face and caught him in the mouth.

Uncle Con put his fingers to the cut and then looked at the blood on them. He shook his head at Enda. "Should've taken your meds," he said.

Enda backed away from him. "Where are they taking Dad?"

"Enda." Uncle Con made calming motions with his hands that just infuriated her more. "Your dad has been verging on a nervous breakdown for some time. He and Selene were very close and with the history we have here of copycat suicides-" he paused, as though pained. "Something like this was bound to happen. It's just lucky I was there in time."

"Yeah, like you were there in time for my mum! You really are an asshole!"

"Please Enda, just calm down. We only want to help you."

Enda felt a nightmarish disorientation, like she'd been in this situation before. The feeling intensified when a woman appeared in the space between her and Uncle Con. Hair that might once have been big and curly straggled in every direction, knotted and unkempt. Cuts and bruises covered every inch of her body not hidden by the bright, torn floral dress she wore. Blood streamed from cuts on her face and arms. Her nose was broken. She took deep, panicked breaths. Each rasp cut through Enda's now pounding head. She reached for Enda. "Don't let them do it." Her voice rose on a note of panic. "Don't let them near you!"

Enda stared at her, for the moment oblivious to Uncle Con. The woman's terror hit her like a ton of bricks. "Who are you?"

The woman curled insubstantial fingers as bruised and swollen as the rest of her around her wrist. "I'm Ada," she said.

"Ada." Enda placed a hand over the fingers she couldn't feel. "Ada what happened to you?" Her mind flit back to the list, but right now she couldn't remember the names.

"They put me in here to die!" Ada's breath rasped louder and louder. The blood made rivulets down her face. She clutched her head, sank to the ground and rocked back and forth, back and forth.

Enda looked over her head at Uncle Con. "What the hell are they doing to the psychiatric patients in here? This woman looks like she's been thrown off Dead Rock!"

She shouldn't have said it. She knew she shouldn't have said it, but pretending not to see ghosts was exhausting. It was hard to account for the recognition on Con's face, though, when she'd said the name.

"There's nobody there Enda." Con looked over her shoulder and made a beckoning motion. "You're not well, but Doctor Howard is going to take good care of you. I'm sorry it had to come to this, sweetheart, but I can't lose you as well."

"Sweetheart?" Enda looked from the rocking, sobbing ghost on the floor to Uncle Con. "Don't you call me that. You're not my father."

"Like it or not, I am."

Enda leaped at him, fist balled, and aimed for his mouth again. "Only because you raped my mother!"

Con caught her fist and held her back. Enda struggled with every last ounce of strength she had.

"A little help!" Con yelled.

Footsteps hurried down the hall. Hands grabbed Enda from both sides and dragged her away. Ada's sobs reached a wailing pitch, hurt her ears, drowned out whatever it was the nurses and Uncle Con were saying. For just one fleeting moment it crossed Enda's mind to wonder if she was, indeed, crazy. The next moment the nurses had hustled her away from Uncle Con, down the hall and into a small room with just one bed and a chair and a little sideboard with a tray of dusty potpourri on it.

One of the nurses, a middle-aged woman with glasses and a strained, tired look, sat her down on the bed. "Come on dear, don't be difficult," she said.

Enda stood up and shook her off. She had a horrible feeling she was on a train without brakes careening towards disaster, but there was no getting off now. "Leave me alone. I need to see my dad."

"You can see him later." The nurse placed both hands on her shoulders and forced her down again. "We're going to give you something to calm you down now."

"What? No!" Enda pulled away, but already the second nurse was ready with a syringe. It stung its way into her arm.

*

She didn't know what they'd given her. Her head felt like it was stuffed full of cotton wool and her limbs were heavy. They'd put her in a hospital gown. The plastic covering on the bed crackled when she turned on her side and curled up into a ball. It was hard to think, to assess her situation, when she was like this. All she knew was she'd fallen back into the nightmare she'd tried so hard to avoid. She squeezed her eyes shut. "I'm not crazy," she whispered. "I'm not crazy. I'm not crazy."

The door opened and shut and a trolley rattled in. Enda watched the nurse through half-closed eyes. It was the same one who'd stuck her with the needle earlier.

"Sit up dear, time for your medication," the nurse said.

Enda slowly sat up. The motion made her head spin. "What did you give me before?"

"It was a mild tranquiliser, just to bring you down."

"What did you give me? What kind of tranquiliser?"

The nurse went a little red. "Now Miss Wilson, please don't take that tone with me. We're here to help. You need to take your medicine and the doctor will be here soon to see you."

Enda took a deep breath. She wasn't even sure her tone had been all that confrontational. She leaned back against the wall because she felt like she was going to collapse if she didn't. "Please tell me, what tranquiliser did you give me, and what is that?"

"We gave you a Benzodiazepine to calm you down," the nurse said. She looked like she didn't think Enda would understand the big words. "This is Haldol."

"Are you insane?" Enda voice rose to a squeak. "Surely you're aware how dangerous it is to inject Benzodiazepines? I could have died! And Haldol? Is that really necessary?"

"I think it's best if we let the doctor decide what's necessary. He's got your best interests at heart." The nurse advanced, carrying a glass of water in one hand and a little cup of pills in the other. "You need to take these. Then you can start getting better."

A wave of cynicism pierced the cotton wool in her brain. Enda shook her head. "Not Haldol. Too dangerous."

"Ms Wilson, don't make me get help. We don't want your stay here to be unpleasant, but Sergeant Wilson is very concerned about you. He said he would do whatever was necessary to ensure you took your medication. He's right outside the door."

"Fine." Enda grabbed the glass. She put the two pills in her mouth, swallowed them and drank the water. "Just don't let him in here."

"Show me."

Enda opened her mouth to show the pills were gone.

"Good girl!" The nurse returned to her trolley and wheeled it out of the room. The door closed behind her.

"Fuck you," Enda muttered at her back. She lay down and closed her eyes.

*

The next time Enda opened her eyes Leda was sitting in the chair next to her bed. Her hair seemed a little greyer and was coming out of its neat bun. Her clothes looked as though she'd simply thrown them on. "Mum?" her voice sounded cracked.

Leda gave her a tired, strained smile. "Hello dear."

Enda manoeuvred herself into a sitting position. "What are you doing here?"

"Conrad rang me and told me what happened. I came straight away."

The flash of hatred she felt at the name was dulled by the

drugs coursing through her system. Enda closed her eyes and leaned her head against the wall. She felt lethargic now, instead of full of cotton wool. It wasn't much of an improvement. "What did he tell you?"

"He said Leo tried to jump off Dead Rock and you were trying to talk him down when Con arrived. Then he said you had an episode when you arrived back at the hospital."

"An episode?"

"You were talking to people who weren't there, getting upset, getting violent for no apparent reason. Conrad is extremely upset about the whole thing."

Enda took a deep breath and stopped herself before she could insist to her mother she'd been talking to ghosts. That would get her nowhere. "How's Dad?"

"He's sedated and under suicide watch. I only saw him briefly."

"I don't think he was going to jump, Mum."

Leda laid her fingers on Enda's wrist. Enda opened her eyes and looked down at the fingers. They were slender, smooth for her age, the nails painted pearly pink. Leda leaned forward and lowered her voice. "I was trying to get you transferred back to the city," she said.

Enda shook her head emphatically. "I want to be near Dad."

"Listen to me." Leda's voice dropped again, so Enda had to lean in close to hear her. Only then did she notice the strain around her mother's eyes, the way the lines were deeper, the flicker of fear. "Conrad has blocked my every effort to get you out of here. He knows he can only hold you for 72 hours, but it won't take much for him to get a court order to hold you for longer if you don't cooperate. This is your second involuntary psychiatric admission in a month, it looks bad."

Enda swallowed hard. "What are you saying?"

"I'm saying Conrad's trying to keep you here. I don't know why and I don't trust him. He's a controlling son of a bitch. Enda please just cooperate with these people until we can get you out of here and away from Dead Rock. I've taken time away from work to be here, I'm not going to leave until you do, alright?"

Enda stared at her mother. "I don't understand."

"Don't make me put it any plainer."

"But you were all about me taking my medication." She was still dull and her brain was not being the least bit helpful.

"And I still am," Leda said, more loudly this time. "Taking your medication is the most important thing."

Enda glanced around the room and saw what Leda must have on coming in; on the roof, a red light blinked at her below a half-sphere. A camera. "They're watching me?" she whispered.

Leda nodded.

Enda leaned towards her. "Why didn't you ever tell anyone about him?"

"Him who?"

"About what Uncle Con did to you."

"I don't know what you're talking about." New lines appeared on Leda's forehead.

"Yes you do. He raped you."

Leda drew back as though stung. "Don't assume things like that, Enda."

"But Alice saw you! She told me!"

Leda's whole face went red and she looked as though she would cry.

Enda stared. She'd never seen Leda cry in her life.

"There was nobody to tell," Leda said in a hollow voice. "Please don't mention that again."

"So he just gets away with that, too?"

"It was over 20 years ago!"

"Mum," Enda said, and she made her voice very, very, quiet. "Dad was on Dead Rock because he thinks Uncle Con killed someone. Someone he was friends with. Listen, I'll do what you say, I'll cooperate and get myself out of here in less than 72 hours if I can, if I did it at City Hospital, I can do it here. But we have to get Dad out too, alright? I'm not leaving Dead Rock without him."

Leda's lips pursed to a thin line. She looked scared. She nodded. "Alright."

Enda laid back down, exhausted. She hated the way the medication made her feel. The Haldol was probably three times worse than the Lithium had been. "I need you to go see Molly," she said. "Tell her what's happened. She lives in the house just near the top of Dead Rock."

"I know where Molly lives."

*

The next time Enda opened her eyes Doctor Howard was in the room with her and there was a thermometer in her mouth.

The doctor gave her a jovial smile that didn't reach his eyes, took the thermometer out and shook it. "Hello Enda. How are you feeling?"

Enda sat up and rubbed her eyes. "Like I've slept for hours."

"You have." He fixed a blood pressure cuff around her arm. "This is going to pinch a little."

Enda waited until he'd finished inflating the cuff, then glanced at the screen. 120 over 70, her blood pressure was perfectly normal.

"We're a little elevated," Doctor Howard said. "But nothing to be concerned about, we'll just keep an eye on it."

Enda tilted her head, watched him and wondered why he was lying. Maybe he wanted to keep her on the back foot. "How long did I sleep?" she asked.

"Almost a day." The doctor settled himself into the chair, clipboard on his lap, and looked at her over his glasses. "You must have needed it. How have you been sleeping, Enda?"

Enda settled herself against the wall. She felt better than she had. "I don't normally sleep that well," she said.

"Any particular reason?"

Ghosts visit me. Shadow things live under my bed. She couldn't see a shadow thing on the doctor. Or any ghosts in the room. "I have nightmares," she said.

"About anything particular?"

"Ghosts."

"Ah." He wrote on his clipboard. "You've mentioned ghosts a number of times before. When you were last hospitalised you claimed to have seen a man at the hospital you were working at suffering severe haemorrhage?"

Enda shifted uncomfortably. "Yes."

"And since then? Yesterday, here, for instance? Sergeant Wilson says you were talking to someone he couldn't see. Was that a ghost too, Enda?"

Enda knitted her fingers and looked at them. She attempted a small, embarrassed smile. "I suppose it seems silly to you," she said.

"Not at all. I believe these delusions are very real to the subject at the time."

"Very real."

"Tell me about this ghost. Did she have a name?"

Enda shrugged. "I don't really remember."

"Can you describe her?"

"She was in her thirties or forties and covered in cuts and bruises. But she was just a delusion, right?"

"Yes," Doctor Howard said, his voice steady. "Yes she was. Tell me, do you see any ghosts with us in the room right now?"

Enda shook her head.

"Good! You're showing a marked improvement on the Haldol, I see. Let me see you take your next dose." He handed her a glass of water and two pills that had been sitting on the table next to him.

Enda took them and swallowed both without comment.

"Show me," he said.

She opened her mouth to show him she'd swallowed the pills.

"Good girl." The doctor stood up and gathered up his clipboard. "Stay on your medication this time and you should be fine. Your uncle will be pleased."

Enda dug her fingernails into the sheets and gave the doctor a forced smile. "Please can I see my dad?"

"Of course. He's under strict supervision, you understand, so you'll have to have someone with you. I'll send someone by to take you in a little while."

The door closed. Enda wondered where her mother was and if she'd gone to see Molly. She looked around the room. Not much to do here. She hopped off the bed and opened the drawers under the table; there was her bag, intact. She took the battered suicide list out of it, keeping her back to the camera, and scanned the names on it.

Ada Winter, 38. Died January 1, 1983. Suffered from a depressive disorder. Police records indicate she was an alcoholic, ejected from the local tavern frequently. Lived alone. Referred to Dr E. Howard for psychiatric help by Sgt C. Wilson shortly before her death.

She replaced the list and sat on the bed. "Ada?" she whispered into the room, and waited.

There was no reply. Not so much as a bump. The silence pressed in.

"Selene?"

Nothing.

Enda threw herself down and buried her face in the pillow. She'd never felt so alone.

*

It was hours before anyone came to take her to see Leo, and when they did, it was her mother and Uncle Con.

Enda forced herself to stay calm. She'd had those hours, alone, to think about the implications of Uncle Con possibly being a murderer, and why Leda had looked so scared. She'd come to the conclusion accusing him outright of anything at all was probably a bad idea. So when he followed Leda into the room she just looked at her feet and shuffled out obediently between them.

Leda said nothing. Enda watched Con out of the corner of her eye. He took up a lot of space, physically and mentally. The sensation of him watching her so closely, waiting for a hint of violence or a conversation with a ghost, was not a pleasant one.

There were no ghosts. Not in the halls, not anywhere. Even the shadow thing was gone from his shoulders, but Enda had a fair idea that was more because she couldn't see it than because he'd shaken it.

They went down two corridors before they reached a door into a ward much like hers, where there was just a bed and a table. This bed was placed by a window that looked into the hospital gardens.

Leo sat up in the bed looking out of the window. He didn't look around when they came in.

"Leo, I've brought you a visitor." Con's voice filled the room.

Leo still didn't so much as flinch.

"Dad?" Enda went toward the bed. She sat on the chair next to it and looked into his face. It was blank; nothing flickered there. The gaze into the garden was unwavering. His hair was brushed and tied back, but he needed a shave. Maybe the nurses wouldn't do that for him. She clicked her fingers in front of his eyes, but they didn't waver.

Enda looked at Con and Leda. Leda just shook her head.

"He's been like this since we brought him in," Con said, from where he stood by the door. "I'm sorry Enda, there's not much they can do until he comes out of it himself."

"But why? Why's he like this? What are they medicating him with?"

Con shrugged. "I'm not a doctor. I don't know."

"Honey I'm sure they're doing everything they can." Leda sounded strained. Enda remembered her earlier warnings.

"Can I have a few minutes alone with him?" she asked. "Please Uncle Con?"

Con shook his head. "I'm sorry Enda, I can't allow it yet, for either of you."

"Okay." The word cost her, when she would have liked to go over there and kick him in the shin. Enda took Leo's hand in her own and squeezed it. "Hey Dad, it's good to see you."

He squeezed back. No other muscle moved. Enda took her cue from him and did not react. "I hope they're looking after you," she said.

Another squeeze.

"As soon as you're better, Dad, we can go home."

Two squeezes. Enda sat there for a while longer, as long as she dared, with Leda shuffling in one corner and Con watching her every move.

Finally Con cleared his throat. "Time to go," he said.

"Alright." Enda stood up. "Bye Dad. I'll come see you again soon." She shuffled back along the corridors with the guard around her. Her biological parents. The thought was bitter and unwelcome. When they reached her room, Leda went to follow her in.

Con laid a hand on her shoulder. "Go on, Enda," he said.

"Can't my mum come and sit with me for a while? Please?"

"Doctor Howard said it was best for you to rest now."

"I'm not tired."

Leda gave her a strained smile. "Go on sweetie. Get some rest. I'll come by later."

Uncle Con reached around and shut the door in her face. His smile was nothing less than nasty when his fingers curled into Leda's shoulder.

Enda pressed her ear to the door.

"Why won't you let me stay with her?" Leda demanded.

"I told you already, she's at a delicate part of her treatment," Con replied. "The doctor wants to minimise her contact with everyone until she's stable."

"But look at her! She's fine, she's on her medication, she's the most stable I've seen her in weeks!"

"Let's allow the doctor to make that call, shall we?"

Enda went over to the bed and buried her face in the pillow. She was heartily sick of this room, this bed, this thin, sterile pillowcase and her own company.

*

The hours dragged by, punctuated only by meal times. When it got dark, Enda slept. When she woke Uncle Con was in the room.

Enda slowly sat up, watching him. It was early. The light filtering into the room hadn't yet reached full strength.

He pushed a glass of water and two pills toward her. "The nurse brought these. I said I'd see you took them."

Enda swallowed them and then waited for him to speak.

Con avoided her eyes. He seemed to be searching for the right words. When he spoke, he spoke to his knees, not to her face. "I'm sorry about all this Enda. I'm sorry you chose to do things this way."

She shifted position on the bed until she was leaning against the opposite wall and didn't answer. She didn't trust herself to.

"I never meant for you to find out I was your father," he said. "Never, and definitely not like you did. I would have died with that secret."

"Why?" the word dropped reluctantly from her lips.

"For Leo," he said. "I gave him the one thing he wanted most, and I was happy to. I gave him a child. You." He leaned forward, elbows resting on his knees. "You've got to understand, Enda, he's my brother. I would do anything to protect him. But now that you know things are going to change. I accept that. You've always been my daughter in one way or another. Don't let all this ruin that, Enda, please. Don't listen to gossip and lies from other people. We're family. The Wilsons have always been strong because we stick together. We're going to stick together now."

Enda regarded him steadily. "What do you want from me?"

"You're going to be discharged later this morning," he said.

"Finally."

"I want you to promise me you'll stay on your medication and stay away from Dead Rock. You've heard a lot of lies." Only then did he meet her eyes and fix them with a deadly serious stare. "I want you to forget everything you've been pursuing since you arrived here. Stay away from it. There's nothing there for you."

"I've no idea what you're talking about."

Uncle Con sighed and shook his head. He took a battered piece of paper from his pocket and held it out to her. "This, Enda."

She took it from him. Her heart hammered. The suicide list. "Where did you get this?"

"I think a better question is, where did *you* get it?" He took the paper back off her. "This is dangerous. It's been fuelling your delusions." He leaned forward and spoke into her face. "Leave it alone, Enda, or people will start getting hurt and I can guarantee you and Mad Molly will be the first in line." He moved back; his voice returned to a normal, even tone. "And I would hate for that to happen. I don't want to lose another daughter. Do we understand each other?"

Enda nodded.

"Tell me you understand me."

"I understand you."

"Good. I'll be keeping a close eye on you." He stood and left, the list clutched in his hand.

Enda stuffed her knuckles in her mouth. Her other hand, the one with the stitches, shook. She watched the closed door. Her stomach clenched so hard she thought she was going to be sick. She hoped to God that was just the fear, and that he hadn't just fed her an overdose of Haldol. Nobody out there would be the least bit surprised if she was found dead at the bottom of Dead Rock in the morning, and it was all his doing.

*

They let her out at midday after taking the stitches out of her hand, giving her a bunch of prescriptions and letting her see Leo for exactly two minutes. Uncle Con walked Enda and her mother into the car park and opened the car door for Leda.

Leda got in without comment. Enda slid into the passenger seat.

Con stuck his head in the window. "Are you sure you'll be alright?"

Leda nodded, her eyes on the steering wheel. "We'll be fine, Conrad."

"Okay. I'll come by and check up later. Enda, you're doing really well. Just remember your promise." He drew back.

Leda started the car and hit reverse. The wheels squealed. They exited the car park.

Enda smoothed down the skirt Leda had brought her to wear. "Maybe we could stay somewhere else than Dad's house," she said. "And not tell him where."

"You know very well he'd find us." Leda's words were clipped. "If you're bound and determined to stay here until your father comes out of hospital we're going to have to put up with him." She turned a corner into town and pulled up outside the chemist. "I'm going to get your prescriptions. Stay here."

"Mum-"

"Enda you are staying on your medication. No arguments." Leda got out of the car.

Enda watched her disappear into the chemist. Then she watched the rear view mirror. The sun beating down on the streets was too hot for there to be more than a stray dog out and about. Leda reappeared after a few minutes clutching a bulging paper bag. She tossed it to Enda, started the car and reversed out.

CHAPTER SIXTEEN

Leda didn't drive straight home. When she missed the turnoff Enda figured she must have another errand to run. When she turned onto the highway, she wondered if Leda had decided to get out of Dead Rock regardless. "Where are we going, Mum?"

"We're going to see Molly."

Enda breathed a sigh of relief. She didn't feel up to the kind of fight that would result from being kidnapped by her own mother right now. "Good."

"Why, where did you think we were going?"

"I thought maybe you were just going to drive back to the city."

"Don't think I didn't consider it. But no, Molly asked me to bring you up to see her as soon as they let you out of hospital. Said she had some things to tell you."

"You went to see her then."

"Of course I did. Molly and I go way back."

Enda stared. "Really?"

"You sound surprised."

"Uncle Con calls her Mad Molly, I didn't think-"

"That I'd see someone he didn't like? My dear, that's practically a recommendation." Leda turned the four wheel drive onto the gravel road that led up the hill. "I started school in Dead Rock not long before Conrad left it. I very quickly figured out I disliked bullies, and Molly and I became friends."

*

1962

Thick, warm drops of rain pelted from the leaden sky. It was like someone had squeezed and squeezed until they wrung the water from the hot, wet air itself. Every raindrop that made it to the ground threw up a little cloud of dust, until the rain gathered enough force to turn the dust into a thin slick of mud.

Leda stood in the rain in the middle of the dust bowl playground and tipped her head back. The warm water slid over her skin, ran fingers of cool over her scalp and through her two plaits. She'd never expected moving schools to be easy, or making new friends in a tiny, dusty town like this to happen fast, but the heat, the heat was awful. This was the first relief she'd had in the two weeks since they'd moved. She didn't care she was going to end up soaking wet on her first day of school, or even if the other kids saw her. She wouldn't be in Dead Rock long.

A shape pushed past her in the rain, so fast it was little more than a blur. Then a second, then a third. The third shape shoved her when it went past and she fell over into the mud.

Leda yelled. She didn't mind being wet, but muddy was another thing entirely.

A fourth shape came running, slowed and stopped in front of her. A boy with black hair and freckles and a pointed face, maybe a year older than her, held out his hand.

Leda accepted it with all the dignity she could muster. She let him help her up and then brushed herself off. She bit her lip to keep it from trembling.

"What are you doing down there?" the boy asked.

"Somebody knocked me," Leda said.

"Probably my brother Con. He's kind of rough." The boy stuck out his hand. "I'm Leo."

"Leda." She gave him her fingertips and they shook. She smiled at him. This boy seemed okay, for a country hick. "Why were those other kids running?"

Leo said a word that made Leda turned scarlet.

"Excuse me?"

"I'm sorry, I forgot. It's Con. I have to make sure he doesn't do anything bad – you stay here." Leo dashed away.

Leda had no intention of staying there. She pelted after Leo and followed him around behind the schoolyard. The rain eased. Her eyes widened at the scene.

The very big boy could only have been Con. He had an Aboriginal boy in an arm lock with one hand, and was holding back an Aboriginal girl with the other while she pummelled her fists at him.

Leo slowed to a halt. Raindrops tumbled from his hair to his mouth. "Con, that's enough," he said.

Con let out a barrage of very bad words at Leo.

Leda's foot nudged a glass bottle. She bent down and picked it up. "You going to do something about this?" she asked Leo.

"He'll stop," Leo said, but he didn't sound like he believed it.

Leda scowled. "My mum says the only person worse than a bully is the one who lets bullying happen. That's why my dad's in Vietnam." And with that sententious remark, she marched around behind Con, wound her arm back and smashed him in the back of the head with the bottle as hard as she could.

The glass cracked. Con whirled around, clutching the back of his head. He raised a fist. "You little bitch!"

Leda, who had never suffered the indignity of being called a name like that in her life, wound the bottle back again and bared her teeth at the boy. "At least I'm not a bully! Get lost! Leave them alone!"

Con swung his fist. Leda jumped out of the way. The hit must have been hard, because the bully swung himself off balance. His eyes rolled back in his head and he pitched forward.

Leo gave her a look of pure admiration, then bolted, presumably for a doctor. Leda put her bottle down and went over to meet the other two kids.

~

Con was out of school for a whole week. Leda fully expected to get in trouble, but nobody said a thing. Leo took to sitting in the next desk over. He told her Con had said he'd just hit his head, rather than admit to being beaten up by a girl a third his size.

Leda decided maybe this place wasn't so bad, at least for now. Sometimes Molly would come and talk to her and then she would feel more at home, because none of the other girls liked her. Apparently they were all scared of being hit with glass bottles.

~

The atmosphere in the classroom changed when Con came back. Even the teacher seemed to tense up. Molly and Tom kept their heads down at the back of the class. When Leo sat next to Leda, Con took a seat on her other side. He didn't try to talk to her, but he looked at her a lot. It made her nervous.

154

1967

Leda leaned toward the mirror in the town hall toilets. It was scratched down the sides and she didn't like to get too close to the cracked and grimy sink below it, but she was more than satisfied with her reflection. Mum had done her hair in cascading ringlets and even let her put on makeup, pale pink lipstick and heavy blue eye shadow. Leda had sewn her own dress, fitted around the bust and with a skirt that went straight from there to just over her hips, like Twiggy. Her chunky platforms added a good three inches to her height.

She rubbed her lips together, made sure her eyelashes hadn't smudged anywhere, straightened her chunky, dangling earrings and nodded. She had no doubt at all she'd be the prettiest girl at the dance tonight. All she had to do was make sure Leo asked her to dance first, and not Emma Lyon, who'd been following him around like a little lost puppy after school ever since she saw him working in Mrs Emmett's garden without a shirt on.

She patted down her dress, took a deep breath, walked out of the toilets and into the hall.

Mr Drew, who played piano in church, hammered out a tune on the big grand piano. The hall rapidly filled with everyone in town. Some of the older people waltzed in lazy circles. The kids didn't dance yet. They'd been promised some records. All the girls stood in a line down one side of the hall. All the boys stood in a line down the other.

Leda walked over to the line of girls, leaned against the wall and studied her nails. She tilted her head, just a little, so the curls cascaded down her neck. She'd practised that in the mirror at home. Then she peeked across the hall to see if Leo was watching.

If only the old people would stop dancing everywhere, she'd have a better view.

There, she spotted him standing almost opposite, keeping one eye on her while he talked with another boy.

Leda smirked, satisfied, and looked for Emma. The smile dropped from her face. Emma's skirt was shorter than hers. Slut.

Mr Drew left the piano for a break. Mrs Emmett, who'd been the teacher at school for the past year, lowered a record onto the turntable set up in the corner. The speakers crackled and started playing the Monkees.

The girls waited, breathless. The boys talked at each other over the other side, daring, pointing, laughing, until Leda wanted to scream at them to get on with it.

Daniel was the bravest. He walked straight over and asked Jenny to dance. Then Tom went and asked Molly, and then Leo finally peeled away from the wall.

Leda waited, breathless. He seemed to take an age. First it looked like he was heading for Emma, then for her. Leda thrust her shoulders back and studied the peeling paint on the back of the bench next to her, just like she didn't care.

The hall doors scraped open to admit late arrivals. Leda cast a glance that way to see who it was. She curled her lip. Conrad was here with his hanger-on, Eric Howard, a skinny little brown-haired thing she despised almost as much as she despised Conrad himself.

Leo had passed Emma. Thank God. Leda finally deigned to meet his eyes and give him a little smile, only to have someone else's hand curl around her wrist. She looked up into Conrad's face, outraged.

He looked down on her and grinned. "Dance," was all he said, and yanked her out into the middle of the floor.

Leda almost tripped over her platforms. She only saved her dignity by running to keep up. She would *not* trip over in a skirt this short. She looked over her shoulder at Leo, who watched them, expressionless. He turned on his heel and went straight to Emma.

Slut!

Leda grit her teeth. Conrad yanked her around to face him, put one hand on her waist, linked fingers with her free hand and pulled her close. He was sweaty and smelled like cigarette smoke. She held her breath and followed his ungainly attempt at dancing, since Leo was practically breathing down Emma's top right now.

"I heard you've been seeing my brother," Conrad said.

"Certainly not." Leda's cheeks flamed.

"What, we're not good enough for you? Rather spend your time with the hired help?" He jerked his thumb at Molly and Tom, who were dancing in a corner on their own. "I saw you talking to her this morning. What do you talk about, the best ways to skin a lizard?" He spun her around a little too roughly. His hand bumped her breast and Leda slapped him away, outraged.

"Keep your hands to yourself!"

Conrad grabbed her waist and pulled her close again. "What I don't understand," he said in her ear, "is how my little brother managed to catch the prettiest girl in town. You should come out with me, I'll show you a good time."

"I'd rather go out with a goat, Conrad Wilson." Leda gave him her coldest smile.

"You're just playing hard to get." He pulled her even closer.

Leda caught sight of Leo, dancing nearby with Emma, but watching her. Good. She was beginning to feel bruised. "Would you let me go? I can't breathe!"

"Only if you come out with me next Saturday."

"No Conrad, and I swear to God if you don't let go of me, I'll hurt you."

He sneered. "What, you're going to sneak up behind me with a bottle and hit me again?"

Leda snickered. "You still sore about that?"

"I'll forget all about it if you kiss me. Just one, come on."

Leda kicked him in the shin with the corner of the metal plate on the bottom of her shoe.

Conrad yelled and grabbed his leg. "Bitch!"

Leda tossed her head and walked away quite fast. She gave Leo a pointed look when she passed him.

He left Emma standing in the middle of the dance floor and followed her, which made the whole night worth it. They went and stood over near the cloakroom.

"Are you okay?" he asked. "You shouldn't have done that, he'll be mad."

"He made me mad first." She folded her arms and pouted at him. "How come you didn't ask me to dance?"

"I was going to, but I-"

"Wasn't fast enough?" Leda gave him a haughty look. "You'll have to do better than that."

"Can I walk you home later?"

That was more like it. "Maybe."

"Will you dance with me now?"

"I suppose." She walked with him back to the dance floor. "Let's just not dance near Conrad," she whispered in his ear.

Leo nodded. They found a spot near the adults and Leo didn't leave her side for the rest of the night.

Leda was aware of Conrad leaning against the wall, watching them, right up until they left.

*

Leda parked the car behind Molly's house, out of view of the road. "Did I get a little side tracked?"

Enda shook her head. "No, it was a good story. But what are you saying, Uncle Con liked you?"

"I don't think he ever really liked anyone. I got his attention because I stood up to him and because I was friends with Molly."

"What about later? After you married Dad and became a Wilson? What happened with Molly then?"

"We kind of drifted apart." The smile dropped from Leda's face. "It's probably not so bad when you're a kid, but as an adult, being a Wilson in Dead Rock's like being in the mafia. Your life's not your own."

CHAPTER SEVENTEEN

Enda followed her mother into the darkness of Molly's house and sat down in the lounge room. Even that short walk left her exhausted. The sooner the Haldol was out of her system the better.

Molly set three glasses of water down and sat across from them. A frown creased the skin between her eyes when she looked at Enda. "You okay?"

Enda nodded and sipped her water.

"What about Leo?"

"Not so much. He's still in the hospital."

"You've got to get him out of there or he's going to get worse."

"He's not responding to anything or anyone," Leda said. "He just sits there and stares into space."

"He responded to me," Enda said.

"How?" Leda looked shocked.

"He squeezed my hand. He's in there Mum, but he's scared."

"What's he so scared of? Not this ridiculous story about a murder, surely?"

Enda sighed and put her glass down. "It's not ridiculous."

"What murder?" Molly asked.

"Kelvin Fraser," Enda said. "He was one of the suicides. Dad thinks Uncle Con killed him."

"Why does he think that?"

Enda flushed. "Because I met Kelvin in the cemetery and he told me how he died. I told Dad about it. I didn't realise it was his friend."

"Enda! Of all the ridiculous stories! Why would you tell your father a thing like that? And how can you sit there and say you met someone who died years ago when you know perfectly well it was a delusion?"

"It's not a delusion Mum!"

"Of course it's a delusion! You're not seeing anything now

you're on the medication, are you? Doesn't that prove none of it was real? Conrad showed me that list you were carrying around, isn't it awfully convenient you were meeting ghosts straight off it?"

"The only thing my medication proves is that chemicals block out my ability to see people who need my help!" Enda rubbed her aching head. "As for Uncle Con – Conrad – that *asshole,* I don't see why you're still letting him manipulate you after all these years, and after what he did to you! Can't you see he knows I'm onto him? He's doing everything in his power to make me look like a complete nutcase so nobody will believe a thing I say! He as good as threatened me and Molly both this morning if I didn't shut the hell up and be a good girl!"

Silence followed her outburst. Leda looked as though she'd been slapped.

Molly cleared her throat. "If you two are quite finished I think I can probably tell you why Leo is scared," she said. "And why you should take Conrad's threats seriously. You can decide what to do after that."

Leda let out an explosive breath and seemed to deflate. "I'm sorry Molly," she said.

Molly brushed away the apology with a wave of her hand. "Just listen," she said. "It's time you heard this, Leda."

*

1968
"Please Mrs Wilson, can Molly come out too?"

Molly slopped the heavy, wet mop onto the kitchen floor. Grey water oozed outward. She pushed the thing along the linoleum, spreading the water further outward, leaving a gleaming slick wherever she went. "Molly can't come out, she's got to work to do," she mouthed, in time to Mum Wilson.

"But *please* Mrs Wilson, she works so hard, surely she's earned a night off. Leo's taking me to the drive in, I bet Molly would love to come."

Leda sure could wheedle when she wanted something.

"I don't know, Leda, I'm not sure that's a good place for Molly."

Molly scrubbed a little faster, just in case. Leda was damn good at getting anything she wanted, especially from Mum Wilson, who thought she was a good catch for Leo. Maybe if she had the floor done she'd get out of here for the night. Conrad was out at the pub with his mates, he wouldn't drop in and ruin things.

"We'll look after her, I promise. It's just my mum said I'm not to go out with Leo on my own."

Molly could almost hear Leda batting her eyelashes. She grinned at the mop bucket and sped through the last part of the floor.

Mum Wilson still sounded doubtful. "What about Con and Betty?"

"Con's out tonight, and Betty's gone to see her family in the city."

"Well, alright, but only if she's finished her chores. Molly. Molly!"

Molly balanced the mop in the bucket and went over the wet floor on her tiptoes. She stopped at the door. "Yes?"

"Have you finished the floor?"

Molly grinned. "Yes I have. And the dishes, and the tables."

Mum Wilson sounded put out. "Alright then. Go and put on your good dress I bought you. Leda and Leo are taking you to the drive in tonight."

Molly tiptoed through the kitchen and ran to her room at the back of the house. She quickly changed into the bright blue dress Mum Wilson had bought her, a hideous thing with a big bow at the back. At least it fit. She smoothed it down, pulled a brush through her hair and put on some sandals. Then she ran back through the house, tiptoed around the edges of the wet kitchen floor and presented herself to Mum Wilson and Leda.

"Very nice." Mum Wilson looked her up and down. She didn't sound terribly convinced. "Leda can't you help her do something with that hair?"

Molly patted her hair. She hadn't thought there was anything wrong with it.

Leda grabbed Molly's hand and started edging her toward the front door. "Yes, Mrs Wilson."

Mum Wilson followed them. "Molly I want you home by ten."

Molly nodded. "Yes Mum Wilson."

"And stay with Leda."

"Yes."

"And no boys, you hear? Especially not that Tom what-his-name, I don't want him leading you astray."

"Don't worry Mrs Wilson, we'll be good." Leda all but dragged Molly through the front door, then shut it.

Molly and Leda stood on the veranda for a moment and looked at each other. Leda burst out giggling first, Molly soon after. They bolted across the front yard and down the street, where a part of the bush had been knocked down last year to make way for the fibro houses now going up.

"Leo's waiting for us at the corner," Leda said. "He's come straight from work. Tom's meeting us at the drive in."

Molly grinned. "Who you gonna lead astray, me or the boys?"

~

Leo had a white pickup truck that was already showing the signs of age. The fenders were rusty and the tray squealed and bounced, but Molly knew he was proud of it.

She and Leda had squeezed into the front with Leo for the drive to the sandy area near Dead Rock, where there was a big temporary screen set up. All the kids in town were haphazardly parked in front of it.

Leo manoeuvred the truck to somewhere in the middle and took a flask from his pocket. He slung an arm around Leda and took a swig.

He'd let his hair grow past his ears, to Mum Wilson's horror, since starting to work. Molly secretly thought he was trying to look like Ringo Starr, except he couldn't for the life of him grow a moustache. She hid her grin behind her hand.

Leo handed the flask to Leda, who took a swig and coughed delicately. She handed it on to Molly.

Molly sniffed it. Whatever Leo was drinking was strong. She tipped it up and took a swig. Fiery liquid burned her throat and she coughed, hard.

Leo chuckled. "Take it easy mate." He slapped her on the back until she could breathe again. "Alright?"

Molly nodded. A pleasant warmth tingled through her fingers and toes.

"Here comes Tom," Leo said, pointing into the rear view.

Molly hopped out of the car, shut the door and waved.

Tom cut a tall, skinny shape striding through the cars. He had on short pants, suspenders, dusty old boots and a wide-brimmed hat. Molly felt sad the Nickels wouldn't even get him nice clothes to go out in. But then again, maybe they didn't know he was out. They could be even stricter than the Wilsons.

Tom put an arm around her shoulders and kissed her on the cheek. His teeth gleamed white in the gathering dusk. "Hi Molly. You look nice."

Molly grinned. "Thanks." She and Tom climbed up into the back of the truck. They settled themselves on the tray, side by side, backs to the movie.

Tom held her hand. Molly stroked Tom's roughened skin with her thumb. They looked up at the sky and ignored the loud opening music of Planet of the Apes. Time together had become so rare since they left school, Molly had no desire to waste it watching a dumb movie. "So how long now?" she said.

"How old are you?"

"I reckon I'm seventeen." Molly gave a tiny sigh. Mum Wilson had argued the point with her a couple of weeks ago, saying she was only sixteen, probably because she didn't want her to take off and leave her with all the housework.

"Next year," Tom said. "Next year you and me are gonna walk up that road and never come back."

Molly leaned into the warmth of his arm. "Where are we gonna go?"

"I want to see that place where the sky meets the land," Tom said.

"I want to find my family. My real family." Molly felt Tom nod. She buried her face in his shoulder. "And yours."

"No more Dead Rock," Tom said.

"No more cleaning." Molly really liked that thought.

"No more Conrad."

There was a moment of silence after that one. "Leo's not so bad though," Molly ventured.

Tom shrugged. "Maybe. When he's on his own."

"Conrad's going away soon," Molly said. "Some kind of school to learn to be in the police. Dad Wilson said it was that or the army, so Con chose the police. He doesn't want to go to

Vietnam."

"I don't think I want to see him in the police," Tom said in a low voice.

"We'll be gone by the time he gets back."

Tom smiled. "That's good. Sooner the better." He bent down and touched her lips, gently, and Molly and Tom kissed, just like Leda and Leo kissed in the front of the car, and all the other kids made out in their cars. The movie played to a heedless audience.

~

Leda got out of the car, swung herself up and balanced at the side of the tray. Behind her the credits rolled. A thin haze of cigarette smoke drifted across the audience of cars, mingling with the faint smell of whiskey and petrol. "Hey kids, how'd you like the movie?"

"Not half so much as you did." Molly pointed at Leda's neck. "What's your mum gonna say when she sees that hickey?"

Leda mock-pouted at her. "That's what scarves are for. Hey, we're gonna go up Dead Rock and smoke weed. Wanna come, or wanna go home and meet Mama Wilson's curfew?"

Molly and Tom glanced at each other. Tom shrugged. "I'll go if you will."

"Good! We're going! Hang on tight!" Leda jumped down and hopped back into the car, less than steady on her feet.

Molly wondered how much of Leo's flask she'd had to drink.

The car started up and turned in a tight circle, manoeuvred past the other cars all trying to leave and went up the highway. Molly and Tom held onto the sides while they bumped up the steep gravel road, curved tightly and then parked at the top of the cliff.

Tom hopped down, then helped Molly to the ground, even though she didn't need him to. They walked hand in hand to the edge to look out at the cascade of stars that went from over their heads all the way to the ground.

"Hey you two! Come over here!" Leo waved them back to the car.

Molly and Tom walked back.

Leo leaned against the side of the tray. Paper rustled in his hands. "Just stay away from the edge, alright? Mum'd kill me if anything happened to Molly."

Leda stood free of the car, looking up at the stars. "It's so beautiful up here." She put her arms out, her head back, and spun in a slow circle. Leo watched her every move with helpless puppy-dog eyes.

Finally he twisted the end of the joint and lit it up with a match. The red end glowed and sparks flew into the air like little stars.

Leda made a smooth arabesque over to him, took the joint from his mouth and drew on it. She exhaled a cloud of smoke and offered it to Tom, who shook his head. She handed it to Molly, who shook her head, too.

"Go on," Leda said. "Who's gonna know?"

Molly shook her head again. "I'll get in trouble."

"Just one tiny little puff. Tom doesn't mind, do you Tom?"

Leda made big eyes at him.

Tom chuckled. "It's up to Molly."

Molly rolled her eyes. Not even Tom was immune to Leda when she wanted something. She took the joint and had a tiny, tiny puff, just to shut her up.

"Come on!" Leda folded her arms. "Take a proper one."

Molly drew smoke deep into her lungs. It burned worse than the alcohol had. She exhaled a cloud of smoke into Leda's face and handed the joint back to Leo. "Happy?"

"I'm so happy." Leda put out her arms as though dancing with an invisible partner.

Leo took a long drag of the joint, then went and joined her. He held her outstretched fingers with one hand and shoved the joint in her mouth with the other. Leda giggled and took a drag and they danced around the grass, under the stars, sharing the joint back and forth.

Molly watched them with a little smile. Leo had been kinder to her since he'd started walking out with Leda. He stood up to Conrad more often too. She hoped they'd get married and have ten kids and be happy after she and Tom left Dead Rock.

Leda was flagging. After a while she leaned on Leo's shoulder and groaned. "I don't feel so good."

Leo swept an arm under her and carried her to the car. By the time he got there she'd passed out. Molly could tell by the way her head lolled.

"Lightweight," Leo said. "Hey Tom, give me a hand getting her in the car."

Tom opened the door and between them, they manoeuvred Leda into the seat and laid her down.

"We gonna take her home?" Molly asked. She was worried. She was glad she hadn't smoked as much as Leda had.

"Nah, she'll be right." Leo gently closed the door. "Besides, her mum would kill us."

"She's gonna kill us anyway for being late."

"Not as bad as she would for smoking pot." Leo leaned against the car with them and rolled a cigarette. He offered the packet of tobacco to Tom, who rolled two cigarettes and handed one to Molly.

Molly only smoked sometimes. Tobacco made her cough. She just sucked in a little bit at a time and practised blowing clouds of smoke into the cold, sharp air. Her blood tingled and her face buzzed.

The feeling drained away, very slowly, when the sound of an approaching car reached them. She started to feel cold. "Who's that?" she whispered.

Tom put a foot in the rung behind him and hoisted himself up to see over the tray. He waited. An interminable minute ticked by. "It's Conrad's car," he said.

Molly's heart thudded against her ribs. "Leo we've got to go," she said. She looked over at him. "Please."

Leo's hand trembled. "It'll be okay," he said. "Don't worry Molly. If we leave now it'll be worse."

Molly glanced at Tom. His jaw was tight and there was a tic in it. "Tom," she said. "Let's just go."

Tom shook his head. "He's right," he said. "If he sees us running away it'll set him off."

"It'll be okay," Leo repeated. "Don't worry. It'll be okay." He glanced in at Leda, who was still unconscious.

Con's car came onto the cliff top fast, circled them twice and screeched to a halt in front of them. For a moment nothing happened. Then Con got out and leaned against the door. He dropped his beer, a little too hard, on the roof. A second man lurched out of the passenger door, bolted to the nearest bushes and threw up.

"Eric, you girl!" Con roared. The sound echoed off the trees. Con turned his attention to the three leaning against the pickup truck. He eyed them with contempt. "Honestly Leo," he said. "I leave you alone for one bloody night and I find you up here with this scum."

Leo shrugged and lit a cigarette. "Go home Con," he said.

"Go home? What, are you my mother, now?" Con picked up his beer and walked around the car, unsteady on his feet.

Molly held Tom's hand so tight she was probably hurting him. She wished them anywhere but here. Con often got home this drunk. Sometimes he'd do things Mum Wilson never seemed to notice, like put dirt on a floor and demand she clean it, and then sit there and needle her with words that hurt, words that humiliated, while she worked. He'd barely touched her since the day he broke her arm, but he'd got bullying with words down to a fine art.

Leo chuckled and shook his head. The sound was friendly, but the nerves bled through. "Go wherever else you want, Con."

"But leave you alone?" Con stopped between the cars and surveyed the three of them. "Where's your pretty little girlfriend, Leo? Maybe I should go and find her, since you don't want my company."

Leo's jaw tightened. His voice came out in a growl. "You so much as touch her, I'll kill you."

Conrad grinned. It wasn't a friendly expression. "Will you, Leo? I don't blame you. She's the only chick worth banging in this hole of a town."

Leo dropped his cigarette on the ground. "Get out of here."

"Funny thing is," Conrad continued, ignoring him, "I could swear the old lady said you were out with her tonight, so where is she? She get bored of you and come looking for me?"

"We dropped her home," Leo said.

Molly glanced at him, involuntarily, because she'd never heard Leo tell a lie before.

"She's here, isn't she? What'd she do, hide? She in the car?" Conrad threw his head back. "Leda!" he yelled. "Come out, come out, wherever you are!" He waited for a moment, then shrugged when there was no reply. "Looks like I'll have to amuse myself some other way. Molly, come here."

Leo's hand landed on Molly's shoulder. "Lay off," he said.

Tom's hand tightened over Molly's fingers.

"Oh, I can't play with your little friends, either? That's just too bad. Molly, get your ass over here. Come on, I won't hurt you."

"No," Molly said in a low voice.

"Really? No? I don't think my parents put a roof over your head so you could say no." Con moved toward her.

Leo stepped in front of Molly and Tom. "Come on Con, leave her alone. You've had your fun."

"I haven't even started. Make your choice, Leo, what's it going to be? Molly or Leda?"

Tom's pulse was jumping. Molly knew he was seconds away from flying at Conrad. She leaned against him with all her weight, willing him not to because he always came off second best. She wished she'd just gone home after the movie like she was supposed to, or taken Tom elsewhere. She could almost smell the fear coming off Leo. He had no idea what to do. Conrad listened to him some when he was sober, but not tonight. Tonight he just reached out his hands, closed them around Leo's neck and pinned him to the car.

Leo made a horrible rasping noise.

Tom broke free of Molly's hold, leaped onto Conrad's back and dug his fingers into his eyes. Conrad yelled and stumbled backwards. Leo fell to the ground, gasping for air.

Molly helped Leo up. "Are you okay?"

He nodded. "Get in the car. I've got to get you and Leda out of here."

"I'm not going without Tom!"

Leo groaned. "Alright. Just wait here." He bolted across the grass to where Conrad and Tom rolled around pummelling each other the same way they had since they were kids.

Conrad had one eye on Leo's approach. "Eric!" he roared. "Get over here!"

Eric stood up from the bushes and wiped his mouth. "What?"

Conrad pushed Tom off him, staggered and gestured at Leo. "Get him out of my face while I deal with this little shit here."

Eric lurched toward Leo and pushed him into the back of Conrad's car.

Molly bit her knuckles. Tears ran down her face to mix with the blood she drew. When Conrad punched Tom full in the face and Tom spit a tooth out of his mouth, she couldn't stand it any longer. Leda was never afraid to stand up to Conrad, why should she be?

She bolted for the pair, put her head down and ran straight into Con's stomach before he could hit Tom again.

Conrad made a sound like all the air had been knocked out of him. He stumbled back.

"Tom come on!" Molly yelled. "Let's go!"

But Tom didn't listen. He was lost in fury, covered in sweat and blood, fists clenched, every muscle coiled.

Behind them Leo and Eric struggled. Leo had the upper hand because Eric was too drunk to be more than a nuisance.

Tom charged at Conrad and drove a fist into his face. Something cracked. Blood flowed from Conrad's nose. He clutched his face and caught Tom on the side of the head with one flying hand. Tom went down and Conrad kicked him in the ribs, again and again, sending him further back along the grass with each blow.

Molly looked beyond Tom to where the sky met the top of Dead Rock. Eric lurched past her. She stuck her foot out and tripped him over, then grabbed Leo's arm and pointed. She could barely hear her own words. "Help him."

"Shit." Leo bolted towards Con, Molly close behind him.

Conrad and Tom were almost at the edge. "Conrad stop!" Molly screamed.

Conrad looked back, giving Tom just enough time to pull himself up off the ground. "Change your mind did you?"

"Please stop this." Molly walked slowly toward him.

Leo put his hands up. "Come on Con. You won. Let me just take these guys home before they get too hurt."

Tom got to his feet, staggered and lurched at Conrad.

The movement caught Conrad's eye. He turned back, put his hands out and pushed hard.

Tom stumbled off balance and teetered at the edge of Dead Rock. Then he disappeared into the sky.

A scream pierced that same sky, so loud it sounded like the spirits of the dead were flying down to meet Tom before he hit the ground. Molly tried to run after him but Leo held her back, wouldn't let her get near the edge. Something inside her kept screaming, screaming, until Conrad came over, pushed Leo away and grabbed her. He pinned her against Leo's car and put a hand over her mouth. "Shut up," he said. "Just shut up, understand?"

Molly nodded, scared he'd kill her too if she didn't agree.

He took his hand away from her mouth, but kept her pinned to the car with an arm braced across her chest. Flecks of spit flew from his lips when he spoke in a low, vicious voice she'd never heard, even from him. "You say nothing," he said. "Nothing, you hear me? You saw nothing. No, you know what? You saw him jump. So you can cry and carry on all you like because that's what happened. He jumped. You ever say anything else about tonight, I swear I will hunt you down and throw you off Dead Rock too. Do you understand?"

Molly nodded.

"Tell me you understand me."

"I understand you," she whispered.

Con let her go. Molly slumped to the ground, her body racked by sobs. She saw Conrad tell Eric to get in the car, then he grabbed Leo, held his face in both hands and talked to him for a long time. At first Leo argued. Molly heard Conrad say something about Leda. After that Leo stopped talking and just nodded. When Leo finally broke away and came to the car he looked like he was staring into the depths of hell. He barely looked at Molly. "Get in," he said.

Molly opened the car door, propped Leda up and sat beside her. Leo got in behind the wheel and waited until Conrad's car had left.

Neither of them said a word.

CHAPTER EIGHTEEN

Leda was in the kitchen throwing up. Enda's stomach clenched with every sound, but she stayed with Molly in the tiny lounge room. The silence stretched out, but it was all on the outside. Inside Enda's skull, a teenaged Molly screamed. Uncle Con sat in a hospital room and said vile things. Selene said *"What's happened is our family's really fucked up, okay?"* and Leo sat in his hospital bed, captive of his own memories.

Enda's voice came out as barely more than a whisper. "Did you tell Selene?"

Molly nodded.

"And then she jumped?"

"Do you think she jumped?"

The sound of water running in the kitchen replaced the sound of throwing up, and then there was a bump.

Enda went in there and found her mother sitting on the floor, her head in her hands, crying. She sat down next to her and laid a hand on her arm. "Mum?"

Leda shook her head. "I guess this explains why he always drank so much." A silence. Then, "I don't remember it," she said. "I don't remember any of it, except the movie and going up to Dead Rock. I never even thought-" she looked up when Molly walked into the kitchen. "You never said anything. Leo never said anything."

"We were afraid. Leo still is." Molly offered Leda her hand and pulled her to her feet.

Enda got up too. "Are you still afraid, Molly?"

"No. What can he do to me that he hasn't already done, a thousand times over? He's made sure I'm isolated in this town, but I've still found people who will listen. One day one of those people will find a way to expose him." She looked at Enda.

"I'm crazy, remember? He's made sure nobody will listen to

171

me either." Enda looked at her mother.

"It's down to me is it?" Leda paced the kitchen, up and down, rubbing at her forehead. "We have to go to the police."

"He *is* the police, Mum."

"Outside police."

"You need evidence. Molly and I can testify, but everyone thinks we're crazy already."

"Then we have to get some evidence." Leda sat on the nearest chair. "My God, I have no idea how to do that. This is a forty-year-old crime."

"What about Kelvin? He was only murdered nine years ago."

"Don't be ridiculous, we're talking about hard evidence, not ghost stories."

Molly's voice was quiet. "The only way you're going to get any kind of evidence is by letting Enda follow her ghosts," she said. "Don't be blind to your daughter's gifts, Leda."

*

It was a relief to be back in the big kitchen, stirring sugar into black tea. It would have been better if Leo was there, but he wasn't. Enda watched her mother putting things away, cleaning things up, reorganising cupboards.

They'd been tip-toeing around each other ever since they got back from Molly's. They'd barely said two words to each other. Not because they were fighting, but because it was hard to know what to say.

She carried the two mugs over to the kitchen table, sat down and sipped her tea. Leda picked up the broom and started to sweep the floor. The motion grated on Enda's nerves.

"For God's sake Mum would you just sit down for one minute!"

Leda leaned on the broom and looked at her. "How can you just sit there? We have to do *some*thing."

"How is sweeping the goddamn floor going to help?"

"It helps me think, which is a damn sight more useful than talking to dead people."

Enda was about to come back with a retort when she heard footsteps in the hall. Her heart thumped with excitement. Maybe the Haldol had worn off already. Maybe she was hearing another ghost.

The look on her mother's face changed her mind. Leda ran two fingers along her mouth, as though zipping it.

Enda understood. She looked over her shoulder; Uncle Con stood in the doorway behind her.

He walked into the kitchen with a smile that reminded Enda of a well-fed shark. She and Leda just watched him. The silence coated them like a blanket of needles.

Con's hand landed on her shoulder. Enda jumped and spilled her tea, but did not dare move.

Leda's voice sounded perfectly confident to Enda's ears, even though she looked white and nervous. She held the broom like a weapon. "Hello Conrad. What can we do for you?"

"Just checking you both got back okay."

Enda wasn't sure if it was his familiar touch or his friendly voice that made her skin crawl. She was so tense she couldn't think or move.

"Yes, we're fine," Leda said.

"And you've got Enda's medication?"

Leda picked up the package off the counter. "Right here. Enda's going to be taking it this time, aren't you Enda?"

Enda nodded.

"Good." He squeezed her shoulder. She flinched. "It's important to keep these things under control."

"Well." Leda's voice was bright. Too bright. "I'm not sure what Leo has in the cupboard here, so Enda and I were about to go food shopping. Weren't we Enda?"

"Yes!" The words galvanised her. She went to move, but Uncle Con's hand got a lot heavier and kept her in the chair.

"No need," he said. "Betty wants you to join us for dinner tonight. You know she's missed your company, Leda. So I'll see you both at six o'clock."

Leda had the look of a rabbit pinned by the glare of headlights. "Alright," she said.

"Good." Con squeezed Enda's shoulder again. "Enda I believe Betty gave you a necklace of Selene's at the funeral. Wear it tonight. It would make her happy." He let go and walked out of the room, just like that.

A second later he stuck his head back in. "I never knew Leo had a cat."

Enda froze.

"He doesn't," Leda said.

"But I heard a cat. Just then, it went down the hall."

Ivy. Uncle Con had heard Ivy. Enda slowly stood up and turned to face him. "There's no cat, Uncle Con."

He shrugged and left.

Enda and Leda stared at each other, silent, until his footsteps had faded and the front door had closed.

"Mum!" Enda said, when she was sure he'd gone. "I don't want to go to dinner there!"

"Well I couldn't think of an excuse!" Leda pushed the broom furiously across the floor. "Until we have some solid evidence he's going to have us dancing like puppets. This is why I left in the first place!"

"I thought you left because Dad was an alcoholic." Leda stopped in the middle of the floor and leaned on the broom. "There was that, too," she said in a low voice.

"You told me we left because of Dad!"

"I tried to get him to come with us." Leda's voice was hard. "I wanted to get him treatment. But he wouldn't leave Dead Rock and I couldn't stay, or leave you here. For over thirty years I had Conrad breathing down my neck, Enda, do you have any idea what that was like?"

"I'm beginning to."

*

The necklace was like ice against Enda's skin. She'd put on a long black dress with a high neck that covered it, but hiding it didn't seem to make wearing it any less unpleasant. She grabbed the pendant through her dress and wrapped the cloth around it to get it away from her skin.

"Would you stop playing with that thing?" Leda hissed. "Why'd you have to wear it anyway?"

"He told me to. I thought we decided not to antagonise him." Enda dodged Betty's rose bushes and started up the path to the back door.

"There's a line between not antagonising and accepting tyranny," Leda said.

"Yeah well I notice you dressed up." Enda eyed her mother, who had on a dress suit, pants and high heels. Her hair was piled up on top of her head.

"It's called power dressing. It's meant to intimidate." Leda squared her shoulders, marched up the path and knocked on the back door.

Enda stood a few paces behind her and waited. She felt a little nauseous and wasn't sure if it was the Haldol in her system or nerves. Coming here was such a bad idea, but there was no getting round the fact neither of them dared say no to Uncle Con.

The door opened. Aunty Betty turned the light on and looked out. "Leda! How lovely, you came. Do come in. Hello Enda darling."

Enda submitted to being kissed on the cheek, relieved it was just Betty to let them in. She felt like a kid again, following her mother through the laundry, along the dim hall and into the hot kitchen, which smelled of roast beef and stewed apples. Betty hustled them through to the lounge room.

"Can we help you with anything?" Leda asked.

"No, no, it's all done. You go sit with Con. Con, they're here!"

Enda's stomach clenched when she stepped down into the sunken lounge room. Uncle Con, out of uniform and dressed in grey pants and a crisp white shirt, rose up out of his easy chair and turned the TV off.

"Good, good, they don't want to watch that dreadful thing." Betty patted her greying curls, smoothed down the apron she wore over her flowery dress and beamed at them all. "I'll be done soon." She disappeared.

Enda stood beside her mother. The reflected light bulb gleamed on Uncle Con's head. The clock on the wall ticked. The fish tank hummed and bubbled.

"Glad you both came," he said. "Leda, why don't you sit on the couch there."

Leda went stiffly to the couch and sat, her back rigid.

Con detained Enda with a hand on her arm. "Enda," he said.

"What?"

"I think yes, Uncle Con would be more polite. I thought your mother taught you manners?"

Her cheeks flamed. "Yes, Uncle Con?"

"I thought I told you to wear the necklace?"

"I'm wearing it."

"Show me."

Enda took the necklace out from under her dress.

"Good. It looks nice on you." Con straightened the pendant and then chucked her under the chin. "See? We can all get along. We might have to look at fixing your hair soon, it makes you look like one of those anarchists from the city. Perhaps you could dye it all blonde, instead of just this bit here." He tugged at the one blonde streak in Enda's hair.

"Why don't you just go-"

"Enda," Leda said. "Come sit down, dear." She patted the couch next to her.

Enda pulled away from Uncle Con and sat next to her mother. She folded her hands in her lap and seethed. The beginnings of a headache niggled at her temples. Con leaned against the mantel, facing them. The silence stretched out. Enda waited for him to say something, then realised he wasn't going to. He was just going to stand there and make them nervous. Beside her, Leda maintained an icy composure.

It seemed hours before Betty appeared in the doorway, although it was probably only minutes. She'd taken off her apron. Her face was flushed with the heat. "Come in now," she said.

Uncle Con gestured for them to go first. Enda stood, sure she'd never been so uncomfortable in her life, and followed Betty to the dining room. She glanced behind her once to see Con with a hand on her mother's shoulder, murmuring something in her ear. Leda looked like she'd swallowed a lemon.

Enda sat in the seat Betty pointed her to in the dining room. She was relieved when Leda sat next to her. Uncle Con disappeared for a minute and Betty went back to the kitchen.

"What did he say to you?" Enda whispered.

Leda patted her hand. "Nothing. Let's just eat and get this thing over with, shall we?"

"I've got a headache coming on," Enda said. "Have you got any painkillers?"

"I don't know if it's a good idea for you to mix medications."

Uncle Con came back in and sat at the head of the table. Betty arrived at the same time and started placing dishes in front of them. "Go on, dish up," she urged, and sat opposite Enda and Leda.

Dinner went about as fast as a car with flat tyres. Enda had trouble chewing the meat because her mouth was dry and the increasing pain in her temples made her feel ill. Every tick of the grandfather clock in the next room echoed in her skull. Betty and Con talked and talked and talked until she thought she would scream, but she just kept nodding and smiling and hoping her answers were appropriate.

Finally, she couldn't keep it up any longer. Her fork clattered to her plate. Even that noise was like being inside a gigantic bell. Enda dropped her face into her hands.

"Enda are you okay?" Leda asked.

"I feel like someone stabbed me in the head," she said. "Side effect of Haldol. In case you were wondering."

"Oh you poor thing, I'd quite forgotten you only just got out of hospital!" Betty put her knife and fork down. "Can I get you something?"

"I think it's best if I take Enda home," Leda said. "She needs to sleep."

"But you've hardly eaten." Con's voice was entirely pleasant. "Enda can lie down on the couch for a little while and rest."

"Nonsense Con, the couch is far too small for her to lie on. Sweetie why don't you go lie down in Selene's room?" Betty's voice wavered on the last word. There was an uncomfortable silence.

Enda didn't care where she laid down, so long as it was close. "Okay." She scraped her chair back and made her way around the dining table.

"You poor thing. Let me help you." Betty rose from her chair.

Uncle Con rose too. "No, I'll go with her," he said, and followed her up the hall.

Lights danced in front of her eyes. Migraine. She'd had one last time she came out of hospital too. She stopped and leaned her head against the wall.

"You're not faking this, are you?" Uncle Con's voice sounded far away. His fingers gripped her shoulder and guided her down the hall. "Are you okay?"

"I think I'm going to throw up," she said.

He pushed open a door to her left and steered her in.

Enda could just make out a sink around the lights. Her stomach heaved and she threw up what little she'd just eaten. Her stomach heaved again and she threw up water. Her hands shook. She gripped the sink tighter. An image of Conrad pushing Tom Nickel from the edge of the cliff flit through her mind. She turned on the tap, washed the sink and then washed her hands and face. Her head still pounded, but she felt a little better.

"Alright?" Con asked from the door.

Enda couldn't see him past the lights. She looked from side to side, but it was no use. He could be standing there with a gun pointed at her and she wouldn't know it. "I've got a migraine," she said. "I can't see a thing."

"Come on." He gripped her shoulder again, guided her down the hall, opened the door at the end and turned on the light. Then he steered her to Selene's bed.

Enda patted down the length of the bed with her hands and lay down. As soon as her face hit the pillow she felt better. She closed her eyes and gave herself over to the pounding. Con said something, but she didn't really listen. The door clicked shut behind him.

The pounding continued. Enda drifted in and out of half-sleep. Selene sat next to her, cross-legged, studying her nails. "Tell her you want the massive dooby I rolled last week. It's in the shoebox under the bed," she said.

Enda pushed herself up and looked around the room for Aunty Betty, sure it was the day of the funeral, but the room was empty. At least as far as she could tell. She was glad the light was on. She didn't want to be alone in the dark in Selene's room.

She buried her face back in the pillow and closed her eyes. The thumping started to subside, at last. She drifted again. Selene's face was inches from hers, taut with anger. "Listen to me!" she yelled. "What's wrong with you?"

Enda started so hard she fell off the bed. She sat up, rubbed her temples and squinted. The lights were very bright, but they were starting to shrink. She could see bits and pieces of the room around them. There was the dresser, the wardrobe and the light on

DEAD SILENT

the roof. It was just directly in front of her she couldn't see now. "Selene?" she whispered.

Silence.

Enda lay down on the floor and stuck her arm under the bed. She hoped to God Selene hadn't left any needles under there, if she really was a drug addict. She patted down the floor and found nothing but dust. She sighed and laid her head on her arm. This would be a lot easier if she could see properly. "Come on Selene," she whispered. "Where did you hide stuff?" She closed her eyes and let her mind drift.

*

1993

Selene and Enda, 10 and 11, flattened under the bed. Selene had been crying. She had a bruise across the backs of her legs because she said a bad word at her dad. She reached up into the springs and eased out a small shoebox.

"One day I'm going to run away," she whispered. "Look Enda, I'm saving up." She turned the box upside down. Both girls giggled madly while coins fell on their bellies. They picked them up and shoved them back in the box.

*

Enda started awake. She wriggled under the bed and felt around in the springs until her fingers touched the corner of the shoebox. It was old now, that box, old and tattered. She eased it out of its place in the springs, her heart thumping. She listened for sounds in the hall but there was nothing. She hoped Aunty Betty was sticking around her mother and Uncle Con and not leaving them alone. She slid out from under the bed, the box clutched to her stomach.

The dancing light was the size of a fist and right in the centre of her vision. Enda got back onto the bed. She sat cross-legged with the box in her lap, staring at it. Then she eased the lid off.

Resting on top was a big fat joint, just like Selene had said. Enda set it aside on the bed.

Underneath was a folded-up piece of paper. Enda opened it

179

up. Her heart beat faster still. There in her hands was the suicide list, torn from the papers Uncle Con had banned. There were numbers and letters handwritten beside each name and little notes she couldn't read through the lights. She folded up the paper as small as she could and secured it in her bra, nice and flat, where it wouldn't move or be seen.

Underneath that was a journal with a lock on it. There was no key in the box and it was way too big to stuff down her bra. Enda turned the book over and over in her hands, wondering what Selene had written about, and why she hadn't thought to wear something bulky with big pockets here.

She crawled to the window, eased it open and peered out into the dark back yard. She could see the path from the back door from here. If she leaned out and tossed the journal just so ... it landed neatly by the third rose bush from the end of the path.

Enda withdrew into the room, eased the window shut and lay down. There were footsteps in the hall. She slid the empty shoebox under the bed and remembered the joint just as the door handle turned. She shoved it down her top and lay on her back, hands folded, heart hammering against her ribs.

Uncle Con leaned in the door. "Enda?"

She watched him and wondered if the look of concern was genuine or part of his power game. Maybe she'd thrown him off-kilter by getting sick. Oh God, if he knew what she'd hidden in her bra, there was no telling what he'd do. Play it cool. Play it cool.

"How are you feeling?" he asked.

"Better, I think," she said. "I can almost see."

He ventured into the room. The end of the bed sank under his weight. "Have you had these migraines before?"

"Once before." Lights the size of a coin danced over his eyes. The shadow of something faint, black, pulsed on his shoulders. The sight made her afraid, but happy at the same time. The ghosts would be back soon.

"Perhaps we should take you back to see the doctor tomorrow. You frightened the hell out of your mother."

Enda shook her head. "I'll be fine."

Uncle Con looked at her for a long moment. "I can't help but feel I've messed things up with you," he said. "All I wanted to do was help. We've all suffered a blow with Selene." He paused. "I just want us to be a family again."

Enda levered herself into a sitting position. She leaned against the bed head and hugged her knees. She didn't say anything. The hammer would fall without her contribution.

"I know your mother needs to get back to the city for work sometime," he said. "And Leo is very unwell, it may be a while before he can go home. Betty and I would like you to think about staying with us for a little while. You could stay here, in Selene's room. It would be such a comfort to Betty to have someone else around. I'm afraid I'm not always the best company for her."

Enda shook her head. "Thank you Uncle Con, but no."

His voice took on an edge. "You can't be by yourself, Enda. Betty and I can look after you."

"I'm 24 years old, I can look after myself. Besides, Mum's taken time off work to stay down here with me while Dad's sick."

"You're going to have to get used to the idea sooner or later he's not your dad," Con said.

Enda flattened herself against the bed head as though it could shield her from the poison in his voice. "You're going to have to get used to the fact I can't be Selene for you," she said, amazed she had the guts to do so.

Uncle Con struggled with something. His fist clenched convulsively. Then he took a deep breath and patted her foot. "You're headstrong, like she was, but we'll get past that. Think about staying. Maybe you'll see sense." He got up off the bed and left the room.

Enda swung her legs over the side of the bed. She sat for a moment with her head in her hands, fighting the dull thump that remained. She could not stand to stay in this house for another moment. She got up, turned the light off and walked down the hallway. She followed the sound of voices to the lounge room where Con, Betty and Leda were drinking coffee and talking about her.

Enda stood in the doorway and rubbed her head.

"Honey how are you feeling?" Leda sounded infinitely relieved to see her.

"I want to go home," Enda said. "Sorry Aunty Betty, I really need to sleep this off in my own bed."

"Of course you do sweetie," Betty said. "We can have dinner

again. Leda, take her home."

Leda gave Betty a peck on the cheek, exchanged a cold handshake with Con and joined Enda in the doorway. She put an arm around her shoulders. "Come on then, let's go home."

Enda could hear Con's footsteps all the way down the hall. At the door he turned on the back light.

"Oh God, turn it off, it hurts my eyes," she said.

"But you need to see your way home."

"We're fine, we know the way," Leda said.

The light flicked off. "Think about what I said, Enda." Con closed the door behind him and disappeared.

Enda breathed a sigh of relief. She walked straight down the path and stopped at the third rose bush from the end. She crouched down and felt around for the journal. At first she couldn't find it, and was terrified Uncle Con would come out here in the morning and see it and know. Then her hands encountered a sharp corner. She snatched it up and hugged it to her chest.

"What are you doing?" Leda said.

"Tying my shoelace." Enda stood up and hurried across the yard.

"You're wearing sandals." Leda was hard on her heels. "What's going on? Are you okay? What did he say to you?"

"Let's just get home Mum, and never go in that house again, okay?"

"Finally, something we can agree on."

Enda squeezed through the gap in the fence and hurried across the yard. She went in through the back door and straight to her room, where she put the journal, the joint and the suicide list under her pillow. Then she went out to the kitchen, where Leda was making tea.

"Sit down," Leda said.

Enda sat at the table and waited. Leda brought two cups over, set one in front of her and sat down opposite. The lines around her eyes and mouth were deeper than they'd been earlier in the night.

"You're tired," Enda said.

"Yes, I'm tired. Are you okay? Conrad said you had a migraine and had trouble seeing."

"I did. It's a side effect of the medication you're all so hot on me taking."

"Probably because you were due to take it two hours ago."

Enda breathed in the steam rising off her tea. "Are you okay? Aunty Betty didn't leave you alone with him?"

"I'm fine. I'm stronger than you seem to think."

"We've got to get this jerk off our backs, Mum."

"I know." Leda took a sip of her tea. "That's why I'm going back to the city."

"What? You can't! You know I'm not leaving without Dad."

"Calm down Enda and let me finish." Leda fixed her with a steely look until she subsided. "We need outside help," she continued. "People who aren't from Dead Rock and who are not under Conrad's influence. I'm going to find a solicitor and I'm going to talk to the police until somebody agrees to come back with me and investigate. I'm going to be gone for one day, maybe two."

"Mum you can't." The thumping came back. Enda rubbed her head. "He asked me to go and stay with him and Betty when you went back to the city. I said no, but he got twitchy. The minute he knows you're gone he's going to be at me again."

Leda's mouth tightened. "Live with them? That's ridiculous. What more does he want from us?"

"Don't you get it? That comment earlier about dying my hair blonde, offering me Selene's room? He thinks I'm going to replace Selene. He's fucked in the head!"

"Language," Leda said. Then she sighed. "He is though, isn't he? I need to go to the city. You could come too."

"And leave Dad alone? No way."

"Then I'll go tonight, since we know he's not out there patrolling. You'll have to cover for me." The lines between Leda's eyebrows deepened. "I don't like this."

"Then don't go."

"I have to!"

Enda dropped her thumping head into her hands. "Look, tell you what. Take my car. Then it looks like you're here, and I'll say my car's gone in for repairs and you're sleeping or something."

Somewhere down the hall, Enda heard a meow and the sound of running footsteps. Her head thumped a little less. Her shoulders relaxed.

"Alright," Leda said. "I'd better go now, before I fall asleep.

We'll have to swap keys. If you go anywhere, don't scratch my car."

"Don't scratch mine." Enda went over to the counter where she'd left her bag and tossed Leda her car keys.

"Keep the house locked so he can't come in like he does." Leda grabbed her bag and left her keys on the counter. "I'll come back as soon as I can, okay?"

"Please do."

"Take your pills." Leda took a box out of the paper bag, popped two pills out of the foil and held them out.

"No."

"Take them, Enda. I don't want you ending up in hospital again while I'm gone."

Enda took the pills, put them in her mouth and went over to the sink. She poured a glass of water, spat the pills into her hand and drank the water. She dropped the pills down the drain and turned back to her mother. "There. Happy?"

Leda looked at her for a long moment, then nodded. "Don't forget your next dose." She walked to Enda and hugged her. "If anything happens, anything at all, call me. Stay away from Conrad if you possibly can."

"You don't have to tell me twice."

"Lock the door after me." Leda walked out of the kitchen.

Enda followed her down the hall. She watched from the veranda while Leda manoeuvred the Magna around the four wheel drive and out of the yard. Only when the sound of the car had disappeared down the street did she lock the door and go back down the hallway. The house creaked around her.

She was alone.

CHAPTER NINETEEN

It was ten o'clock at night. There was a depression at the end of her bed she knew was Ivy, because she could hear her comforting purr. Her head still throbbed. In front of her lay Selene's joint and journal. She wasn't ready to look at the journal yet, because reading wasn't a big help for a migraine.

She wasn't big on smoking pot, but she knew it would rid her of the headache. She also knew it would open up receptors in her brain the Haldol had pretty much closed down. There were things she needed to know from the ghosts of Dead Rock and who knew when Leda would next leave her alone?

Her mind made up, Enda slid the journal underneath the mattress, put the joint and the suicide list in the pocket of the jeans she'd changed into and went into the kitchen. She took a box of matches from beside the stove, tip-toed down the hall and left the house. She re-locked the door behind her and put the keys in her other pocket.

She ran from the yard, jumped the gate and hurried down the quiet street until she reached the alley that led to the bush track.

When she was safely in the darkness under the trees, Enda held a match to the end of the joint and sucked until the paper glowed. Then she walked along the track, very slowly taking deep drags of sharp, bitter smoke into her lungs. This thing had been rolled with tobacco. She coughed until her throat hurt, then stubbed it out and threw it away when she couldn't take it anymore.

The drug made her light-headed. She could feel the effects creeping up in her blood, her skin, her head. She wondered if this had been such a good idea after all. Then she realised her head was no longer thumping. God, what if Leda came back for something and found her gone? Or found her out here stoned? She'd go ballistic.

Enda closed her eyes, took a deep breath and got a grip. She reached the end of the bush path. No moon tonight. Dark sand crunched under her sneakers. A faint, cool breeze teased her hair. She felt exposed and alone in this space, the bush at her back, Dead Rock a black wall in the night ahead of her.

Somewhere high up there was the sound of an engine revving. Enda waited, barely daring to breathe.

The revs built to a roar and came closer. A faint glow at the top of the rock exploded into blinding headlights that jumped, soared, sailed down through the air in an endless silent arc, just like Thelma and Louise, except the movie didn't end.

Enda shielded her face from the glare. The car landed and threw up a wave of sand. Pieces of twisted metal flew off in every direction. Flames leaped from the bonnet.

Enda saw a woman in there, shaking, hurt. She bolted for the car but before she'd gone two steps it exploded. She threw herself to the ground to shield herself from the blast, but there was none.

Enda got to her feet. No car, no fire. Someone lit a cigarette; the tiny glow shook like a firefly in the darkness.

"Are you okay?" Enda went towards her.

"What?" The voice was female.

Enda struck a match. The glow cast a dim light around her and the woman. She was in her thirties, pretty, wearing dark red lipstick. Her hair was neatly curled and pinned back and she wore a long-sleeved paisley dress. "What's your name?" Enda asked.

"Felicity," The woman said. She took a drag of her cigarette.

"Felicity Brown?" Enda shook out the match when it burned her fingertips, and they were in darkness again. She'd read the suicide list so many times tonight she'd memorised the names.

"Who are you?"

"I'm Enda." Enda took a step closer. The cigarette end still shook. "What happened to you?"

"Oh. I heard about you." Felicity dragged on her cigarette. "You're next, right?"

"Next for what?"

"Anytime anyone comes looking for us, they end up jumping." She stuck her fingers up in fake quotation marks around the last word.

Enda wrapped her arms around her shoulders to keep out the sudden cold. "I'm not going to jump."

"Course you're not. Nobody ever did."

"What do you mean?"

"Except me." Felicity leaned closer. "I murdered my husband because he was a prat. That makes me the only suicide here."

The glow of the cigarette disappeared. There was silence in the darkness. A pool of cold air spread outward.

Enda backed out of the coldness. Excitement flickered in her belly. It had worked. The ghosts were back. She started to jog, not towards Dead Rock, but down the highway toward the cemetery. The exercise set her blood racing and her head spinning. She knew she'd have to eat something soon to ease the effects of the pot, but right now she needed to see dead people.

She paused at the gates to the cemetery. They were padlocked. Damn. She picked her way down the side of the stone wall and around the corner to where it gave way to fence. Here the trees crowded close. She pushed her way through scratching, clawing branches in the dark until she found a section of wire that had come away from the ground.

Enda dropped, pulled the wire as far up as she could and slithered under it. She emerged into the still, quiet graveyard. Lamp posts with round ball lights cast an ethereal glow over the paths of lush grass and the march of headstones.

She walked down the nearest row, as quiet as she could be. Did ghosts sleep at night? Not in her experience. Just like last time, it took a few minutes until she began to see movement here and there.

Before long Selene fell into step beside her, but she didn't say anything.

"Hey," Enda said.

"Oh, so you're talking to me now? Lucky me."

"Don't be a bitch, Selene. The drugs they gave me at the hospital stopped me from seeing anything."

"Wow. Sucks to be you."

"They're out of my system now. At least I think they are." Enda stopped under a lamp post that shed light on a row of headstones. Right at the edge of the row, there was a small plaque with the letter E on it. Interesting. Enda got the suicide list out of her pocket and unfolded it.

"Hey," Selene said. "That's mine, right?"

"Yep." Enda ran her finger down the list to the final entry, which was handwritten in, next to the characters *V47*.

Sadie Thorne, 27. Died January 6, 2001.

"Wanna tell me about these numbers?"

Selene shrugged. "I don't remember."

"You remember this but not what you wrote on it?"

"Search me. You're the detective. I'm dead, remember?"

"Fat lot of help you are." Enda walked along the rows and counted off the letters. At *M* she had to go to the next block of graves and find a light so she could count the letters down to *V*. Then she walked along the row and counted headstones until she got to 47. Selene followed close behind, humming something under her breath that sounded a lot like Yellow Submarine.

Sure enough, number 47 was a headstone with the name *Sadie Thorne* on it. It had her birth and death date and nothing else. The stone was weathered and the grass around it so dead it was as though nothing dared to grow there. Enda shivered in the icy cold air. "Sadie Thorne?"

The shape seemed to simply melt out of the night. First there was nothing there, and then there was a human-size shadow. It shifted slightly and became the figure of a woman sitting on the headstone. She wore heels, a black pencil skirt, tailored jacket and a white blouse. Her hair was cut into a short, sleek bob and her face was perfectly made up underneath a huge gash across her left cheek that dripped blood. "Who wants to know?"

"Enda Wilson." Enda resisted the urge to stick out her hand. No point trying to shake hands with a ghost.

"Boo." Sadie arched an eyebrow and looked over Enda's shoulder at Selene. "Friend of yours? Not scared?"

"This is my sister," Selene said. "And no, she's not scared, so you can get rid of your dead head."

"Oh, fine." All at once, Sadie's face was smooth and perfect. "Better?"

"Much," Enda said. She couldn't help but feel it was rude to comment on an injury like that, but at the same time it was hard to look away from it.

"What do you want? I'm very busy you know."

"Yeah, busy being dead. It's a cracker." Selene hopped on top of the next gravestone and threw her arms out. "Sadie!" She sang.

"The cleaning lady!"

"Shut up Selene," Enda said.

"Oh, fine. I'll go amuse myself elsewhere. She wants to know how you died, Sadie." Selene disappeared.

"Sorry," Enda said. "I think she's put out because I couldn't see her for a few days."

"Why not?" Sadie crossed her legs and studied her nails.

"Psychiatric medication."

Sadie gave her a sharp look. "Have you been tended by the charming Doctor Howard?"

"Yes."

"And does Sergeant Wilson know you talk to us?"

"Yes."

"I expect you'll be joining us soon then." Sadie hopped off the headstone and walked down the line of graves.

Enda followed. "Why do you all keep saying that? I'm not going to jump."

"None of us jumped, darling."

"Then what happened? How did you die?"

"I got shot by terrorists in a breathtakingly exciting helicopter chase."

"What?" Enda stumbled and ran to keep up. She almost fell over a headstone when Sadie abruptly stopped walking and looked her in the eye.

"It's more interesting than what really happened," the ghost said. "I mean, I was going to do amazing things. I was going to go to Libya and be a foreign correspondent. I was going to do stuff that mattered. And what happens? I get myself thrown off a cliff by a small town cop because I uncovered the skeletons in his closet. Death sucks."

"He killed you too?" Enda's voice was almost a squeak. "Because of this?" She thrust the suicide paper at her.

Sadie glanced over the paper. "Yep. That's what happened. And if you haven't figured the rest out, then you're dumber than you look. Always check for patterns, Enda Wilson. And try not to die." She vanished.

Enda stood alone in the cemetery, her heart thudding so hard her ribs hurt. The pot had almost left her system, leaving her shaky and breathless. Selene appeared in front of her so suddenly she started. "Jesus!" She hissed. "Do you have to do that?"

"Daddy's here," Selene whispered.

Enda glanced over her shoulder. Across the other side of the cemetery, a powerful torch swept up and down the graves. "Shit." She dropped to the ground and crawled across the graves toward the nearest fence, over brick borders and dead flowers and grass stubble that stabbed the palms of her hands. She hissed a curse when she knocked a jam jar over and spilled a bunch of dandelions onto the grass. The jar clattered onto a brick. The sound rolled through the night. Enda glanced over her shoulder in time to see the light turned in her direction.

"Nice one," Selene said. "Hurry up, would you?"

Enda gained the cover of some bushes. She stood up behind them and bolted to the fence, but it towered over her head. She didn't like her chances of climbing it. She ran along it, tugging at the bottom, looking for holes. Nothing. *Nothing.* Shit, how did Con even know she was here? Her breath escaped in a sob when she came to the end of the fence, where it turned a corner and became a much lower stone wall. She wasn't much of a gymnast, but she had enough adrenalin coursing through her veins to hoist herself onto the wall and fall down the other side onto a gravel road. She grazed her hands and her hip and ducked down low when the beam of light went overhead.

"Keep going," Selene hissed beside her.

Enda crawled over the road and into the bush behind it. She flattened herself behind the nearest big tree. Her hands stung. Her lungs heaved. She kept her mouth shut tight to avoid making a noise.

Two sets of footsteps approached the wall and the light swept the bush around her.

Uncle Con's voice carried on the night air. "You're right, there was definitely someone here."

"Long gone by the looks of it," a second voice said.

"They could still be here." The light swept the bushes again.

"Probably just kids up to mischief. Let it go, Sergeant, they've left the cemetery, that's the main thing. I just don't want to get up to find graves desecrated."

"Rest assured, there'll be hell to pay if any of that starts in my town."

"You're a good man, Sergeant, I don't know what this town would do without you. Why don't you come back for a cup of coffee?"

"Don't mind if I do. Already been a rough night."

The light swept around once more. Enda waited, tense, against the tree. The footsteps faded into the night. It was minutes before she could summon up the courage to move. When she did, she crept back to the road, terrified she'd find him waiting there for her.

But the road was empty. Even Selene had gone. Enda ran all the way home.

*

Past midnight. Enda locked every door and window in the house before she went to bed. She locked her bedroom door, just in case, and sat in there with the light and the glitter lamp on. Then she took a needle to the lock on Selene's journal.

The mechanism clicked and popped after just a minute. Enda flicked through the pages. About a third of the book was filled, the rest blank. She went back to the first page; a sigh escaped her.

Dear Enda, it began.

There was no date on the page.

Here's the thing. I can't write to you in real life, because I figure you still hate me and you don't know half of what I know. So I'm going to write to you here, because you're the only one who's got a hope of understanding anything, partly because we're sisters – not that you know it – and partly because you never fell for all the bullshit junk about being a Wilson like Alice did. I'm so fucking jealous your mum took you to the city. I wish she'd taken me too, I can't stand it here. This town suffocates me. Mum and Dad suffocate me. Well, mostly Dad. He was so pissed when you left. We thought he was going to crack a blood vessel. Mum had to talk him out of going to the city and dragging you and Aunty Leda back.

Enda looked up from the book. Selene perched on her dressing table, watching her. "I'm reading your journal," she said.

"Anything interesting?"

"I'll let you know."

The next entry was dated: March 1, 1999.

I wonder if you heard about the suicides up there in the city. Maybe not, Dad seemed to make sure it was kept quiet. Apparently papers aren't allowed to report on suicides in case they inspire copycats. Everyone at school is really upset. Tina, Amanda and Alyssa all went to school here. I knew them. Hell, I used to score pot off Amanda all the time. It's weird, it's like you and Aunty Leda leave and all hell breaks loose. At least Dad has calmed down some. I was getting sick of dodging him all the time.

October 10, 1999

Shit, I meant to write in here all the time, but I keep forgetting. There was another suicide last week. Some old alcoholic jumped off Dead Rock. Your dad is really upset about it, apparently it was some kind of friend of his, but my dad said good riddance to bad rubbish, just like that. Kind of heartless. Maybe that's what being a cop does to you.

January 1, 2000

Happy new fucking century, Enda. I got wasted. What did you do?

January 7, 2001

Shit, over a year. Not that you care. You could call. Another suicide yesterday. This one is freaking me out. This journalist jumped. Apparently she published a story about all the suicides and then next thing you know, she's dead. Is it just me, or is there something not right about that? I said as much to Dad and he told me to shut up and do my homework, I know nothing about policing. Sometimes I hate him. He could listen.

October 30, 2001

I graduated from school this week. I guess you did last year. I'm going to apply for university. Maybe I'll get out of here. Maybe I'll come see you. Hey Dad gave me a necklace for my graduation present, it's really expensive. Really pretty. He wants me to wear it all the time now, which is actually kind of creepy. Maybe I'll hock it when I get to the city.

March 15, 2002

I can't fucking believe I got rejected from university. My grades weren't that bad. Did you get in? What are you studying? I told Dad I wanted to move to the city and get a job anyway, but he went ballistic. Looks like I'm stuck here until I can save some money up.

July 20, 2002

Do you know what it's like to be depressed, Enda? Really, really, depressed?

April 12, 2003

Four years it's been and you haven't called. You've barely even spoken to Uncle Leo. What's with you? Have you turned into some kind of prize bitch, living up there? I know I gave you shit in school, but come on, get over it.

August 16, 2004

Enda I met this woman. You're not going to believe this. Her name's Molly Wilson and she's our aunty. Nan and Pop adopted her when she was little, but then she ran away later and now my dad and your dad don't even talk about her. I had no idea our family was so fucked up.

May 30, 2005

See? I remember to write to you once a year. You could return the favour, bitch.

February 18, 2006

I'm turning 21 in a couple of weeks. I'm going to have a big party at the hall. Dad's going to be there checking everyone for drugs. Shit, isn't that going to be fun. Nobody's even going to turn up because they know he'll be there. Come to my party. We can stand in an empty hall and be fucking sober.

March 30, 2007

Hey Enda, I've been talking to Molly a lot. She tells me stuff about her past, real interesting stuff. I never knew half of what your mum and dad used to get up to, they were hard core.

July 7, 2007

Fuck. Fuck. My dad found my pot. He just accused me of all this other stuff, smoking crack, snorting cocaine, injecting speed, everything. It would never happen. I've got a black eye. I hate him. I've got to get out of here.

September 6, 2007

You wouldn't believe how fucked up things have got around here. I can't put a foot right anymore. Dad won't let my friends near me. I have to have drug tests every week. And that's not even the half of it. I have to sneak out to see Molly, he went psycho when he saw me with her yesterday. Another black eye. I'm going to run away. I swear I am.

December 30, 2007

Enda I don't even know where to start. I snuck out to see Molly and she told me a story. I think she's been building up to this one. She didn't want to tell me, but I made her. Dad killed her boyfriend. Pushed him off Dead Rock. He's a fucking murderer and nobody even knows.

January 2, 2008

I can't get this question out of my head: Why would Sadie Thorne jump off Dead Rock?

January 10, 2008

I dug up a copy of Sadie's report into the suicides at the library. Half the names on there were being treated for psychiatric disorders on my Dad's referral. I've stopped believing in coincidence.

January 17, 2008

Enda I'm coming to get you and then we're leaving. We're going into hiding. It's not safe. We're not safe. I can't ignore the evidence anymore, or the coincidences. There were no suicides at Dead Rock. I'm going to confront him. I'm going to make him tell me and then I'm going to leave, because I have finally faced the truth: our father is a serial killer.

CHAPTER TWENTY

Early morning sunlight flooded through the window. Ivy was a dark shape curled at the end of the bed. The journal laid on the covers, just past her fingertips, solid, unavoidable evidence that she was in deep shit.

She felt curiously calm and clear-headed. Detached, even. It was much easier to know what to do now she knew the whole truth. She dressed, went straight to the kitchen and dialled in Leda's mobile number on the phone. It rang eleven times, then went to message.

"Mum, call me as soon as you get this," Enda said. "It's urgent." She hung up the phone, made herself some tea and leaned against the counter drinking it. Her medication glared at her. At least that was easily fixed.

She went into the bathroom and searched through the medicine cabinet until she found a box of paracetamol. She grabbed the two foils out of it, went back to the kitchen and swapped them with the Haldol. Then she took the Haldol to the sink, popped each pill out and washed them down the drain. There. Now nobody could force her to take anything except painkillers.

There wasn't much else she could do except go see Leo, at least until Leda got back. She hoped she was planning to come back with a whole pile of police.

*

Enda sincerely hoped Uncle Con was busy catching up on all the police work he must have missed while breathing down her neck over the last few days. Surely, surely there must be something to keep him away from the hospital, at least for this morning.

When she pulled into the hospital car park in Leda's car, it looked like her prayers were answered because there was no police vehicle there. She found a parking spot in the far corner where the car wouldn't stand out too much, then walked over to reception.

The nurse at the desk gave her the same blank, professional smile Enda used to bestow on her patients before she got fired for being crazy. "Hello Enda. Everything okay?"

Sure. Peachy. My biological father is a serial killer. How's your day going? Enda stretched her lips into a smile. "Fine. Can I see my dad?"

The nurse pursed her lips and ran her finger down a list of names. "I'm sorry, he's sleeping at the moment."

"Then I'd like to just sit with him."

She shook her head. "Look, Doctor Howard said he's not to have visitors unless they're supervised by a member of staff. He's in a very delicate condition."

Enda leaned on the counter. "You know I'm a registered nurse, right? I'm not going to do anything to put my dad at risk. Please."

The nurse studied her closely. "How's the medication going?"

"Fine. Really good, actually, I think it's working better than the other stuff I was on."

The nurse kept studying her, as though trying to determine if she was on the level. Enda kept her face straight.

She sighed. "Alright, but only for five minutes, okay? I'll take you."

"Thank you." Enda followed her down the hall and through the maze of passages that made up the sprawling building. She kept her eyes on the nurse's feet and ignored everyone else they passed. Hospitals were fraught with ghosts who looked like the living. She couldn't afford to give herself away in here.

They stopped in front of Leo's room. The nurse went in first and tactfully busied herself cleaning up around the room.

Leo was just where she'd left him, sitting up in bed, staring out of the window. His stubble was longer and his hair needed a wash. Enda felt tears prickle her eyes. She sat down next to him. "Hey Dad."

No movement. Nothing. She wished he'd just turn his head and smile, or ask for a smoke, anything, anything but this vacant apathy.

Enda glanced over her shoulder. The nurse was busy in the

bathroom. She went to the end of the bed, picked up the clipboard and leafed through it. It was hard to read Doctor Howard's handwriting. It was almost like he scribbled on purpose. There was no understanding what was on the first page. She flipped the paper over, frowning. What she saw on the other side was of even more concern.

The nurse came back into the room at that moment. "What are you doing?"

Enda looked up from the clipboard. "Why is my father being given such a high dose of tranquilisers?"

"To keep him calm." The nurse walked over, took the clipboard from her hand and replaced it at the foot of the bed.

"Any calmer and he'll be dead!"

The nurse folded her arms and looked Enda square in the eye. "Please calm down Ms Wilson," she said. "I can assure you Doctor Howard knows exactly what he's doing. If you have any questions, direct them to him. In the meantime, I think it's time we left Mr Wilson alone. He's not to be upset."

Enda looked askance at Leo, who hadn't so much as twitched during the exchange. "Fine," she said. "I'll talk to the doctor about it." She sat in the chair by the bed. "Here."

"You'll have to wait in reception."

"No." Enda curled her fingers into Leo's. "I'm going to wait right here."

The nurse flushed bright red. "Fine. I'll get the doctor." She hurried from the room.

"Like hell." Enda grabbed the wheelchair from the corner of the room and brought it over to the bed. "Come on Dad, let's get out of here." She peeled back the covers, grabbed Leo under the arms and dragged him backwards into the chair. He landed off centre and slumped forward. Enda straightened him up, set his feet right and wheeled the chair towards the door. She peered out. The corridor was empty. Her blood pounded through her veins. She'd be straight back in psych if she was caught now.

She backed through the door and pushed the wheelchair into the hall. Footsteps approached. She saw a fire alarm, hesitated over just exactly how bad she was going to be today, then thumped the big red button. An alarm shrilled overhead.

Enda increased her pace. She pushed the wheelchair down the

hall, dodged the first running person, kept her head down. Soon there were nurses and patients and wheelchairs everywhere. Chaos. Fantastic. Three more halls to go. She picked up her pace to a slow jog, jostled with another wheelchair and dodged a bed with an old lady in it left in the middle of the hall. Three nurses rushed past. People yelled. Enda slowed and walked as casually as she could through reception, then out the sliding doors and into the bright morning sunshine. There were patients gathered on the grassed areas at the front of reception, some in wheelchairs, some on foot, and some in their hospital beds.

"Oh good, good, there you are Mr Wilson, just stay with him here," a nurse said, then rushed on.

"Sure." Enda skirted the grassed area and kept going to Leda's car. Still nobody came after them. "Hey Dad," she whispered. "Let's get the fuck out of here, yeah?" She wheeled him up to the back door and opened it. Holy shit. This wasn't going to be easy.

Enda took a deep breath, grabbed Leo under the shoulders and lifted him out of the chair. "Come on Dad, help me out here." She lifted his leg at the knee, put his foot on the step and then pushed him into the back seat. He landed face down.

She climbed in after him, turned him on his side, grabbed the blanket Leda always kept in the back and covered him with it. She watched for a moment, but he just stared at the back of the seat. A low, explosive breath escaped her. "Fine," she said, shut the door behind her and crawled over to the driver's seat.

She turned the key. The car roared into life. She sat there, hands on the steering wheel, staring at the bed of geraniums that lined the parking lot. Holy shit. What now? She hadn't thought this through, but it was too late to go back. She reversed out, drove slowly past the patients on the grass and turned onto the road.

"Alright Dad," she said. "You're out of hospital. What now? I can't take you home, that's the first place they'll look. If Uncle Con pulls me over we're completely fucked. So where do we go?"

Silence.

"You're right. Molly's." Enda changed gears, took the back roads to avoid town and drove the few minutes to the highway. Her hands shook on the steering wheel and she checked the rear view mirror every five minutes, but no flashing lights appeared. She turned up the gravel road, followed the twists and bends to the little house nestled in behind the bush and parked where the car would be at least partially out of sight. Then she scrambled out, opened the back doors and checked on Leo. No change. Shit, she should've brought the wheelchair.

She peeled back the blanket. "Hey Dad. This time I really need your help. If I just drag you out of here, you're probably going to hit your head or something."

Still nothing. Christ, how long were these tranquilisers going to last?

"Enda Wilson, what the hell are you doing?"

Enda jumped and turned to face Molly. "Molly I'm really sorry, I just didn't know where else to bring him. We won't stay long, I just need to get some things from home and then we'll go."

"What are you talking about?" Molly peered over her shoulder into the back seat. "Is that Leo? Why's he staring like that? What have you done?"

"I took him from the hospital," Enda said in a small voice. "They were dosing him with dangerous levels of tranquilisers and I don't know why. I couldn't just leave him there. Please don't be mad."

Molly's breath hissed through her teeth. "Alright," she said. "We'd best get him inside. Come on, you take one arm, I'll get the other."

They pulled Leo backwards from the seat. He landed awkwardly, but Molly caught him. Then they draped an arm over each of his shoulders, half-carried, half-dragged him inside and laid him on the lounge. Enda ran back outside for the blanket to cover him with. She locked Molly's door behind her when she came back in.

Molly watched her cover Leo and put a cushion under his head. "Kitchen," she said, when she'd finished.

Enda went into the kitchen, sat at the table and stared at her hands.

Molly shut the door and leaned against it. "Explain," she said. "Why you would bring him to my house in that state. Are you insane?"

Enda flinched. "No."

"Bad choice of words." Molly sighed. "Come on Enda, spit it out. What's going on?"

"I talked to Sadie Thorne last night," Enda said. "And I found Selene's journal. They both said the same thing." She looked at Molly's face and found an expression there she dreaded.

Molly knew.

"There were no suicides off Dead Rock," Enda said. "Selene thinks Uncle Con is a serial killer."

"And what do you think?"

Enda glanced out of the window. From here she could see the yard, Leda's car, a little forest. Everything was quiet and peaceful. Waiting. Waiting for the hammer to fall. "I think he killed her to stop her telling anyone else or coming to me."

Molly pushed herself off the door and sank into the chair opposite Enda. "I've suspected it for a long time," she said. "But I couldn't prove it."

"Molly." Enda leaned forward. "Sadie said I was next. She said to look for patterns." With a shaking hand, she pushed the suicide list across the table. "Look at this. Read it. Half the people there were referred to the hospital for psychiatric help by Uncle Con weeks before their death, that or they had problems with drugs or alcohol. I don't know what the hell links them all except that. It was Uncle Con who put me in the psych ward this week. It's what he does. He isolates you and calls you crazy so when you're found dead, nobody questions that it was suicide."

Molly read down the list. Her mouth set into a grim line. "I can tell you what else links them," she said. "These people were misfits. Conrad has never hidden the fact he doesn't like people in his town who don't do things his way." She hesitated. "But not all of them. Sadie, that must have been to cover his tracks. She was onto him. It's always been these three girls I didn't get. Amanda, Tina and Alyssa."

Enda massaged her temples and thought about that. "What are the dates?"

"February 1999."

"Mum and I left not long before that." Enda closed her eyes. A thought presented itself that made her cold. "Selene said he was furious when we left. He was, I remember, he tried to stop us. But she said he calmed down after the suicides – the murders –"

"Are you trying to say these three girls died because Conrad was pissed at you and your mother?"

Enda groaned. "I don't know. I just don't know. Molly what are the chances Selene was wrong? I mean, we know he killed Tom, Sadie and Kelvin, but what if all the others were coincidence?"

"I don't believe in coincidence."

"Neither do I." Enda met Molly's eyes. "Which is why I have to get Dad into hiding."

"You think he's next?"

Enda knit her fingers together. "Yes. No. Maybe. He wouldn't kill his own brother, would he? But he killed Selene. I can't take the chance."

"What if it's you?"

The kitchen was silent. A fly buzzed over their heads. "It'll be me if I don't do what he wants."

"What does he want?"

"He wants me to bleach my hair and pretend to be Selene."

Molly gave a low whistle. "Alright. Agreed, you and Leo need to hide. Where's Leda?"

"She's gone to the city to get the police down here."

"Smart woman, your mum. You know you can't hide here, Enda. He'll come looking."

Enda nodded. "I was thinking of going into the bush. We could camp out somewhere until Mum comes back."

"You got what you need for that?"

"No. When I left the house this morning I was just kind of expecting to sit with Dad for the day." Enda contemplated. "I have to go home and get some stuff. Can Dad stay here for half an hour?"

"Alright." Molly jerked her head at the door. "Go. Be as quick as you can and for God's sake don't let him see you. I'll look after Leo."

CHAPTER TWENTY-ONE

January, 1999

Forked lightning cracked the leaden sky. The wind bent the trees in fierce arcs across the road, but there was no rain. It would come any minute. It had to, no clouds could hold back that amount of water forever.

A single, fat drop exploded on the windscreen. Then nothing.

Enda pushed back her hood and leaned her face against the window. She watched Dead Rock disappear. She wished she'd been able to say goodbye to Dad properly, but he'd drunk too much and passed out on the kitchen floor. She dragged her finger across the dust on the window, made the shape of an arrow, pointing ahead to the city, to a new start. She wasn't going to miss anyone else. Not Selene, bitch. Not cranky pregnant Alice and definitely not Uncle Con.

The revs dropped out for a minute and the car stuttered. Her mother put her foot down and they shot forward.

"This bomb going to get us there?" Enda said.

"This bomb will get us there even if I have to plant rockets in the exhaust," Leda said.

Enda grinned. Mum sounded mad, but she knew she was excited. They'd planned this in secret for weeks, after finally agreeing there was no point in sticking around. She rifled through the bag at her feet for her walkman. Behind them, the back seat and the boot were jammed with everything they could fit, the bare minimum they needed to start fresh. "Hey Mum can I cut my hair?"

"You can wear your hair however you want."

"Sweet. Can I dye it pink?"

"No."

Enda stuck a cassette into the walkman and fitted the earphones on. They passed a sign announcing they were leaving Dead Rock.

She whooped. Leda grinned.

Less than a minute later, Leda cursed, jammed on the brakes and pulled over.

Enda yanked off her walkman. "What the hell?" She glanced in the rear view mirror. "Oh." Uncle Con's police car pulled in behind them, lights flashing. Leda's mouth had disappeared to the single line she always got when she was really, really pissed.

Enda twisted around and watched Uncle Con walk over to the car. He walked like a tough guy in a B Grade movie. How embarrassing.

He bent down and stuck his head through Leda's window. "Hi Enda."

Enda folded her arms, buried her face in her hood and watched the adults from the shadows.

"What do you want, Conrad?" Leda kept her hands wrapped around the wheel.

"Going somewhere?" Uncle Con's voice was even, friendly. Enda had heard him sound like that just before going ballistic at Selene once.

"Obviously," Leda said.

"Without saying goodbye?"

Leda kept her eyes on the steering wheel and said nothing. Enda thought she probably had quite a lot to say, but didn't dare.

"Would you step out of the car and talk to me?" Uncle Con said.

Don't do it Mum, Enda wanted to say, but she didn't. Instead she watched Leda undo her seatbelt and get out. A split second later she did the same. She sat on the bonnet and watched them from under her hood. They stood like old adversaries, inches apart on the gravel shoulder of the road.

"Get back in the car, Enda," Uncle Con said.

"No."

"Tell her, Leda."

"No," Leda said. "Anything you have to say to me you can say in front of her."

Uncle Con's cheeks turned pink. "What do you think you're doing?"

"Leaving."

"You can't."

"Who are you to say I can't go?"

"You know very well who I am." He stuck his face closer to hers. "You can't just kidnap a child from her father."

"Her *father* is currently lying on the kitchen floor passed out because he drank himself into oblivion. Again. Tell him I kidnapped her."

"It's not kidnap if I agreed to go," Enda said.

"Shut up." Uncle Con spared her barely a glance.

"Don't you talk to my daughter like that."

Yay. Go Mum.

Leda jabbed him in the chest with her finger. "You can't do anything Conrad, so don't try. Just go back to Dead Rock and scrape your brother off the floor, because I'm done with him."

"I'm not going to let you leave him. Like it or not Leda, I'm here to do what he doesn't have the balls to. Again."

Leda's hand snapped up and struck Uncle Con across the face, hard. Enda gaped. She'd never seen her mother hit anyone.

Uncle Con put a hand to his face.

"Don't you ever talk about that again," Leda said in a low, furious voice. "And don't you threaten us. Ever." She yanked the door open and got into the car.

Enda scrambled off the bonnet and into her seat, eyes wide. She jammed down the lock on her door like Leda did.

Leda started the engine and wound up the window. Uncle Con grabbed it when she'd got halfway. "You'd better turn around and go back," he said.

"Or what? Remove your hand unless you want it broken."

"I'll have you for assault on a police officer."

"Fine. I'll go to court and tell them everything. You really want to play this game?"

Uncle Con's lips curled back over his teeth. "I'll get custody."

"Your name's not on the birth certificate, remember?" Leda yanked the winder and the window inched up.

"Slut!" the word exploded from him, filled the car with poison. He snatched his hand away just before Leda crushed it against the top of the window. There was the thud of a boot in the door. The car shook.

Enda uttered an involuntary scream.

Leda gunned the accelerator. The wheels spun and sprayed up

gravel, the car swerved onto the highway and sped forward.

Enda twisted around and watched out of the back window. The man beside the police car dwindled, faded, vanished. "He's not following," she said.

Leda's mouth remained a thin, angry line. The speed crept higher. "He will," she said. "Sooner or later, he will. Don't ever go back to Dead Rock, Enda."

*

Enda shook off the memory of leaving Dead Rock. She'd be doing it again soon enough. She pulled into the driveway, stunned she'd made it home without a single glimpse of the police car. So far so good. She scrambled out of the car and ran to the front door. The veranda gave an alarming creak underfoot. Something cracked. No time to investigate. Enda unlocked the door, relocked it behind her and ran down the hall. Tiny footsteps pattered behind her, followed by a meow.

Enda glanced back at Ivy's lithe black form. No time to pet the dead cat. She yanked the telephone out of the receiver and dialled Leda's number. It rang and rang and rang until she thought she'd scream, then the message bank kicked in.

"Mum, you need to call me!" Enda yelled. She took a breath and lowered her voice. "Don't come back without help. Uncle Con has murdered like seventeen people that we know of. I'm taking Dad and hiding until you get here. Don't come home, go to Molly's house, okay? And pick up your fucking phone once in a while!"

She slammed the phone down and went to her room for Selene's journal. Then she went into the kitchen and started grabbing food from the pantry and piling it into a box. Christ. She had no idea what they'd need to go into hiding in the bush, she'd never camped in her life. She had no idea how long they'd be out there. Not long, surely, but what if Leo's condition deteriorated?

Matches. Can opener. She went into Leo's room and got him a change of clothes, and put her own change of clothes with it. A blanket. That would have to be all, she couldn't afford to spend another second here.

There was a knock at the front door.

Enda froze. It wasn't Uncle Con, he would have thumped. She tip-toed down the hall and peered through the keyhole. Doctor Howard stood on the other side. Shit. He must be looking for Leo. Why would he come himself?

She put the chain on and opened the door the two inches it allowed.

"Enda?" Doctor Howard leaned forward, peering at her. His glasses magnified his eyes. His bald spot shone. His smile was friendly and fake. "Everything okay?"

"Just fine," Enda said. "Is this a house call?"

"If Leo's here it is. May I come in?"

"It's not a good time, I'm kind of busy."

Doctor Howard took his glasses off and polished them on his shirt. "Please, Enda, let me in. Leo's condition is very serious. I need to talk to you about it."

God. Why now? Enda took the chain off, held the door open for him and then locked it behind him.

Doctor Howard gave her an odd look. "Are you sure everything's okay?"

"Just fine. Can we make this quick?"

"I know you took your father out of hospital," he said. "We saw it on camera. What were you thinking? Where is he? Is he here?"

"I was thinking you had him on way too many tranquilisers." Enda glanced up and down the hall, mentally calculating how many trips it would take her to get stuff out to the car. Two, maybe.

"Are you on your medication?" he asked.

"Yes!" Enda ran her hand through her hair.

He shook his head. "I don't think you are. You're too strung out."

Enda took a deep breath. She sized up this doctor. He seemed a sensible man. Well-meaning, if a little dense. "I'm not strung out," she said. "I'm scared. I'm not telling you where my dad is, so you may as well go. Now. Please."

"Enda." He looked at her over his glasses. "Bipolar is a tricky thing. Delusions and paranoia are par for the course. Your uncle and I are very worried about you."

"Doctor Howard," she said. "Listen to me carefully. You're a doctor, you need to know what's going on. Uncle Con is not what he seems. He's been killing your patients. All those people who jumped off Dead Rock, they were pushed or thrown. He could be here any minute and I do not intend to be around. You need to get out of here and tell someone. Please. Go."

Doctor Howard sighed. He took out a hanky and mopped his glistening forehead. "I'm so sorry it's come to this," he said. "I suspected it would from the moment you came in, of course, but I tried. I really tried. For your uncle's sake."

"What?" Enda took a step toward the kitchen.

"I never like watching young people get sucked under this way. Luckily there's a court order pending for your indefinite involuntary admission to the psychiatric ward. Although he might have other ideas by now."

"What the hell? I'm not going back there." Enda took another backward step. His babble was messing with her head.

A fist thumped the other side of the door.

"See?" she whispered. "He's here."

Doctor Howard walked to the door.

"What are you doing?" Enda backed toward the kitchen. "Don't open that door!"

The doctor unlocked the door and opened it wide. "She's here," he said. "And worse than we thought."

Enda met Uncle Con's eyes across the hall. Something in them made her skin crawl.

He extended a hand to her. "Come on Enda," he said. "You're unwell. Let us help you."

Enda turned her back on them, bolted down the hall and locked the kitchen door behind her. She hesitated in the kitchen. No way could she get the food and clothes out to the car now. She just had to get out of the house.

The kitchen door shuddered under a heavy blow. She stared, fascinated, imagined Uncle Con slamming his bulk against it to get to her. Shit. She fled into the hall. She could hear the doctor at the back door, he must have run around the house. She ducked into Leo's room and threw herself under the bed.

The space was small, dark and dusty. She covered her nose and mouth with her hand so they wouldn't hear her breathe. Or sneeze.

Footsteps went up the hall. There was a muffled crack when the kitchen door broke, just in time for the doctor to open it from the other side. Great. Thump, thump, thump. Uncle Con walked like a herd of elephants when you had your ear pressed to the floor.

Their voices floated through to her from the hall.

"She didn't go out the back," Doctor Howard said.

"Then she's hiding. Check the rooms."

Enda inched herself as close as she could to the wall. Footsteps went off into the other rooms. She could crawl out and make a run for it if she was quick enough. Where the hell was her mother with the police?

A footstep outside the door. Then, of all things, her own voice, slightly muted as though she was playing on loudspeaker on someone's phone. She sounded shaky and panicked.

"Mum, you need to call me! Don't come back without help. Uncle Con has murdered like seventeen people that we know of. I'm taking Dad and hiding until you get here. Don't come home, go to Molly's house, okay? And pick up your fucking phone once in a while!"

Enda gasped. She couldn't help it. She pressed her hand harder against her mouth, but it was too late. Uncle Con's face peered under the bed at her seconds later. He reached in one big hand, hooked her shirt and dragged her out. When she was all the way out he hauled her to her feet.

"Eric!" he yelled.

Enda could only stare at the phone in his hand. Leda's phone. "Where did you get that?"

He looked down at her and shifted his grip so that he had her by the scruff of the neck. "I took it off your mother," he said. "I didn't think it would be a good idea for her to be making any calls today."

"Where is she?" Her voice cracked.

Doctor Howard came into the room. There was a syringe in his hand.

"I caught your mother speeding on the road out of town last night," Uncle Con said. "Now that's not like her at all. Of course, being in your car, I thought she was you, so I went to pull her over and make sure she was okay. But she kept going. She engaged me in a high speed chase. Very, very risky that, and she broke a lot of laws. Then she crashed your car."

Enda couldn't breathe. Panic ate away at the back of her brain. "Is she okay?"

"She's fine, just fine. Got off with a few scratches and bruises. But I couldn't let someone that dangerous wander the streets. She's cooling her heels in the cells, waiting for you to come and bail her out."

Relief flooded her, but it was relief tinged with fear. She didn't want to think what he might have subjected Leda to between then and now. "Is that where we're going now?"

Uncle Con's mouth twisted into a cruel line. "No sweetheart," he said. "Sit down." He pushed her onto Leo's bed.

She looked up at him and the doctor. "Please don't hurt me."

Uncle Con bent over and looked into her face. "You've got a choice, Enda," he said. "You can be a good girl, tell us where Leo is, then go with Doctor Howard and stay at the hospital until he says you're better. After that you'll stay with me and Betty and be a good daughter until we're sure you can make it on your own. Betty needs someone to look after and I'm happy to give her that. We want this for you. I don't want to lose another daughter." He paused. "Or you can try and run. I'm a fair man. I'll give you, shall we say, three minutes lead? Then I'll find you. I'll find my brother. And I'll consider exactly what I should do with Leda."

Enda blinked back the tears that stung her eyes. She couldn't believe she'd failed.

"Don't cry." Uncle Con's knuckle brushed her cheek. "We're only trying to help you. Eric."

The doctor approached her with the syringe. Uncle Con took a step back. The doctor took her arm with one hand and rubbed a finger over the veins on her wrist. "There's just going to be a little sting," he said.

Enda looked up at him. "Wait."

"What?" The needle hovered over her arm.

Enda smacked her head into his forehead as hard as she could and pushed him into Uncle Con. Both men fell to the floor in a tangle of arms and legs. Enda grabbed the syringe off the floor and fled the room.

"Three minutes Enda!" Uncle Con roared behind her.

"Go fuck yourself!" she yelled. She pocketed the syringe,

grabbed Leo's clothes and Selene's journal when she flew past the kitchen table and dodged through the broken door. Three minutes bullshit, they were already out of the room.

She bolted down the hallway and out of the front door. The veranda cracked again under her pounding feet, then she was down the steps and out of the door. She stopped beside Leda's car, momentarily frozen. Something was wrong with it. What was wrong? Her gaze fell on the tyres. They were flat. No, they'd been slashed.

Asshole!

Behind her the front door opened again and Uncle Con pounded onto the veranda. The crack this time echoed across the yard. He yelled, but not at her. Enda took a few steps back and saw the floorboards cave in under his feet. A dust cloud flew up and the man was waist deep in rubble, Doctor Howard trapped in the house behind him.

Enda took off again. She found the police car sitting on the verge outside the house. The keys were in the ignition. Her heart thudded so hard against her ribs she thought there was a good chance she should be heading to the hospital after all. Damn, this was no time for indecision. She flung her things into the passenger seat, jumped behind the wheel and started the engine. She was in deep shit now. She wound up the windows so she couldn't hear what Uncle Con was yelling, did a tight U-turn and sped up the street.

There were so many buttons, bells and whistles on the car she hardly dared touch anything. Holy shit. She didn't know how much time she was going to gain like this. The doctor's car was still in front of the house. Stealing a police car was probably even dumber than kidnapping her dad from the hospital. Maybe she was insane. Shit. Who should she get first, Leda out of jail or Leo into hiding?

A single breath came out in a sob. Panic still bled into her mind, but she sat on it. Think. Think. Right now he was more interested in going after her and Leo, so she had to get Leo to safety first. He'd know to go to Molly's, he'd listened to the message she left her mother.

A long black skink crawled out from the side of the road in front of her. Enda swerved around it, overcorrected and bounced off the gravel. The car fishtailed down the road before she had it under control. Damn! It was touchy, far more powerful than her Magna or even Leda's four wheel drive.

The radio crackled. Enda looked at it askance. She wasn't game to touch.

It crackled again. "Sergeant Wilson, please respond," a female voice said.

It hadn't occurred to Enda there would be somebody else at the police station. Dead Rock was a one cop town, had been for years, but that didn't mean there wasn't someone in admin, watching the cells.

"Hey," she said. "Can you hear me?"

The voice went sharp. "Please identify yourself."

"My name is Enda Wilson."

"And where is Sergeant Wilson?"

"At my house, stuck in broken floorboards. That wasn't my fault, by the way."

"And why are you in the vehicle?"

"Because it was the only way I could put any distance between us, I never stole a car before, but he slashed my tyres and tried to inject me with something! He's got it in for me, I think he's trying to kill me!"

"Ms Wilson, please calm down." The voice on the radio was level and stern.

"Please, you have to believe me," Enda said. "He's a killer. Do you have a woman in the cells there?"

"I'm not at liberty to give out that information."

"He said she was there. Leda Wilson, she's my mother, she'll back me up, she was going for help last night. Please, we need police out here before he kills again."

"Ms Wilson I want you to listen to me. I'm going to check your information and I'll be back on the radio in a minute. You need to bring that car back to the station right now. Do you understand?"

"Yes."

Silence.

Then a ring tone, right by her leg. Uncle Con's phone. Enda picked it up. The number on the screen was the number of the house. She pushed the answer button, even though she knew she shouldn't. She wondered what she'd get for talking on the phone while driving a stolen police car. She held it to her ear.

"Enda," Con said.

She yanked the car around the corner and headed for the highway.

"Enda I know you can hear me," he said. "Tell me where you're going."

"Not bloody likely."

"You're really fucked now." His voice was low and vicious. She'd never heard him swear before. "Stealing a police car, assault on a police officer, abduction. There's not much I can do to help you if you don't stop the car, stay with it and wait for me."

"How about you ring the police, tell them about all the people you murdered and wait for them to come get you?

A pause.

"I'm coming for you," he said.

Enda yanked the wheel hard right, jammed on the brakes and came to a halt with the bumper touching the cemetery gates. She grabbed Leo's clothes and the journal, scrambled out of the car and threw the keys into the cemetery. Then she set off at a run down the road towards the highway, keeping to the trees and the shade. The sun beat down around her. Her throat was dry.

The quickest way was up the steep path at Dead Rock itself. Enda felt exposed on the highway, but she just kept her head down and ran faster until she was in the shade of the cliff. Obviously Uncle Con had got out of the broken veranda, but he still had to find the car and the keys and with any luck search the cemetery for her.

She took a moment to catch her breath, tucked the clothes and book into her belt and then pulled herself hand over hand up the path. She didn't pause to allow herself to think, because if she thought about anything, she was going to get scared.

Selene waited at the top of the path.

"Where the hell have you been?" Enda pulled herself toward the ghost.

Selene's eyes were wide. "He's coming, isn't he?"

"Yes." Enda dragged herself onto the top of the cliff. No time to rest. She got to her feet. "So tell me, do you remember how you died yet?"

"It's all happened before. Just like this."

Enda had no time to stop and strangle Selene for being obtuse, and she was dead anyway, so there was no point. She set off in the direction of Molly's at a fast walk, the most she could manage right now. Selene was beside her every step of the way and she thought she could feel Tom at her back.

When she reached Molly's back door Enda collapsed against it, closed her eyes and let exhaustion take her until Molly opened the door and all but dragged her inside.

"Where have you been?" Molly demanded. "You said half an hour, that was three hours ago!"

Enda stumbled down the hall after her, collapsed in the lounge room across from Leo and dropped the clothes on the floor. "Molly it's not just Uncle Con." She put her head in her hands. "Please can I have some water?"

Molly disappeared. Enda peered through her fingers at Leo. She was surprised to find him looking at her, not through her. She took her hands away from her face. "Dad?"

He turned his face away.

Enda was off the couch like a shot. She knelt beside him and grabbed his face in her hands. "Dad, look at me."

Molly came back in and handed her a glass of water. Enda drank it fast to put out the fire in her throat. Then she returned her attention to Leo. "Dad, you've got to come back to me. It's very important. You have to do it now, because they're coming for us. I slowed them down some, but we don't have long."

"I think you'd better tell me what happened," Molly said from behind her. "You look like hell."

Enda sighed. Leo looked up at her, *at* her. The drugs must be leaving his system. "Doctor Howard came to the house while I was there," she said. "He brought Uncle Con. They tried to inject me with something. I ran away. They slashed my tyres, Molly, so I took the police car. It was the only way to get some time."

"You stole his car?" Molly made a sound that was somewhere between a snort and a cough. "Oh my God. You're crazy."

"I'm not crazy!" Enda ended on a yell.

Molly cracked first. She started to laugh. Enda couldn't help it; she laughed too. The tension was broken.

It only took a minute for them to sober up. Enda returned her attention to Leo. "He's got Mum at the police station," she said.

"He took her phone and listened to her messages so he knows to come here. I left his car at the cemetery, but it won't keep him there for long. We have to go, Dad. Now."

Leo exhaled a long breath and made a movement with one hand. Enda helped him to sit up on the couch; he leaned forward and dropped his face into his hands.

"He's in no state to go anywhere," Molly said.

Enda looked at his chest. The shadow thing that pulsed there had grown bigger, darker. She could see how its tentacles curled around him, dug into his flesh, entangled. The way it pulsed, breathed, fed, made her feel sick. "This thing is killing you Dad," she whispered.

Leo spoke into his hands. "He killed him," he said. "He killed him because he was my friend."

"He's killed a lot more than Kelvin," Enda said. "Everyone you ever thought jumped off Dead Rock."

Leo dropped his hands and looked at her. "Even Selene?"

"Even Selene." Enda hated the look in his eyes, the resignation, the fear. It was the same look she'd seen from Molly earlier. He knew. He'd known for a long time. "I've pissed him off," she said. "I'm next."

"No." He shook his head. "Not you. He wouldn't."

"Yes, he would. We have to go now."

"Too late," Molly said from the window. "They're coming."

"Shit." Enda could see the dust cloud approaching. "Where do we go?"

"Under the house. Come on Leo." Molly hauled him off the couch and they hurried out the back door, Leo staggering between them. Molly steered them down the side. She moved a sheet of tin away from the supports of the house to reveal a way under. The rest of the way around was completely enclosed by wooden beams. "Get under there," she said.

Leo crawled under first and collapsed on the dirt. Enda followed him. Molly replaced the tin.

"Molly!" Enda hissed. "Come back! You need to be under here too!"

"I'm not hiding from Conrad anymore," Molly said. "You just stay there and be quiet until I come get you out." She walked away.

Enda bent down to Leo. "Are you okay?"

He nodded, eyes closed.

Enda could see the shadow thing even in the semi-dark. "I'm going to ask you to do something," she said.

He nodded again.

"There's a thing attached to you, Dad, a very bad thing. It's feeding off you right now and it's going to kill you soon. I can help you get rid of it, but you have to let go."

He opened his eyes. She could see he wanted to argue, but hadn't the will. "Let go of what?"

"Whatever you're feeding it. Guilt. Anger. The murders weren't your fault, okay?"

A tear trailed down his face and into the dust. "Yes. Yes they were. I should have stopped him."

"Dad." Enda bent down close to him and dropped her voice. "You couldn't have. He's the crazy one, he would have done it anyway. You need to shake this thing off and then you and I can stop him from killing anyone else. You understand? If you don't you may as well just give up and die right now."

"Don't you see, Enda?" his voice was barely a whisper. "I deserve this. I deserve to die. I failed you, I failed Leda. I knew what he was doing and all I could ever do was drink to dull the pain."

"Don't be an asshole," Enda hissed. "Fine, you drank and did nothing. Well do something now, because if you don't and I end up dead I'm coming back to haunt you."

"I failed Tom," he said. "I failed Tom."

Behind Leo a shadow stirred. Enda met Tom's eyes; the ghost bent over Leo. His face was solemn.

"Tom's here," she whispered.

"I'm sorry Tom," Leo said. "I'm sorry."

Tom leaned over and placed his hands around the shadow thing. Enda followed suit.

"Dad, Tom and I are going to take this thing off you," she said."You've got to help us. Just-" Christ, she was no shrink, she was supposed to be the crazy one. "Forgive yourself or something."

His eyes closed. He nodded.

Enda curled her fingers around the shadow thing. It latched on.

She went cold. Leo was breathing too fast; she could almost hear his skipping pulse. She raised her eyes to Tom's again.

The ghost nodded his head, once, twice, and handed the shadow thing to her.

Enda backed away from Leo. It throbbed in her hands. Each tendril attached to her the moment it detached from Leo. The panic that had been bleeding into her brain all day grew. She felt suffocated. Terror sat on her back. She heard, as though through a vacuum, the sound of wheels crunching on gravel.

Tom raised his hands and plunged them into the earth.

Enda raised her hands. Through the shadow thing she saw Leo watching her. His eyes were fixed on her hands and she wondered if he could see it. She plunged her hands down, hard. Even though they hit the dust, the shadow thing sank into the dirt, fell from her fingers and disappeared.

Enda curled over, shocked by the way the terror slid away with it. She caught her breath. She thought she felt a hand on her shoulder. Then Tom was no longer under the house with them.

CHAPTER TWENTY-TWO

Footsteps crunched on the gravel.

Enda crawled over to the side of the house and peered through the gap between the planks. A pair of blue trousers passed so close she could have breathed on them. Uncle Con. Jesus, this was it. She hoped Molly knew what she was doing.

The trousers disappeared. He hammered on the door. Voices. Footsteps went overhead. Enda followed the sound until they stopped; she couldn't quite stand up under here, but she could kneel and press her ear to the boards. Wait. There, right above her, was a little knot in the wood. She peered through it, but all she could see was the bottom of the kitchen cabinets.

A pair of sneakers went past. Molly. So far so good.

Uncle Con sounded like he was right overhead. "Now Molly, I know you know where they are," he said.

"Why would I know a thing like that?" A kitchen chair scraped; perhaps Molly was leaning on it, keeping it between her and Con.

"Because she said she was coming here."

Molly shrugged. "I told her to stop doing that. I know you don't like me seeing my nieces."

His footsteps paced closer to Molly. Enda shifted positions, trying to see what was happening.

"You've got to understand Enda is very unwell," he said. "She suffers from an acute form of bipolar disorder and she won't take her medication. She's delusional, Molly. I have to find her and Leo before something terrible happens. You wouldn't want another tragedy on your hands, would you? You wouldn't want to think Enda was able to do something terrible because you refused to aid a police investigation?"

Enda made a face at him through the floor. Fucking liar, she wanted to yell.

"Look Conrad," Molly said. "She was supposed to come back here with Leo but she never did. I've been waiting all day. You have to know she's scared of you. Real scared. Maybe she went to ground somewhere else."

"Where would they go? Anything you can tell me, Molly, anything."

"She said something about the graveyard. She was talking about   ghosts."

Smart, Molly, very smart. Mess with his head. Had he searched the graveyard already? Enda held her breath and wondered if he'd take the bait.

There was a long silence.

"See," Con finally said, "This is what I never liked about you, Molly. You always thought you were smarter than the rest of us. But if you were so smart you would have hidden that blanket in your lounge room, because I saw it not long ago in Leda's car. Not to mention the clothes Enda took off with earlier that are now lying on your floor. I know they're here."

A pause. A click. Enda pressed her hand to her mouth. The scene she couldn't quite see played out in her mind; Molly, framed against the window. Uncle Con aiming his police-issue gun at her. The click as the safety was released. "Now tell me where they are."

Shit. Enda scrambled over to Leo, who was lying on his side, eyes closed. His colour was better. He opened eyes that were alert and present when she leaned over him.

"What's going on?" he said.

"I'm going to distract Uncle Con. When he's gone tell Molly to go bail Mum out of jail, then come and find me. I don't know how long I can hold him off. Give Mum this." She placed Selene's diary in his hand.

"Enda no! Wait!" Leo grabbed for her leg. "It's too dangerous!"

Enda knocked out the sheet of tin, scrambled out from under the house and bolted up the side. She stopped only to pick up a lump of wood. Great, a lump of wood versus a gun. Good thing she could run fast.

She eased open the back door and walked softly through the lounge room. She could hear their voices again.

"You're not going to shoot me Conrad," Molly said.

"How do you figure that?"

Wow. If anything Uncle Con sounded more flustered than Molly did.

"Because you can't pass me off as a Dead Rock suicide if I've got a bullet hole in me."

Enda went through the door and peered into the kitchen. Uncle Con stood two feet in front of her and held the gun in both hands, pointed at Molly's head.

"Good point," he said. "But then, who'd miss you if you were gone?"

Molly turned her head to the side. Enda saw Tom was in the kitchen. "Who is it?" she said.

"What? Who is what?'

Enda took a step closer. She could see sweat trickling down the back of Con's neck.

"I wasn't talking to you," Molly said. "I was talking to Tom. He said there's help coming."

"Tom's dead, you stupid old bat."

"I know. He wants you to know he's met what's waiting for you when you join him."

Enda took another step closer, lifted her lump of wood and slammed it into the arm holding the gun.

Con yelled. The gun flew across the kitchen. He hit out and caught a glancing blow on Enda's mouth. She stumbled into the wall, caught herself and pressed her fingertips to her lips. They came away bloody. She got to her feet, a little unsteady, while Con clutched his arm to his stomach. It obviously wasn't broken but with any luck there'd be a nasty bruise.

He stared at her. "You little bitch!"

Enda edged towards the door. "Surprise. Come and get me, Uncle Con. Or are you going to give me three minutes?" She bolted out of the door, ran through the lounge room and out the back. She could hear him lurch after her. She went straight across the yard and headed for the trees. She'd never been into the forest before, but surely, surely there'd be cover in there.

She caught sight of the police car out of the corner of her eye and muttered a curse when she realised the doctor had been leaning against it the whole time, probably waiting for her to come flying out of somewhere. He was on her heels in seconds.

But she was young and fast. He was old and less than fit. Enda ducked into the tree line and kept going. Now she had to dodge tree roots and find her way through the undergrowth, which slowed her. She didn't look back. She didn't want to know. It was enough to hear Uncle Con yell something behind her, to know they were both in pursuit and Molly and Dad were safe for the moment.

She hit a kangaroo trail, which made the going easier except that it twisted and turned every which way. Soon she had to start pushing through thorn bushes and close-growing grass trees and oh God, what if there were snakes out here?

Enda spotted a dense thicket of balgas not far off the path. She ran towards them and dropped to the ground to catch her breath. Cockatoos screeched in the tree tops. Bees droned, crickets chirped, branches groaned when they rubbed together. The smell of fresh soil rose up to her face. She closed her eyes and wished she could just stay here until it was all over. This place wasn't so bad.

Footsteps pounded along the trail. Enda took deep, slow breaths to stay calm. She peered through the leaves and watched Uncle Con go past. Boy, could he run. Must be all those years as a cop. Doctor Howard came soon after, slower, panting. Think, think, she had to be smart about this. She could go back while they searched the bush for her and hope they didn't think of that. She could try to take out the weaker pursuer and then just keep Uncle Con busy. Christ, who did she think she was, Xena?

She backed out of her hiding spot, kept low and made her way through the bushes in the opposite direction to the path. Spindly leaves scratched her face. Rocks scattered under her shoes. Christ, she was going to have no idea how to get back if she kept going this way.

The ground abruptly fell away in a short, rocky slope. Enda yelped, tripped, slithered down it on her rear end and grazed her hands yet again. She landed at the bottom in a clearing and swallowed hard.

Uncle Con and Doctor Howard were already there.

"Get her," Con said. He reached out a big hand and closed it around her shoulder.

"Christ, what are you, a cartoon bad guy?" Enda tried to pull away, but he tightened his grip and grabbed her face in the other hand. "Enough, Enda," he said. "It's all over now."

Time for the hammer to fall. Finally. Doctor Howard fumbled with another syringe; he was out of breath, smudged with sweat and dirt, the knees of his pants torn. The syringe reminded her of something. Enda very carefully eased a hand into her jeans pocket, where she'd put the last syringe he'd tried to jab her with. She withdrew it and knocked the cap off with her thumb. She kept her head down so Uncle Con would think she'd given up and watched the doctor from the corner of her eyes.

He came closer. She shifted the syringe in her fist.

"I was going to say I'm sorry about this, but I'm not anymore," Doctor Howard said. "This one's given us more trouble than all the rest put together."

Uncle Con chuckled deep in his throat. "That's my girl."

Sick bastard.

The doctor braced his leg against her feet and leaned over her. Enda drew back her fist and jabbed the syringe straight through his pants, into his calf muscle. The man screamed and stumbled backward. He swayed, his eyes rolled back in his head and he collapsed on the gravel.

Enda took advantage of Con's surprise to break free. She put distance between them.

"What did you do?" he roared.

"That all depends." Enda couldn't look away from the collapsed body, which might have been her in another second. "What was in that syringe?" A horrible thought occurred to her. "Holy shit Uncle Con, was it some kind of poison? Is he dead?"

Con came slowly toward her, arms out like a man trying to herd a wild beast. Enda backed away.

"What would you do if he was?"

"I don't know." Enda stepped carefully around a rock. She didn't dare look for an escape route in case he chose that moment to pounce. "I sure as hell wouldn't throw him off Dead Rock and say he did it himself."

"But think about it Enda," Con said. "You're 24. You've got your whole life ahead of you, so much possibility."

"Not the way you figure it."

"Is his life worth more than yours? Would you spend twenty years languishing in jail for him?"

"I'm not you," she said. She came up against a tree and edged around it. "Is that what you figured out, forty years ago? That your life was worth more than Tom Nickel's?"

"Of course it was!" the roar echoed off the trees and for a moment there was perfect silence.

"He was never going to amount to anything," Con said. "He was nothing. Did you think I was going to let him stand in the way of my future? Or Eric's, or Leo's? We've spent the last forty years serving the community, me and Eric, and what would Tom have done? Lived off the dole?"

"You never gave him the chance to find out," Enda said. "And as for you and Doctor Howard, you haven't served the community, you've turned into serial killers!"

"I did the community a favour," he said. "Think about it Enda, all those people were draining the community of anything good in it. Drug addicts, alcoholics, nutcases, all of them. Wastes of space. I kept this town clean and crime free!"

"Alcoholics and nutcases like me and my dad?"

He went bright red. "Leo is not your father!"

"What about those three girls?" Enda could feel the path behind her getting steep; she backed up it. "Those three girls you killed right after Mum and I left? What was that all about? Were they drug addicts and nutcases too?"

"Yes," he said. "Such a shame. Such pretty girls, to go to waste like that. I said to myself, what would I do if my daughters ended up like that?" He lost focus for a second. "I wanted to kill Leda for leaving and taking you."

"So you killed them instead? Is that it?"

He snapped back. "Yes."

"God. I was right. You're the nutcase." Enda decided to take her chances. She turned her back on him and bolted up the hill, but the chance didn't pay off. He was on her in a minute. A hand closed in her hair. He yanked her backward, threw her to the gravel and planted his boot in her ribs. He went for something bright yellow in his belt. "This is for taking my car, you little bitch."

Something crackled. Pain so intense it felt as if every bone in her body would shatter, as if her skin would burn off. Every muscle contracted. She could hear a horrible scream of agony.

*

"Hey," Selene said. "Nice view?"

Enda opened her eyes. All she could see was gravel. Trees, upside down. A pair of police boots, then a pair of strappy red high-heeled sandals under a floaty red dress. What an awkward place to be. She appeared to be slung over Uncle Con's shoulder. She twisted her head up and squinted at Selene.

Selene put her finger to her lips. "This is how it happened."

The gravel turned to grass. There were no more trees. Enda twisted her head from side to side and decided they must be back on top of Dead Rock. Shit. Tasered and thrown off a cliff, what a way to go. She did what any girl in her position would do and booted the nearest piece of soft flesh.

That got an instant reaction. Hands lifted her off and dumped her on the ground.

Enda squinted upward. The late afternoon light made a halo around Uncle Con's head and cast his face in shadow.

He planted his boot on her ribcage and laid a hand on the taser, now back in his belt. "Are you going to make me hurt you again?"

She shook her head. Anything but that.

He bent down and placed something around her neck. Enda closed her eyes in horror, thinking she was going to be strangled, but no; he fastened a chain and laid a pendant on her ribs. Selene's necklace. Ew, he'd searched her room. He laid a hand over the pendant and studied her.

"Enda Wilson," he said. "Psychotic, prey to delusions, jumps off Dead Rock to be with her dead cousin. Another tragedy. Another copycat suicide. I warned you this might happen if you insisted on coming up here." He hauled her to her feet and twisted both hands up behind her back.

Enda had to move where he pushed her or fall. The edge of Dead Rock embraced her feet. Tiny rocks clattered over the edge. She looked down, but couldn't see a thing for the after-reflection of the sun. She took a shaky breath in.

"This is it," Uncle Con said. "I'm truly sorry it had to be this way, Enda. I had high hopes for you."

"But it doesn't have to be this way," Enda said. "Please Uncle Con, think about what you're doing."

"I have thought about it. I can't allow someone like you to go on. You have no regard for rules or laws or even looking like a normal person." With his free hand he touched her blonde lock in what could almost have been a fatherly gesture. "You came out all wrong and refused to change. I knew it years ago. I thought if only you would listen to me, your true father, be put under my guidance, I could make you right. But she took you away. Everything about your life failed. Now it's up to me to put you out of your misery."

Enda gulped for air. For one dizzying second she remembered she'd come to Dead Rock with no job, no home and no friends, seeking to escape her mother. But she'd never sought an end.

Never.

Selene stood by her on the cliff and reached with one hand toward the horizon. "You're not going to kill your own daughter," she said. "I'm leaving and never coming back. And I'm taking Enda with me. You'll never get near her."

Enda couldn't take her eyes off the sight. Selene's body, incorporeal, became suffused with light in the setting sun. "Is this how it happened for you?" she asked.

Selene nodded.

"How what happened?" Con's fingers dug into her like needles.

"I was just asking Selene if this was how she died."

His voice shook. "You can't see her."

"You're not going to kill your own daughter. I'm leaving and never coming back. And I'm taking Enda with me. You'll never get near her," Enda said.

His breath caught. He shook her, pushed her closer to the edge. Showers of grey dirt spilled from under her feet. "What did you say?"

Enda squeezed her eyes shut, terrified, but she couldn't stop herself. "The sunset makes her hair look red and gold," she said. "She's wearing a red dress with a long skirt and red shoes with high heels. Red lipstick. She's beautiful, Uncle Con, and you can see the sunset through her!"

"You can't control everything," Selene's voice was low, angry. "Sooner or later someone will stop you. If you kill me now, it'll be her. I'll make sure of it. I'll stick around. I know she sees them, clearer than you do."

Enda gasped. "He sees them?"

He shook her again. "Stop it!"

"What are you going to do, kill me? Get it over with!" Enda's words bounced down the cliff. "Who do you see? Who do you see, Uncle Con? I know you saw Ivy, how many others?"

"Who the hell is Ivy?"

"My dead cat!"

He yanked her back from the edge, let her go and stuck a meaty finger in her face. Unsteady words jerked from him. "I – do not – see anything."

Enda staggered away. "You do. You do see them. So does my dad, but not like you. I bet you see Tom, Selene, Kelvin and Sadie and all of them! That's why I see ghosts all the time, it's in my genetics!" she yelled the last word. "Did you see that woman in the hospital? Did you see Ada and still throw me in psych for it?"

"Stop it!" Con clutched his head as though he could tear her words out of it.

Enda took another step away. "You can't pretend forever," she said. "Not once they know. Hey Selene!" she raised her voice. "Selene he can see you!"

Selene appeared beside Con. She peered into his face. "Dad? Can you see me?"

CHAPTER TWENTY-THREE

He looked at Selene for a split second. Enda thought something trembled, cracked, but then he reached out for her.

She ducked. When he grabbed her she fought him, fists, teeth, nails, everything she had. He hit her with an open hand so hard she almost blacked out. She returned with a kick to the shins, resisted his pull toward the edge, but he was twice her size and weight. She landed face first on the ground and got a mouthful of dirt. He hauled her up again and pushed her toward the edge. "Goodbye Enda."

"Take your hands off my daughter," said a voice behind them.

Enda almost cried.

Con turned slowly, bringing Enda with him. She stared over the barrel of a gun into Leo's face. He was upright, healthy, a miracle with lines of exhaustion etched into his face.

"She's not your daughter," Con said. "I brought her into this world, I'll be the one to take her out of it."

Leo held the gun steady. "I won't let you take the last good thing I have."

"Oh, but you will," Con said. "You can't change the habits of a lifetime. I've got your wife. I'll take your daughter. And if you don't want to bury it all in the bottom of a wine cask you can follow them."

One hand moved from Enda's throat to his belt. Con kicked out the back of her legs. Her knees buckled and she landed on the ground. An arm wrapped around her neck, the other pressed a metal tip to her forehead. She knew it was the taser the same way she knew what the dirt would taste like at the end of the fall off Dead Rock. She looked at Leo but dared to say nothing.

"This could kill her," Con said. "See this, little brother? The power is all here, 50,000 volts. Is this what you want for her? Shock therapy? Couldn't do her any harm."

"No!" Leo put out a shaking hand. "Conrad, stop. It has to stop now. She's not the one you're angry at. She's done nothing. Look at yourself, look at what you've become, it's not her fault!" Leo's voice rose. "It's yours! It's your fault, Conrad, you killed Tom and you were never right again!"

Con's hand clenched on her arm. The promise of death by electricity kissed Enda's temple. Enda tried to communicate telepathically to Leo, for all the good it would do, to shut the hell up before he got her killed.

"Why don't you go talk to a cask of wine?" Con's voice was low, acid. "You don't think you're going to survive much longer, do you, brother? I tried with you. I tried so hard, but in the end you're just another derelict alcoholic feeding off society. Your last few days catatonic in the psych ward were the most useful of your life."

A noise that had been growing in the distance, like wind or thunder, turned to the roar of an engine. Molly's car sped onto the cliff top behind Leo and braked sharply. The wheels made deep grooves in the grass. Molly and Leda bolted from the car almost before the engine died.

"Welcome to the party, ladies!" Con yelled. "I was expecting you, Molly, but I thought I put this other bitch where she belonged!"

"I have a good lawyer." Leda strode towards them and took in the situation at a glance. She grabbed the gun out of Leo's shaking hand and pressed it against Con's temple. "Take your filthy hands off my daughter or I will do what I should have done twenty-four years ago."

"Leda." Con pressed the taser into Enda's skin a little harder. "It was always you. From the minute you hit me with that bottle at school I wanted you. I wanted to hurt you. Keep you. Make your life hell. You're just like your daughter. Or she's just like you, rebellious and non-conformist and different. No respect. It's your fault she came out so wrong. It's your fault she has to die. I only have to twitch and she's gone."

"Tell that to the twenty police on their way here from the city," Leda said.

Enda closed her eyes and imagined dying. When she opened them Tom was kneeling in front of her, his hands around her face.

There was a sensation of cold where those hands were. "Tom," she whispered.

Footsteps approached. Molly's beat up sneakers stopped by Tom, who rose to his feet.

Enda looked up at them. She saw Tom place his hands on Con's face, while Molly very gently took the hand with the taser and moved it from her head.

Leo dived under Molly's arm and grabbed her hands. Enda scrambled out of reach with him and collapsed on the grass, every limb shaking. She couldn't move; she couldn't look away from the way something in Uncle Con's eyes had cracked wide open when Tom touched him.

He didn't seem to realise there was a gun to his head. He stared right into the ghost's eyes. Then he looked from Tom to Molly. "Stop it," he said. "Make him go away."

"No." Molly's voice was harder than Enda had ever heard it. The single syllable quivered with rage.

"I did it for you, Molly," Con said. "You had no future with him."

"That's not why you did it."

Leo left Enda's side. She watched him very gently fold his hand over Leda's, draw her away from Con and the edge of the cliff. Leda kept the gun trained on Uncle Con from a distance.

Far, far away, Enda thought she could hear sirens. Her shoulders drooped. The nightmare would be over soon. She wasn't going to die.

Molly grabbed Con's face and forced him to look into her eyes. "You're sick," she said. "This thing's been sitting on your back ever since you killed Tom, making you crazier and crazier. You have to make amends, Conrad, with me, with Tom and with yourself. You hear me? You have to take responsibility!"

Con's eyes were drawn like magnets back to Tom, whose hand hovered over his face. And then he began to talk.

*

1968

Petrol fumes and beer had Con's blood thumping in all the right places. The wheels spun on the gravel and the steering screamed when he put it on full lock to make the turn onto the cliff top. Eric, skinny bespectacled bastard, had stopped hanging out of the window yelling and was lolling against the seat looking green.

Con kept the wheel on lock and cut up in a circle around the car already up here. He should've known where Leo would be, the little bastard. He'd spent all afternoon drinking to get up the balls to go and win Leo's little girlfriend off him only to find he'd already taken her out.

The second circle made his head spin. Con slammed on the brakes. The car stopped but it felt like everything else kept going. There were two steering wheels. He swayed, rubbed his eyes and got out. Fresh air slapped him in the face. When he put his beer on the roof it landed hard and almost broke.

Eric lurched out of the passenger door, bolted to the nearest bushes and threw up.

"Eric, you girl!" Con roared. The sound bounced back at him, a disembodied roar, his own voice turned to pure power. Yeah.

Con peered across the car at the three figures leaning against the pickup truck. At first he thought the girl was Leda, but when he finally focused, he realised it was just Molly the match girl and her boyfriend. So where was Leda? "Honestly Leo," he said. "I leave you alone for one bloody night and I find you up here with this scum."

Leo lit a cigarette. The end made streaks of light. "Go home Con," he said. There was a streak of contempt in his voice.

He'd be laughing on the other side of his face when Con found Leda. "Go home? What are you my mother now?" Con picked up his beer and closed the distance between himself and the other three.

Leo chuckled. "Go wherever else you want."

Con grinned in the darkness. Little brother was scared, he could hear it in the rapid back down. "But leave you alone?" He tried to focus on Leo's faces and make them into just one. "Where's your pretty little girlfriend? Maybe I should go and find her, since you don't want my company."

Leo's voice came out in a growl this time. "You so much as touch her, I'll kill you."

Better and better. Didn't take much to get a rise these days. "Will you, Leo? I don't blame you. She's the only chick worth banging in this hole of a town."

Leo dropped his cigarette on the ground. "Get out of here."

Con ignored him. "Funny thing is, I could swear the old lady said you were out with her tonight, so where is she? She get bored of you and come looking for me maybe?" For the fiftieth time that night he pictured Leda slapping Leo upside the head and waiting on the side of the road for someone to rescue her.

"We dropped her home," Leo said.

Con narrowed his eyes. He saw Molly make a nervous movement. He didn't believe it for a second. "She's here, isn't she? What'd she do, hide? She in the car?" He threw his head back. "Leda!" he yelled. "Come out, come out, wherever you are!"

Silence. Leo looked at him like he was nothing. Skinny little shit. He'd show him who had the power here. Him and Molly and that other little bastard, all three of them.

"Fine," Con said. "Then I'll have to amuse myself some other way. Molly, come here."

"Lay off," Leo said.

"Oh, I can't play with your little friends, either?" Con leaned back against his car, enjoying himself now they were all sweating. "That's just too bad. Molly, get your ass over here. Come on, I won't hurt you."

"No," Molly said in a low voice.

"Really? No? I don't think my parents put a roof over your head so you could say no." Con took a step toward her, determined to wipe the defiance off her face. The movement made his head spin.

Leo stepped in front of Molly and Tom. "Come on Con, leave her alone. You've had your fun."

"I haven't even started. Make your choice, Leo, what's it going to be? Molly or Leda?"

Leo shaped up to him. Little shit, he'd put a stop to that. Con wrapped his hands around Leo's neck and pinned him to his piece of shit car. He squeezed. The anger seeped into his fists, his clenched teeth, his brain, bastard, what did she see in him that Con didn't have anyway?

He didn't see Tom move, but all of a sudden he was on Con's back, gouging his eyes. Con lost balance and went back, half-roaring, half-laughing, because he was on familiar ground now. He flung himself backward to get Tom off and then lurched onto him and pinned him to the grass. He had brute strength on his side, but

Tom was a slippery little bastard; his fist caught him in the eye. They rolled around on the cold grass, each trying to get a handle on the other. Leo streaked toward them to spoil his fun.

"Eric!" Con roared, remembering he had backup. "Get over here!"

"What?" Eric sounded like he wasn't finished throwing up.

Con pushed Tom off him, staggered to his feet and gestured at Leo. "Get him out of my face while I deal with this little shit here."

Eric lurched toward Leo and pushed him into Con's car.

There, sorted. Con punched Tom full in the face. Tom spit a tooth out of his mouth and looked at him with pure hatred.

Con grinned and went for him again, only to have the wind knocked out of him by a small flying shape. At first he thought it was Leda. Leda would do that. But when he regained his focus only Molly was there.

"Tom come on!" Molly yelled. "Let's go!"

Her words disappeared into the air. Tom drove a fist into Con's face. Something cracked. Pain blinded him. Hot blood flowed from Con's nose. He yelled, clutched his face and caught Tom on the side of the head with one flying hand. Tom went down. Con kicked him in the ribs again and again, sending him further back along the grass with each blow. He spat blood from his mouth, furious the little shit had got that hit in. He'd pay for that. He'd pay.

Footsteps pounded towards him. A girl screamed and he thought again it was Leda, but he could only see Molly. He looked back at her, foot poised over Tom. "Change your mind, did you?"

"Please stop this." Molly walked slowly toward him. She looked scared.

Leo was beside her. "Come on Con," he said. "You won. Let me just take these guys home before they get too hurt."

Movement under him. Tom got to his feet, staggered, lurched at Con.

Blinding fury. Con shoved him in the chest. His own forward momentum took him by surprise and for a minute he teetered on the edge of the darkest, most complete night he had ever seen.

But it was Tom who fell into the night.

A scream split Con's head in two. He clutched it in both hands, standing on the edge of the darkness, waiting for Tom to reappear, climb back up, but there was nothing. The screaming went on and on and it made something in him snap. Tom wasn't coming back. Shit. Tom wasn't coming back. He struggled to comprehend. When he finally did he pushed Leo away from Molly, propelled her back to Leo's car and put his hand over her mouth. He saw the whites of her eyes roll in terror.

"Shut up," he said. "Just shut up, understand?"

She nodded. Through the haze of fear, confusion, he registered she was terrified of him. Good. Good, keep her that way.

He took his hand away from her mouth but kept her pinned to the car with an arm braced across her chest. He barely knew where the words came from, just that they would save his life. "You say nothing," he said. "Nothing, you hear me? You saw nothing. No, you know what? You saw him jump. So you can cry and carry on all you like, because that's what happened. He jumped. You ever say anything else about tonight, I swear I will hunt you down and throw you off Dead Rock too. Do you understand?"

Molly nodded.

"Tell me you understand me."

"I understand you," she whispered.

Con let her go. He swayed and saw Eric standing there staring at him, gaping like the yokel he was. "Get in the car," he said.

Leo was crouched on the ground nearby, his head in his hands, rasping for breath. Con hauled him to his feet and grabbed his face in both hands. He looked into Leo's eyes, eyes the same as his. He dug his fingers into the stubble on his face. "We're family," he said. "You have to stand with me on this one little brother, you know you do."

Leo looked terrified and disgusted at the same time. His lip curled back. "No, Conrad. You went too far. We have to tell the police."

"Listen to me Leo, it was just one little prick the world can do without anyway! Are you going fuck my future for him? What about yours and Eric's? You were here too, you were part of it. What about Mum? It'll kill her!"

"You can't cover up a murder!"

Leo's skin got hot and sweaty under his fingers. Con tightened his hold. "Sure we can, come on, Leo, all you have to do is say nothing. You were never here. I'll look after you, I promise. He jumped, alright? He jumped off, he committed suicide."

"No!" Leo tried to push him off, but Con kept him pinned.

He grit his teeth and dropped his voice. "You like your little girlfriend, Leo? You gonna marry her? You say one word, I'll go after her. I'll make her wish she was never born, you want that for her?"

Leo's hands were around his wrists, trying to force them off his face. "Con," he said. "Con, you're drunk, don't talk like this."

"I'm not that drunk," Con snarled. "You know I'll do it, you know I want her more than you do. You say one word and she'll end up worse off than Tom and it'll all be your fault, you little prick, because you didn't do what you had to for your brother!"

Leo's face went down and he stopped struggling. Con pressed his victory. He softened his voice. "Just back me up on this one little thing, Leo, and I swear to you I will never touch her. Never."

"Her. Or Molly." Leo's voice was hard.

"I won't lay a finger on either of them."

Leo nodded. Con let him go. His breath came hard and fast. He could barely believe he'd dealt with this. Something woke up in him, exultation, victory. He staggered to his car, got in and started the engine.

Eric stared at him.

"What?" Con jerked the car into gear, ignored the grind and put his foot on the pedal. The car jerked forward. He slammed it around the corner. Gravel sprayed the window.

"Nothing." Eric leaned back in his seat.

Con drove down the gravel road silently, concentrating everything he had on getting there, not thinking, not thinking, not thinking. They hit the highway. He skidded to a halt under the cliff and got out of the car, leaving the headlights on.

"What are you doing?" Eric hung out of his door, his legs still in the car. "Come on Conrad, let's go!"

Con rubbed his pounding head. "I have to see." He stumbled into the pool of light in front of the car. There was nothing there, nothing, until he reached the very edge of the light. Then he saw a darker shadow in the darkness, an upright form, a man.

He went closer.

The man took a step towards him. The headlights picked up the shine on his black skin. Eyes like tar bore into him. Then cracks appeared in his face. A map of gashes, like termite tracings on old wood, seeped blood down the skin.

"Tom," Con whispered.

The man lifted a broken, mangled arm and pointed at him.

Con's breath came hard and painful. "Tom," he said. "I never meant-"

"I know what's waiting for you," Tom said.

Con fell to his knees, face in his hands. He couldn't get his breath. The dead man reached out for him and now he was going to die too.

A pair of hands grabbed him by the shirt, dragged him back into the headlights. Eric slapped him across the face.

"Get a grip Con!"

Con looked up at the bespectacled face, then back into the darkness.

"It's just a body," Eric said. "Look. Look!"

But Con couldn't look. He shook his head.

"Get in the car. Now." Eric pointed him at the passenger door.

Con got in the car and slumped in the seat. Eric took the wheel. The tyres screamed. He wrenched the car around and drove them away from Dead Rock.

*

The silence on top of Dead Rock was like creeping ice. Far, far in the distance sirens wailed. Leo's hand was on her shoulder. Enda wondered if he realised his grip hurt.

"Is it true?" Leda said, in a low voice not meant for Con's ears.

Enda hugged her knees and watched Uncle Con. She wasn't ready to move yet, even though she wanted to be far, far away. Molly and Tom had walked away near the edge, watching perhaps for the police.

"Is it true?" Leda repeated, this time more forcefully. "Did you cover up the murder to protect me and Molly?"

"It's true," Leo said.

Enda covered his hand with hers to offer him mute support.

"Why? You knew I could look after myself. And he's never dared to lay a hand on Molly."

"Can you look after yourself, Leda?" Leo's voice was rough,

drawn. "Because one day when I couldn't stand myself any longer I told him I couldn't live with the secret. That same day he left you bleeding and pregnant."

"I can't. I can't deal with this. I'm going to meet the police."

The gun landed near her foot, a gleaming, heavy lump of metal in the grass. Leda walked away.

Enda watched Con lift his head. His hands dropped and their eyes met. Enda slowly, slowly moved the gun behind her. She thought about all the other murders, about Uncle Con reliving that first kill over and over again. "Did you see all their ghosts?" she said.

His face tightened.

"Did you?" Enda rose to her feet. She wanted to look down on him, but he rose with her and was silhouetted against the sunset.

He darted at her and Leo, grabbed her by the hair, knocked Leo back and dragged Enda with him to the edge of the cliff.

Enda had no time for fear. All she could see was Selene. The red light of the sinking sun set her hair ablaze. She stood at the edge of Dead Rock, back to the sunset, framed in gold, arms out like she was going to fly.

Con stopped dead.

"Look at her," Enda said, since there was nothing to lose but time and her life. "She's your daughter, not me. You fucked up, Uncle Con. You killed your own flesh and blood. Where does it stop now?"

"Shut up." He dragged her another step forward.

Selene's face cracked. Fissures appeared in her skin and blood seeped from them.

"No," Con whispered. "No."

The setting sun gave one last blaze and turned Selene to pure light. Enda jammed her elbow into his ribs, kicked back into his shin and somehow freed herself. Uncle Con grabbed for her with one hand and dived at Selene with the other. A shot blasted into the air, ricocheted off the cliff, made the blades of grass shudder. The sun dipped from blinding gold to crimson. A body knocked them flat and hands grasped Enda's feet, but Uncle Con had already dived straight through Selene. She rippled and disappeared into the light.

Enda scrabbled for a hold but he had her arm. His weight

carried her over the edge. For a split second she was poised in midair, a bird in flight, dragged down by sharks, but someone still had her feet. She slammed into the cliff face upside down. Con's grasp slid from her arm to her hands. His weight wrenched her shoulder. Somebody screamed from far away.

Enda stared down into his blue eyes. The madness she'd glimpsed had cracked all the way through. There was nothing familiar left. Blood poured from a deep gash on his face, a bullet hole, holy crap, who'd fired the gun?

Underneath him shadows crept up the cliff. The sun died into a pool of dull crimson.

"Enda," he said. "Don't let me go."

Enda closed her eyes for a split second. Her shoulder was on fire. She could feel the grip on her feet slipping. The weight was too much. "I never wanted it to be like this," she said.

"What?" The mad eyes widened. "I'm your father! Help me!"

"It's just that you came out wrong," she said. "No respect for life. Really, it's your fault. You have to die."

Con stared. Blood flowed from his face onto his shoulder, dripped into the darkness below. "Don't you dare let go you bitch!"

Her hand was sweaty and slippery. She relaxed it, made her fingers straight so there was nothing to hold onto. His grip slid away and Uncle Con fell into the gathering night without a sound.

Enda snapped the chain around her neck and dropped Selene's necklace down after him.

The hands on her feet tightened. She felt like a fishing float freed from a snag and was hauled up over the rock face and to safety.

CHAPTER TWENTY-FOUR

The babble of voices sent a shockwave through Enda's brain. What the hell was going on? She opened her eyes and looked around. A nurse bent over and shone a torch in her eyes. She could feel the rattle of the wheels on the bed she was on. The roof streaked past. She tried to sit up, but shooting pain went from her shoulder into her head. Hands pushed her down again. She rolled her head to the side. Selene raced alongside the bed, looking anxious and excited all at the same time.

"Enda, oh my God, I can't believe you did it," she said.

"Selene? I thought you disappeared!" Enda tried to clear the cobwebs from her head, but with all this babble it was next to impossible. The nurse peered into her face again. Hands pressed her down.

"She's delirious," the nurse said to someone she couldn't see. "Have to get her into emergency. What the hell is going on? Where's Doctor Howard?"

A surge of panic. Enda tried to sit up again, but the nurses held her to the bed.

Sadie pressed in between the nurses. Excitement flushed her skin a dull red. "I came as soon as I heard," she said. "I can't believe it. How'd you do it? Do you know what this means?"

"Sadie?" Enda squeezed her eyes shut and opened them again. When she did, Kelvin leaned over Sadie's shoulder, the cricket bat still in his hands. "What are you doing? Why are you all here?"

The bed rolled into the emergency room. Enda squinted under the bright lights. The noise grew more intense. Hands lifted her onto another table, a swift, practiced operation that sent pain right through her shoulder. She groaned.

"Please tell me you've found the doctor!" a voice yelled out behind her.

Panic stabbed through her again. Enda squeezed her eyes shut.

The hands holding her down had disappeared. She sat bolt upright and screamed, a sound helped along by the fact the motion hurt like hell.

There was a brief, shocked silence.

"Get out!" Enda yelled at the ghosts filling the room. "Just shut up and get out! Oh my God!" She fell back onto the bed.

The ghosts filed out, one by one, shadows in her peripheral vision.

The nurse leaned over her. "Ms Wilson?" her voice was cautious. "We're just trying to do our jobs, if you would please calm down."

"I wasn't talking to you," Enda said. "You had like sixteen ghosts in here and I couldn't think for the noise. Why the hell am I in so much pain?"

"You have a dislocated shoulder," the nurse replied, with remarkable composure. "We're going to have to set it ourselves unless we can find Doctor Howard within the next three minutes."

Enda closed her eyes and took a deep breath to calm herself. "Set it," she said. And then, with a little less certainty, "Is my mum here?"

"She's just outside." The nurse disappeared.

Leda leaned over her a few seconds later. Her hair had escaped from its bun. Her eyes had the wild, hungry glint of a mother tiger defending her young.

Enda held up her good arm, the one that didn't hurt. Leda clasped hands with her.

One nurse braced the injured arm and the other performed a swift manoeuvre. Enda closed her eyes, held onto Leda's arm, grit her teeth and tried not to scream. When it was over she breathed easier.

"We need to put this in a sling," the nurse told Leda, apparently content to ignore Enda now someone else was in the room. "But we need the doctor here, now, to check for further trauma and other injuries."

"Can't you get another doctor?" Leda demanded.

"There is no other doctor in Dead Rock!"

Enda thought about Doctor Howard lying in the bush somewhere, a syringe lost in the leaf litter beside him. Uncle Con had never said whether he was dead or not. "He's not coming," she said.

"This really is a very bad situation." The nurse's voice rose. She didn't even look at Enda. "Your daughter is obviously off her medication again, she's severely injured and babbling about ghosts, we are not equipped to deal with this!"

Leda's voice was cold and clipped. "None of us sitting out there could have failed to hear what you call babble. If my daughter says there are ghosts in the room, then there most probably are, whether you and I like it or not. Now I suggest you get her on a plane or an ambulance to a hospital that can treat her. Right now."

"But the police said-"

"They can send someone with us. Get on the phone. Now!" Leda looked down at Enda and squeezed her hand. "What were you saying sweetie?"

But Enda couldn't answer. Behind Leda stood Doctor Howard. Her heart beat faster and faster until she thought it might stop altogether. He was cut and bruised, his glasses were cracked and his pants still torn at the knees. He looked at her with a complete lack of expression. She had no way to tell, none at all, if he was alive or dead. "Get away from me," she said.

"Dear dear." The doctor walked into the room, scrubbed his hands at the sink and pulled on a pair of gloves. "Back again, Ms Wilson? You really do have the most terrible luck."

"Oh Doctor, thank God you're here!" the nurse almost yelled the words.

"What seems to be the trouble?" he loomed over the bed. His mouth curved, a cruel smile in a bland face.

Enda tried to get off the bed. "Get away from me! Mum, help!"

"Hold her down," he said to the nurses, then turned to Leda. "Leda, I'm going to need you to leave the room, I'm so sorry, but I need absolute calm to bring her out of this episode quickly and examine any injuries."

"Mum don't go!" Enda bucked against the hands and yelled when the pain streaked through her head again.

Worry creased Leda's forehead. She resisted when he tried to lead her to the door. "I'm not leaving," she said. "Just give me a moment Eric, I'm sure I can calm her down."

"Leda I understand this has been a difficult day already, but I need you to trust me on this one." Doctor Howard put his hands on her shoulders and moved her backwards. "Her condition is very complicated and currently very dangerous."

"Don't listen to him Mum he tried to kill me!" Enda yelled. "He's been helping Uncle Con!"

Leda said something to the doctor, but Enda couldn't hear it. The door shut and she was alone with him and the nurses holding her down. He locked the door and put a chair under the handle.

Enda opened her mouth and screamed so loud she thought her vocal cords might break.

The doctor moved toward her. He chuckled. "That's not going to help you."

Enda caught the nurses exchanging a glance of bewilderment, perhaps even concern. "Help me," she said to them. "He tried to kill me, look at him, look at the state of him, please, please keep him away from me."

"Shhh." Doctor Howard laid a calming hand on her forehead and brushed hair out of her face. "You're perfectly safe now, you're in hospital. Nobody's going to hurt you, least of all me." He glanced at the nurses. "I'm going to need a tranquiliser here and someone needs to get plaster for that shoulder."

Both nurses hurried away. The doctor smiled at Enda. Then he drew his finger in a line across his throat.

She opened her mouth to scream again. He clapped a hand over it and bent down to whisper in her ear. "I don't know how you got away from Conrad and I don't care. I'm going to make you hurt for what you did to me."

Enda sunk her teeth into his palm and spit blood when he snatched his hand away. "He's dead," she hissed. "It's over."

"Is that why all the police are here? You killed him?" his eyes widened, but he didn't seem shocked. "Seems you're the only one who knows about me then. What a shame you died of your injuries." He leaned one hand on her injured shoulder and clapped the other over her mouth and nose this time.

She couldn't move. Somewhere in the room something vibrated under a steady, violent thud. Pain kept her immobile. She couldn't scream, couldn't breathe. Stars exploded in her eyes.

A female scream. Outrage. "Doctor Howard what are you

doing?"

A crash. Footsteps. The hand torn away from her mouth, oxygen, sweet oxygen flooding her lungs. Enda took deep breaths until she could see and feel again. Only then did she realise the room was full of blue uniforms, none of them Uncle Con. The doctor was pinned to the floor. One of the nurses sat on the floor with her head in her hands, while the other slumped in the chair next to Enda, breathing hard.

"Christ," Enda said, when she could talk again. "Maybe you people will start listening to me now?"

*

One year later

There was something about staring death in the face that just changed things so absolutely and completely you could never, never go back.

Enda pulled her car off the highway and parked in the sand across from Dead Rock. She got out of the car, taking only a handful of yellow dandelions with her. The hot summer sun beat down all around, but did not seem to penetrate the shadow thrown by the cliff. It would always be cold here.

Everything had changed since she'd left Dead Rock in an ambulance one year ago today. Nobody tried to force medication into her anymore. Leda finally believed in her ghosts, and kept any doctors who thought differently far, far away.

Unfortunately doctors had been a big part of her life since then. Enda wouldn't have believed a dislocated shoulder would be so much trouble, but only after a year of physiotherapy was she beginning to approach normal. Apparently Doctor Howard had done a hell of a lot of damage to it in his two minutes alone with her.

The court case had dragged on for nine months and ended with Doctor Howard going away for a long, long time, while newspapers splashed lurid details of the small town serial killer cop and the attempted murder-suicide of his niece all over the country.

Nobody informed them he'd been Enda's father. She, Leda and Leo had agreed to leave that one buried. They'd had to cover their faces outside the courthouse for months because of the cameras, until finally Leda snapped and took out a court injunction to protect their identities.

Charges of being an accessory to murder had eventually been dismissed against Leo. The fact Leda had shot Conrad in the moment before he went off Dead Rock had taken longer to clean up, but she was okay now.

Enda crossed the highway with her bunch of flowers and stood under Dead Rock, looking up. Those last few moments still replayed in her mind from time to time. Leda returning to the fight, picking up the gun and grazing Con's face with the bullet, a poor repayment for years of terror. Leo grabbing Enda's feet to stop her going over, Molly grabbing Leo, the police swarming onto the cliff top...

Enda took a deep breath in and out. It was the only sound under the rock. Then a crow cawed from somewhere high up, wind rustled dry leaves and traffic hummed in the distance. She went to Selene's cross, battered by a year of weather, and laid flowers there.

Molly had left Dead Rock after it all happened and gone in search of her missing sister. She hadn't been in touch for a while, so Enda hoped she'd found her. One day she'd come back, she'd said, because Tom was still here waiting for her.

Leo wasn't coming back. He lived with Leda and Enda and hadn't had a drink in almost a year. He and Leda weren't back together, but they weren't apart either. Enda wasn't sure if her mother would ever forgive him for making her the unwitting catalyst of all those deaths. But then, she didn't think Leda would ever forgive herself, either, for never knowing.

They never spoke of it.

"About time you came back," said a very pissed off female voice.

Enda grinned at Selene, who stood under the rock, arms folded, scowling. "Wasn't sure you'd still be around."

"Where am I gonna go, into the light? I'm an atheist, you know."

Enda sat with her back to the rock and looked up at the deep blue of the sky. "Sorry. I was in hospital for ages. I couldn't come back right away."

Selene flopped down beside her. "Yeah right. I'm surprised

they let you out. You should've seen those nurses faces when you yelled at us all to get out of the room."

Enda chuckled. "I stay away from psychiatric units these days."

"So what are you doing then?" Selene studied her nails.

"Reading, mostly." Enda didn't elaborate. She'd read everything she could get her hands on about ghosts and the supernatural over the last few months. She wasn't sure where it would take her, but there had to be a better job out there than selling people crap they didn't want. "How's your mum?"

Selene shrugged. "I see her sometimes. She doesn't go out much. She misses Dad, you know. I think she was the only one he ever treated nice."

"And Alice?"

"Still a prize bitch. It's how she deals with everything." Selene fidgeted with her dress. "It's been boring since you left. Kelvin went."

"Went?"

"You know, to the other place. One day he was there, the next he wasn't. Sadie said she saw him walk into this bright light. Then she saw this newspaper article all about Dad and it mentioned her, said she was murdered. Then she was gone too."

"But you're still here."

"Told you, I'm an atheist."

"That's not really why though, is it?" Enda turned her head to look at Selene. "Have you seen Uncle Con?"

Selene shook her head. "Not once. Tom said he became part of something dark." She gestured around them. "He's here, but he's not here."

"He's part of the cold," Enda said.

"Yeah."

"Selene, I'm sorry I never spoke to you for all those years. I wish I'd known you were my sister. I'd have come and got you. We could have gone to uni together and stuff."

Selene smiled at her. "Really? You would've done that?"

"Really." Enda reached over the cross and rested her fingertips on Selene's hand, lightly, gently, because there was nothing there. "You saved my life."

"No I didn't. I stood on the edge of the cliff and tried to make my dad jump, and that almost got you killed."

"I don't mean that. I mean you made me see I could speak to you and all the other ghosts for a purpose. You made me grow up and stop taking shit from doctors."

"Really?" Selene reached a hand toward the sky as though seeking the warmth of the sun. "I did that?"

"You did that." Enda watched a spark of light grow in front of Selene. It was a beautiful thing, like a mirror without borders, light that was there and yet not there. "Now it's time for you to move on."

"But I don't want to go." Selene's lower lip trembled. "I don't know what's waiting."

"Me neither." Enda tried to memorise every last feature on Selene's face. "Maybe it's something really cool."

"Maybe." Selene stood up and walked toward the light. She'd almost reached it when she stopped and looked over her shoulder. "Hey Enda."

"Yeah?"

"Thanks."

And then she was gone.

Dead Rock's shadow spread across the highway, across the sand. Enda shuddered in the cold and hurried back to her car. There she stood with the driver's door open for a minute, looking around. The cold crept into her skin. For a bare second it felt as though someone breathed down her neck. Fine hairs prickled. Her blood raced. Dark blue eyes. Her hand, stretched out so a man would die and she would live. Murder.

She stiffened. "You're dead, Conrad Wilson," she said aloud. "And you have no power over me."

Then she got back in the car, slammed the door and tramped the accelerator. She only looked in the rear view once. The top of the cliff cut across the sky. A tiny figure in a wide-brimmed hat stood up there and raised a distant hand.

"Bye Tom," Enda said, and drove away from Dead Rock.

THE END

ABOUT THE AUTHOR

Nina Smith is a writer, belly dancer and costume designer who lives in Western Australia with her partner, her son and a menagerie of winged and furry friends.

23551496R00133

Made in the USA
Charleston, SC
28 October 2013